TARRAGON WAR

Book Three of the Tarragon Series

Elizabeth James

Thrall of Darkness

ISBN-13: 978-1-944969-02-8

THE TARRAGON SERIES

CONTENTS

PROLOGUE

Derek awoke with the memory of Scott's lips against his. He ran his fingers over his lips and smiled. In just a few days, he would be back on the same campus as Scott, and his body had been sending him very pleasurable reminders of their time together just a few months ago, as if he needed the reminders. Scott had not only soothed Derek's body, he had soothed his mind and they had grown close in the short time they were together. Derek knew that he would be able to pick up where they had left off and start the semester as friends, and perhaps more.

He wasn't sure how much physical intimacy to expect from Scott, however. Although Scott had willingly seduced him and they had made love – Derek's first time and an incredible experience all around – Scott did have a boyfriend to deal with. The boyfriend had been out of the picture last spring during the prospective student weekend when Scott and Derek had gotten together, but he would be a problem this fall. Derek's smile faded, but his fingers continued to stroke his lips, remembering Scott's kisses. Scott was so incredibly sweet. Derek would do anything to get him away from his boyfriend so he could have the man all to himself.

Derek sat up and looked around at his room. Most of his belongings were packed for the trip to Portland, but he still had a few things out for his last days in Spokane. It was only a six-hour drive and his mom had promised to bring him anything he forgot, but he didn't want to inconvenience her. Plus, he didn't want her intruding on his first independent adventure.

The prospective student weekend had been an invigorating experience for him. Always before, his mother had hovered over him, watching like a hawk to make sure everything went perfectly for him. If he came in second place in a science fair, she would bully the judge into changing his ruling. If he ran home with a split lip, she would find the boys who did it and make sure they paid the price for beating up her son. Derek didn't know how or why she was so influential, although he suspected it was because of his absent father, Peter Ashton, the head of the Tarragon council.

He and his mother lived in a community of Tarragon graduates on the south hill of Spokane, Washington and Ashton's word was law. As Ashton's son, Derek was considered a privileged child even though he had never really known the man. Ashton didn't leave the campus and Derek hadn't met him until the prospective student's weekend, but the other mothers all said he looked just like the man and after seeing Ashton in person, Derek knew it was quite a compliment. Still, he would have preferred to be in one of the other families, with a father who lived with his family and took care of his children. There were plenty of ball games where his mother looked all alone sitting in the stands without a husband at her side, alone among the couples cheering for their children. She missed Ashton, too, and although she frequently had boyfriends, none ever lasted more than a month or two.

Derek began putting some of his remaining items into boxes. He didn't know what his mom would do once he was gone. She got misty-eyed whenever he talked about leaving, and kept mentioning how he would only be six hours away. He hoped she would be able to find her own life, because as much as he loved her, he didn't want her intruding on his new life on campus. He had big plans, after all: he wanted to seduce Scott and make him realize that they belonged together. And perhaps most importantly, he wanted to earn the respect of his father. He had never had the chance to be with his father before, but soon he would be near his father all the time, living and working and playing on the same campus, and Derek would not let it go to waste. He would find a way to impress Ashton, no matter what the cost. He would show Ashton that he had grown into a fine young man, a young man worthy of his attention. He still remembered with pride how Ashton had fingered the medals on his chest at the prospective students' fair on the last day after Derek and Scott had won so many competitions. Ashton had been impressed then, and he would be again. But his mother would only get in the way.

Derek sighed. He didn't resent his mother, but he sometimes wondered if she were the reason Ashton stayed away. He wondered what would have happened if she had chosen to live closer to the campus so that Ashton could have visited regularly. He wondered if there were some reason Ashton never spoke to his mother or even tried to communicate with her until he let her know about the prospective student weekend. She had mentioned once that Ashton had other children by other women, and Derek wondered if Ashton took part in their lives or if he was equally absent in all of them. He would feel better if Ashton neglected all of his kids, even though that was a horrible thing to hope. But it would mean that Derek wasn't being singled out for the isolation, and above all else Derek feared that he might have done something wrong to make his father never want to see him or speak to him. He had no memories of Ashton, but what if, as a child, he had done something to his father and Ashton had decided to cut all ties to Derek and his mother? What if their abandonment was Derek's fault?

He shook his head sharply. These were not good thoughts to be having. They were distracting him from the happy thoughts of Scott that had awoken him and had kept him pleasantly awake at night. He heard footsteps outside his door, then a knock. He groaned and called for his mother to come in. Thoughts of Scott would have to wait even longer.

"How are you doing?" his mother asked, coming in and sitting on his bed, looking around at the boxes.

He was dressed only in his boxers but he supposed as his mother she didn't care much what he was wearing. He, however, was embarrassed and pulled a shirt on.

"I'm ready to go. I can't believe we don't leave until tomorrow."

"Is there anything you want to do before we go? Any friends you have to say goodbye to, or places you want to go? You won't be back for a long time."

Derek shook his head. It was true, though. Freshmen weren't allowed to go home their entire first year, not even for winter break. It was a strange rule, but then again, there were lots of strange things about Tarragon Academy. There were lots of strange things about Tarragon society in general and he had learned not to ask questions. Now that he was going to school, however, he knew that his questions would finally be answered. Graduates of the college all seemed to share a secret that bound them together, and Derek was determined to find out what that secret was.

But as for friends to see or places to go, he didn't have any. Although he was good at socializing and pretending to be a socialite, in reality it was a defense mechanism from the years and years of bullying he had endured. Most of the bullying stemmed from the fact that he was Ashton's son, and everyone viewed him as special. Being special in any school was sure to single you out for bullies, and it was especially true in Tarragon society. He had been beaten up more times than he could count and when his mother took care of the situation for him, the bullying became worse. By high school, the physical bullying had all but stopped, but it was replaced by verbal abuse. No one would speak to him except to make fun of him or gossip about him, and vicious rumors were started that made even his paltry few friends turn against him. By the end of his senior year he didn't have a single person that he could genuinely call a friend, but he had learned to navigate their world. He had learned to smile and turn the other cheek, and then gossip behind their backs as revenge. His new abilities gave him many pseudo-friends, but none that he truly trusted. He was looking forward to Tarragon Academy as a place to finally meet people who wouldn't judge him based on his father, or his past mistakes, or the fact that he was gay. He wanted people who could truly see him and appreciate him, and befriend him. Scott had done it; Scott had even seen his vicious side and still become his friend, so perhaps others at the academy would do the same.

"Are you sure there's nothing in Spokane you want to do?" his mother asked again, almost desperately.

Derek could tell that she wanted him to say yes, as if by wanting something in Spokane he would be validating her decision to live here all these years. But there was nothing for him here aside from her and the house he grew up in. Maybe he could go downtown to the mall, but he didn't want to shop or see a movie, and maybe they could go out to dinner, but the Mexican restaurant they normally frequented had new owners and the food had gone downhill even as the prices had gone up. And that was about it. He didn't have friends, so he couldn't hang out with them. It was just him, his mom, and their home. That was his world right now, and he was itching to expand it.

"I'll just be online," he said.

He had joined a group of students who would be starting at Tarragon Academy in the fall and had already formed what might be the beginnings of some friendships there. Even though the internet was tightly controlled on campus, it was free now and a lot of students were taking advantage of it to get to know each other, especially their roommates. Derek hadn't heard yet who his roommate would be; his dorm was last in roommate selection. He likely wouldn't find out until he arrived, but he didn't mind surprises. He was used to faking his way around people thanks to his years being bullied, and he could fake it a few more months if he needed until he could change room assignments. He wished he could room with Scott but he knew freshmen were housed separately from upperclassmen. Freshmen did everything separately, it seemed. It was going to take some effort to meet up with Scott, but Derek would figure it out.

"Honey," his mom said. "I know you've had a rough couple of years."

Derek forced a smile. She didn't know or understand how bad he had it. She had dealt with the physical abuse, but he had never told her about the psychological torture the students had put him through. She had no idea what she was talking about.

"But things will get better at college, and maybe you'll look back at high school and be able to remember the good times."

As if there were good times, he thought. He couldn't remember a single happy memory from high school, aside from his memories of finally getting home each day and being able to escape that place each summer.

"I'm looking forward to college," he said. "It's going to be different."

"Just remember that it will be some of the same kids," his mom said in a worried voice. "But you don't have to worry about that. The school is small, and everyone takes care of each other."

Derek's heart sank slightly. He knew that some of his enemies were coming with him, but he tried not to think about it. The worst kids weren't coming, luckily. They hadn't been accepted into the prestigious academy, despite the protests of their parents. Some of those parents had been almost hysterical about their children's rejections, as if the kids would die if they didn't get in. But prestigious or not, it was just a college and there were plenty of others, even though families from the Tarragon society tended to only apply to Tarragon Academy. Derek often thought the school should expand, since there was clearly a need for a larger school, but apparently class size had remained the same for centuries even though every child in Tarragon society worldwide was raised to believe that they would attend the school.

"I can take care of myself, mom," he said.

"I know. I wish you didn't have to."

"I need to," he said. "It's part of growing up."

She sniffed, and he realized she was about to cry. He wrapped an arm around her and pulled her into a hug.

"I'm sorry," he said, unsure if he said something wrong but knowing an apology never hurt.

"No, I'm sorry," she said, tears leaking from her eyes. "I've spent so much time protecting you, I've never let you live. And now you'll be on your own, facing the test on your own, and I don't know what I would do without you."

"What test? And I'm only going to be six hours away," he said. Then, regretfully, he added, "If you need to visit me, you can, you know. Anytime."

She pulled him tighter and began to cry in earnest, as if she were giving him away forever. He let her cry, puzzled and a little frightened. Did she think he was going to die? He shivered and a sense of foreboding swept over him. What if he went to the college and instead of impressing Ashton, he disappointed Ashton and his attempt cost him his life? No, he would never let that happen. As much as he wanted Ashton's approval, he valued his life too much. He would never pull a stunt like that. Yet the feeling of foreboding remained, long after his mother apologized and left him to find a handkerchief, even after he finished packing and began moving things to the car so they could get an early start the next day. For the first time, Derek realized his life could end. But it couldn't, not yet. He still had so many things to do.

CHAPTER ONE

Summer's Farewell

J amie pulled on a shirt and was surprised at how foreign it felt to be wearing something on his torso. It had been months since he and Scott had started going shirtless in the perfect weather of the hatching grounds, and Jamie had finally grown accustomed to being without some sort of protection from prying eyes. All his life he had tried to hide the scars on his body for fear that someone would recognize them and realize what a mess he was, but now he had scars to be proud of: the scars from his fight with Marisol.

He hadn't realized it when he was first attacked by Marisol, but Tarragon society valued scars highly and the three long streaks across his belly were proof that he was a tried and true member of the society. The other, older dragon partners who came to hear about the revolution he was starting looked at him with more respect when they saw his scars, one of the many reasons he and Scott had ditched their shirts. They needed all the help they could get in persuading people to turn against Ashton, and Jamie was prepared to let people see his scars if that's what it took.

"How is the packing going?" Kale asked, peeking into the large tent that Scott had bought on one of his trips back to the campus. Scott hadn't been enthused at the idea of sleeping out in the open, so on one of his first trips to the campus he had ordered all sorts of camping supplies at the academy's expense, and now he, Jamie, and Kale had an elaborate campsite with many modern amenities.

"Good," Jamie said. "I wish you could come."

Kale had joined them in Marisol's hatching ground a couple of weeks after Jamie and Scott moved to the hatching ground for the summer. Only two people came to visit Jamie and Scott, and they were both sworn to secrecy about Kale's presence. Of those two people, Jamie knew that Eric would never breathe a word. Eric had been the one to save Kale's life when Ashton attacked the man and tried to kill him on the mountaintop, and if Ashton found out about Eric's interference, not even Eric's position on the Tarragon council would protect him.

Jamie wasn't as sure about the other man who came to visit, Mike Ferrin. Mike used to be one of Jamie's teachers and Jamie knew that he still harbored inappropriate thoughts about Jamie, but his heart had been swept away by Ashton. Everything he did seemed to be for Ashton, but there was always a bitterness when he spoke of the man. It was impossible to tell if Mike loved him or hated him, and Jamie couldn't predict when or if Mike would reveal Kale's presence to Ashton. He hadn't so far, but he still might. Mike's dragon was a similar conflict of desires, though Eraxes was firmly of the belief that Ashton was an evil person. Jamie just didn't know if that belief extended to Mike or not. It was puzzling.

Jamie knew he was walking into danger by returning to the campus, but he also knew he couldn't stay at the hatching grounds forever. As much as he had enjoyed spending the summer alone with only a few friends and visitors, he needed to be surrounded by people again. He had always considered himself an introvert, but perhaps there was a little extravert in him after all because he was starting to crave being around people. Not a lot of people, just enough so that he wasn't the center of attention. Maybe that was it. Maybe it was an introvert impulse after all. He was just tired of having everyone coming to visit him, and he wanted to be able to sink into the background for once.

After all, every week or so Scott would bring new dragons and new people to speak with Jamie. All were people who hated Ashton and believed he needed to go, and they needed to know that Jamie was capable of leading them through the battle. Jamie had to be strong and commanding, and Marisol had to be on her best behavior. It was exhausting work, and at night Jamie often wept and worried that he would disappoint everyone because no matter what he made those people believe, in truth he wasn't strong enough and he knew deep down he would fail. Scott would rock him then, and hold him, and whisper encouragement in his ear. Sometimes it would silence him, but the doubts remained.

Jamie finished packing some of their souvenirs from the summer into a small backpack and looked up at Kale.

"You'll be okay on your own here?"

"Don't worry about me," he said. "I'm about to get the big tent."

Jamie smiled. With Jamie and Scott gone, Kale would be moving into the circus-like tent they normally stayed in. They would be leaving a lot of their gear for Kale to use, as well. With Marisol protecting the boundaries of the hatching ground from intruders, there was no threat of theft, and Marisol had assured them many times that there were no animals larger than the squirrels on the island. She would not allow it.

Which also meant that she had barely fed all summer. Scott's dragon Narné had brought her several cows over the long months, but couldn't bring too many because it was so difficult to fly with a living, struggling creature. Marisol had learned to fish from Mike's dragon, but didn't enjoy the fish at all and only ate them as a last resort. Kale's dragon Vestis had attempted to persuade her to eat some of the greenery, but she spat it out and insisted that only meat would work. She had enough to eat, but the longer she stayed, the grumpier she was becoming and Jamie knew it was in direct proportion to the amount she was eating. Unfortunately, even though he and Scott were returning to the campus, Marisol insisted on remaining with her eggs. She planned on staying with them until they hatched, which would be another three months or so. Jamie just hoped she could last that long with the meager food supplies she was getting.

Kale would be in charge of her, and Scott would continue to attempt to bring her cows to eat. It was as good a plan as any, since Jamie and Scott couldn't stay at the hatching ground any longer. Jamie hated to admit it, but they were needed back at school. It was time to return to class.

The familiar scent of honey washed over Jamie's senses and a smile softened his face as he looked around for Scott. Sure enough, Scott was just hopping off Narné's back outside the tent. Jamie zipped up the backpack and slid his arms through the straps. He was mostly bringing sentimental items, leaving the practical things in case they had to return in a hurry and couldn't pack. Besides, they had everything they needed back at their apartment in dragon canyon on campus.

"I guess this is it," Jamie said, looking around at the large campsite, with its firepit that the dragons lit every night, the two small tents beside the large tent that had been his home for the past three months, the worn places in the grass from where their feet had trod so many times it left a trail. His eyes followed the trail for a minute. The only thing he wouldn't miss was the outhouse. Jamie was grateful to be able to go somewhere with running water for a change. His eyes swept the campsite. It was the only thing he wouldn't miss; the rest was dear to him. But he knew he would be back, and he dreaded coming back. When he returned, it would be to lead an army, not for pleasure. When he returned, it would be because there were no other options. He hoped it would be quite a while before he returned.

He and Scott said their goodbyes to Kale, then mounted Narné. The great dragon leapt into the air and circled the island so that Jamie could get a good view of Marisol, still circling her eggs. He wasn't allowed anywhere near her or her eggs, and he was grateful for this last look in what might be a long time.

I am always with you, Marisol said, her voice ringing through his head. He grinned and acknowledged the sentiment.

But sometimes, he replied, *it is nice to see you.*

I will see you again soon.

He waved, knowing she was probably too far away to see but knowing she would feel the gesture, and then Narné let out a beautiful song that allowed them to travel from whatever alternate dimension the hatching ground existed in to Mount Tarragon. As the mist cleared around them, it began to rain, a light, Portland rain. By the time Narné made it into their home in dragon canyon, both he and Scott were soaked and freezing. The hatching grounds had been warm, and Portland was significantly cooler, even though it was probably quite warm for normal Portland weather.

Ashton and half the council waited for them and for a moment, Jamie panicked and thought they were about to be arrested for their attempts to undermine Ashton's control. But when they slid off Narné – having no other options – Ashton instead embraced Jamie.

"Welcome back, Queen," he said. "We have missed you during your absence. Should you need anything, you have only to ask me or the council."

Jamie nodded, too frightened to say anything. He had forgotten how imposing Ashton was, and how handsome. Were they really trying to go up against this man? He was a charming, charismatic leader who already held the loyalty of Tarragon society, and Jamie was nothing, would be nothing if he hadn't happened to hatch a Queen dragon. Why were people agreeing to help him? Sudden thoughts of traps and lies filled his mind, but he pushed them aside. Everyone who had agreed to join Jamie's cause was sincere. He had looked into the minds of their dragons and read their sincerity. Ashton might be behaving right now, but Jamie had to remember how manipulative the man could be. This was an act, nothing more.

The other council members welcomed Jamie as well and shook his hand, and he allowed it numbly, barely feeling the firm grasps of the men. It was all men; none of the women were present. That made sense, he thought. It was the start of the school year and they were likely on their separate campus getting the new students ready. It was probably a great honor to be greeted like this, and here he was acting like a scared animal. He took a deep breath.

"Thank you, Ashton and council members," he said, trying to regain his confidence from the last time he had met with the council. "I look forward to working with you this school year."

Ashton's lips quirked as if in amusement, and Jamie realized he had just placed himself as an equal to the council. But none of the other council members seemed fazed by what he had just said; they seemed to expect it. They filed out of his room, Ashton last. Ashton took his hand before leaving.

"I look forward to working with you, too, little one," he said.

Jamie could feel Scott tensing behind him and he released Ashton's hand, hoping the man would take a hint. It almost felt like Ashton was hitting on him, but surely Ashton wouldn't hit on him so soon after arriving, not after everything Ashton had already done to him. Ashton let go and left the room.

"That jerk," Scott muttered, grabbing Jamie's hand and kissing it as if his lips could rid Jamie's skin of Ashton's touch.

Jamie said nothing, just made exaggerated gestures towards the ceiling corners. Scott took the hint. If the council were waiting for them in their quarters, it was almost certain that the council, or Ashton at least, had gone through their things and planted bugs to listen in on their conversations. They had swept the place once, before leaving, but now they would have to start from scratch. And until they felt confident about getting every bug, they couldn't complain about Ashton. It would give away the game. Although a few odd comments wouldn't be amiss,

Jamie thought. It was well-known that Ashton and Scott hated each other, so nothing Scott had said was out of place. But if they let anything slip about the war, or recruiting, or anything like that, it would be all over.

Jamie shivered. Having a modern bathroom was nice, but he had forgotten what it felt like to be caged, to be under the constant scrutiny of others. It was the reason he and Scott had run away to the hatching grounds in the first place and now that he was back, he could feel the iron bars tightening into a noose around him. But he wouldn't give up. He would find some way to escape.

He turned to Scott to express some of his thoughts, but Scott held up a hand to silence him, a vague look on his face meaning that he was talking to Narné. Then he kissed Jamie's forehead.

"I have to go, sweetheart. You can get settled without me, can't you?"

"Go? Go where?"

"I'll have Narné send for you when we're ready. Be prepared."

He left without another word. Jamie slid his backpack on the ground and stared at the door, then at Narné, who went to the ledge and jumped off into the dragon canyon. Five minutes home and already he was alone again. Where had Scott gone?

CHAPTER TWO

Recruitment

"Guten tag," Scott said in his best German, shaking the German representative's hand firmly. He had met the man twice before and tried to feel out whether or not he supported Ashton, but he had never been able to get a read on him. Now that Jamie was back, he was hoping Jamie and Marisol would be able to give some insight on the man.

"Wie geht es Ihnen?" Scott continued, hoping he got everything correct as he asked the man how he was doing.

Dieter grinned and shook his hand enthusiastically before releasing it.

"I see you have been studying your German," he said in flawless English. "I am doing fine, thank you. And you?"

"I have just returned with the Queen," Scott said. "We are back to living on the campus full-time."

"I have excellent timing, then," Dieter said.

"Jamie has only just arrived, but will be ready to accept visitors soon. Until then, can I offer you anything to eat or drink? You must have had a long flight."

"I came by jetliner, not dragonback, so I have had all the amenities of travel. However, a home-cooked meal would not be amiss."

"Of course," Scott said, gesturing for Dieter to follow him.

Scott had quickly become an expert at navigating the dragon

canyon and had been surprised to find out that there was a large cafeteria-like eating area on the ground level of the canyon for anyone who didn't have time to cook. Since many of the residents of the canyon were students and teachers who had homework to do and papers to grade, it was heavily frequented and the food was excellent. There was also a sit-down area for guests and other visiting dignitaries, and that was where Scott had been brought when the other foreign representatives had arrived. Normally Ashton would be present for a visit from the German representative, but with school starting tomorrow he had too much to prepare and Scott was on his own with no council support. It showed a level of confidence in Scott's abilities that Ashton was willing to leave him alone with a representative, and perhaps it also showed that Ashton didn't see him as a threat anymore, which would be ideal.

The cafeteria was filled with excited students at one end of the room and frazzled teachers at the other, and very little mixing going on between them. Occasionally a student would wander over to the teachers, but the teachers were busy planning their first days and weeks and weren't as interested in helping students as they usually were. Scott spotted Mike in the chaos, sitting by himself in a corner. Scott hesitated, almost tempted to ask Dieter to wait a moment and go over and talk to him. Mike had changed in the past few months, drawing inward and losing some of the spark that made him so irritating and irresistible. Scott knew it had to do with Ashton, and suspected it had to do specifically with Jamie's decision to go to the council and try to get Ashton kicked off the council. Mike had shown up a day after that incident with bruises and a limp, and only Ashton could have given them to him. But Mike said nothing, and there was nothing Scott could do if the man refused to ask for help. Scott tore his eyes away from Mike and returned his attention to the task at hand.

They finally arrived at the sit-down area and were promptly seated and given menus. Scott and Dieter ordered from the limited selection and then leaned back and stared at each other.

"I can hardly wait to meet this Queen," Dieter said. "I've heard many things about Jamie, not to mention what I saw during the mating flight."

Scott flushed on Jamie's behalf. During Jamie's mating flight, Jamie had inadvertedly projected an image into the minds of everyone in Tarragon society, male and female, straight and gay, of himself writhing in agonized pleasure, desperate to be touched. Everyone who saw and felt that image had experienced an intense instinct to be the one to touch Jamie and fulfill his need, which was a disturbing experience for the straight men who felt it and made it awkward for Jamie when he met nearly everyone. Time had dulled the experience for most people, but it was seared into their minds and everyone who met Jamie had that image in the back of their minds. It was something Jamie had to live with, and something he was still adapting to. Scott was embarrassed on his boyfriend's behalf, but also because he suspected Dieter felt some jealousy; after all, when Jamie had summoned the world to chase him in the mating flight, only Scott had been victorious.

"Jamie is young, but he has matured a lot over the past year," Scott said. "He is already a good leader."

"But the council does the leading, do they not? Jamie is a fig-ure-head, nothing more."

Scott was silent. This was dangerous ground because he still didn't know the man's feelings about Ashton. He reached out to Narné and asked if Marisol could read the man's true intentions. There was a silence, then Narné responded that the man could be trusted. Scott let out a sigh of relief. But even with that, there were ears everywhere and he couldn't speak openly.

"The council leads, true," Scott said. "But Jamie is their equal."

"I see," Dieter said, then looked around. "Perhaps we can dis-cuss this further with Jamie present."

"That would be best."

Dieter changed the subject and began talking about the dragons in Germany and how they hid in castles, just like the dragons of old who used to lie on vast heaps of treasure and protect the treasure from wandering knights.

"Only now," Dieter said, "They sleep atop thumb drives and the entrances to rooms filled with servers. The currency of information is primary now, not gold, but dragons are still used as protection against any prying eyes and ears."

"How many dragons are in Germany?"

"About two thousand, although some live on borderlands."

"How do they all stay hidden?"

"The mist hides them, partially. It grew thin for several years, but has recently thickened again. And we are careful where we fly. Life away from Mount Tarragon has its disadvantages, but it is our home."

"I understand," Scott said. "I'm lucky that I grew up nearby. I can't imagine growing up in a foreign country, then being carted off to this school, then having to decide whether to remain here or return home. It must be a difficult decision."

"It is, but of course there are communities of us everywhere and we all share the same secret. That makes it easier. We live together, hide together, raise our children together. The only requirement that sets our children apart is that they must learn English so that they can do well in school here. Other than that, they are ordinary children."

They chatted more about Tarragon society in Germany and elsewhere and slowly Scott gleaned more information about the army that he was potentially gaining. When the representative of a country didn't agree with Ashton, it was likely that many of the other dragons within that country didn't agree with Ashton, so it was important to find out how many of those two thousand German dragons would join with Jamie in the upcoming war and how many would stay out of the fighting or, worse, join with Ashton. Scott rather suspected that most would side with their representative and Jamie, but it wasn't a sure thing until Jamie read the situation and Marisol did a deeper examination. He glanced at his watch. An hour had passed since he had left Jamie's side. He felt bad about abandoning Jamie like he had, but he had never been called to greet a representative by himself before and he couldn't refuse the honor, especially with someone like the German representative who was so hard to read. He hoped Jamie would forgive him, and he hoped Narné had warned Jamie that they were coming to the apartment because he and Dieter were finished with their meal and heading to the top level of the dragon canyon where his and Jamie's room lay.

Jamie must have gotten Narné's message, however, because just as they approached the door, it opened and Jamie stood on the other side looking beautiful as always, this time in a clean white button-up shirt with a pair of dark jeans. His normally too-white skin was a cheerful tan from his months in the sun and he glowed with health. He extended his hand to Dieter and the other man lifted it to his lips. Jamie covered his surprise well and Scott had to stifle his jealousy. Obviously Dieter, like so many others, still had lingering lust from the mating flight.

"A pleasure to meet you at last, Jamie," Dieter said.

"This is Dieter Ulmann, representative of Germany," Scott said, interrupting any romantic scene that might have played out.

"Pleasure to meet you, Mr. Ulmann," Jamie said.

"Please, call me Dieter."

"Of course," Jamie said, blushing as Dieter still held his hand. With a final caress of his thumb against Jamie's skin, Dieter finally relinquished his hand. Jamie cleared his throat. "The Queen dragon is not here, but you are welcome to come in."

"I didn't come to see the dragon," Dieter said, smiling at Jamie.

Scott huffed to himself, unable to voice his impatience out loud for fear of offending Dieter. He couldn't afford to lose any allies, even when those allies were hitting on his boyfriend in front of him. Still, a show of possession wouldn't be amiss. It would remind Dieter that Scott was Jamie's mate. Scott entered the room and put his hand on Jamie's back possessively as he gestured for Dieter to enter. Dieter's mouth quirked as he recognized the possessive display and he dipped his head as if acknowledging Scott's claim.

Jamie opened his mouth to speak, but Dieter held up a hand to silence him. Scott frowned. Normally Dieter wasn't rude, but silencing Jamie was very impolite. Dieter had the glazed look in his eyes that indicated he was speaking to his dragon, however, and great leeway was given to people in that circumstance in Tarragon society. There was a popping sound, then smashing sounds from the corners of the room. Scott leapt up and ran to one of the corners. A small camera, now smashed beyond recognition, had fallen to the ground. Scott looked at Dieter in disbelief.

"What happened?"

"I wanted to talk to you without being listened to," the man explained. "Each of us has dragons with different talents. My dragon's talent is to destroy electronics in a limited range around me. I use it frequently to get rid of listening devices. You'll find that your entire chambers are clear except for the dragon sleeping chambers. Those are too large. New devices may be added, of course, but for a time you are safe."

"Thank you," Jamie said, sounding a little dazed.

Scott sat next to him on the couch and stared at Dieter in awe. Destroying electronics was an extremely valuable gift.

"So," Dieter began, nearly spitting out the word. "You have set yourself up as equal to the council. That makes you equal to Ashton. A dangerous position to be in."

"Tarragon society must change," Scott began, but Jamie placed a hand on his arm to silence him and Scott fell silent. Scott had been doing all of the recruiting all summer, but perhaps it was time to let Jamie do the speaking, since Jamie would be leading the war. Scott just hoped Jamie knew what he was doing.

"I am equal to Ashton," Jamie said. "But I should be more than equal, according to Tarragon tradition."

"You both make good points," Dieter said. "But what is your plan? You hope to bring down Ashton by manipulating the council?"

"No," Jamie said. "I've tried using reason and going through the council. The time for peaceful means is over. Only a war will fix this problem."

Dieter's lips went white and he licked them nervously. "A war? Dragon against dragon? Do you have any idea what you're asking?"

"I'm asking for your allegiance against an evil that is sapping our society of strength and honor. As Scott pointed out, our society must change. Ashton must be killed in order for our way of life to continue and to prosper. You understand this, I know, but do you have the courage to face it?"

Dieter stared at the floor, at the ceiling, at the walls, at anything besides Jamie. Then he took a deep breath. "I've known for a long time that Ashton must go, but is a war really necessary?"

"If it were possible to take Ashton down individually, I would do it," Jamie said with a fierceness that Scott had never seen. "But you know he's going to call on his allies, and unless we can defend against that, we won't be able to get near him."

"We could lose our dragons."

"You could lose them now."

"But Arion can sever the link between a dragon and his partner. What's to stop Arion from severing that link in everyone who opposes him?"

"I've spoken to the dragons and they agree that Arion can't do more than one a day, so if we can keep the battle short, overpower our enemy, and kill Ashton quickly, the casualties will be limited. But I'm not denying that there will be losses."

Dieter sighed heavily. "Give me time to think. If it were just me, I would be with you in a heartbeat. But I speak for the people of Germany, and I cannot pledge all of our support without further thought."

"Ashton cannot know about this," Scott warned. "You cannot ask your people, because they might turn against you and inform Ashton of our plans."

"I will contemplate in private," Dieter promised. "I will consider what is best for Germany, and when you are ready to fight, I will summon our dragons and those who listen to me will come to your aid."

"Thank you, Dieter," Jamie said.

They stood and escorted Dieter to the door. As they left, Dieter kissed Jamie on the cheek. He surprised Scott by kissing Dieter on his cheek in return. Normally Jamie was shy about shows of affection, even clearly non-sexual ones like this, but perhaps he was doing it to persuade Dieter. Either way, Scott was more than a little jealous as he shut the door on the other man and turned to Jamie.

"You," he said, "are incredible."

Jamie flashed a wicked smile.

"I've been waiting to get you alone. Do you think the cameras really are gone? Because there're some things I want to show you."

Scott grinned as Jamie led him towards the bedroom where, sure enough, there was smashed glass from destroyed cameras in several places around the room. Jamie laughed and leapt in the bed.

"We haven't been in a bed together in months. You're not going to run off again, are you?"

"No," Scott said. "Right now, my only concern is you."

CHAPTER THREE

Together

J amie grinned as Scott sat on the bed beside him and took off his shoes and socks. Jamie did the same, and couldn't keep his grin from getting wider. They had slept together over the summer, but only on the hard, rocky ground. Being in a bed would be an incredibly luxurious experience after so much time away. He was a little worried that something would drag Scott away like the representative had earlier, but Scott seemed to genuinely think that nothing could interrupt them. They had already dealt with the council and the representative, so there shouldn't be anyone or anything else until classes in the morning. Until then, it was just them.

Scott pulled his shirt over his head and Jamie admired his hazelnut skin once more, and the muscles that rippled beneath it. His tongue ached with the need to taste that skin and feel Scott's nipples growing hard under him. He ached for the feel of Scott's cock as well, but that was still hidden. Jamie placed his hands on Scott's shoulders and pushed the man backwards, straddling him and lowering his head so that he could lick a stripe down the center of his chest. Scott sighed in pleasure. Jamie let his tongue wander to Scott's nipples and the difference in texture intrigued and enticed him as always, the feel of the nubs playfully rubbing against his tongue a marvelous sensation. Scott tasted of rain from their flight back to dragon canyon, a heavy taste with echoes of darkness unusual for his lover and Jamie scoured his tongue across more of Scott's body, wanting more.

Scott's hands pulled at Jamie's shirt but he couldn't reach the buttons to undo it, so he ended up twisting it into his hands rather than removing it as he sighed and moaned at Jamie's licking. Scott curled around Jamie and Jamie could see and feel the hardening mound in his pants. Jamie let one of his hands slip down and stroke him through the thick material of his pants and Scott jumped and groaned.

"Too much, you're too much for me," he whispered, trying to pull his pants off.

Jamie stroked him a few more times, exalting in the power he had over his boyfriend before finally allowing Scott to disrobe and release his cock from the confines of his pants. As soon as the pants were gone, Scott's beautiful cock bobbed up against his belly and Jamie's mouth went dry. He wanted Scott inside of him. He wanted to be cushioned on this comfortable bed as Scott was inside of him. Just the thought made him shiver with desire and his fingers stumbled as he tried to unbutton his shirt with no more success than Scott had had earlier. Scott laughed, a smoky laugh, and helped him. Now that Scott was naked he seemed much more in control of the situation. Or perhaps Jamie's need had grown greater than Scott's now that Scott's cock was revealed in all its glory.

Together, they managed to unbutton Jamie's shirt and as they pulled it off, Scott kissed Jamie's shoulders where the old scars were as well as his abdomen where the new scars were. Jamie flushed and felt some embarrassment, but mostly overwhelming love and joy at having found someone who accepted him so thoroughly. Jamie's pants were next and Scott made quick work of them, whipping them off in no time. Scott let out a sigh of awe as he stared at Jamie's arousal and Jamie's blush grew deeper. He knew that Scott loved looking at him naked, but he still didn't understand why Scott thought he was beautiful when Scott was the most beautiful man alive. He didn't care too much, though – as long as his boyfriend was happy, he was happy too.

Scott pulled him down until they were embracing on the soft bed, bodies pressed against each other, cocks rubbing up together. Scott grabbed one of the blankets at the foot of the bed and pulled it over them. Jamie was surprised; they had never had sex under a blanket before, instead having sex in the open. But it was cold, he thought, and the blanket trapped their heat. It was also exhilarating feeling the soft cotton of the blanket caressing his skin even as Scott's hands began travelling up and down his back.

Jamie kissed Scott and as their lips met, any remaining cold in the room melted away and was replaced by the heat of their love. Jamie rubbed against Scott, longing to be closer, knowing he wouldn't be satisfied until Scott was inside him but wanting to enjoy every single moment of this experience. Scott's tongue mapped his mouth as Jamie gave himself over to the pleasure of the kiss and clutched Scott tightly, grinding against him to create friction between them. His cock was aching with need and as he rubbed against Scott's, he knew they were both finding satisfaction.

Some nights during the summer this was the furthest they got, grinding against each other until they reached completion, stroking each other off without Scott entering Jamie. But tonight Jamie wanted everything, he wanted to feel that special connection between them that only formed when Scott was fully inside him. It was a type of bonding, just like the bonding he and Marisol had endured, and while neither Jamie nor Scott understood why it happened, both agreed that it meant they were destined to be together. Occasionally Jamie worried that he would feel the same connection with anyone he had sex with, but he always pushed those thoughts out of his mind and he did tonight as well. Tonight was about Scott, and the comfortable bed, and preparing for the school year.

As Scott kissed him and they rubbed against each other, Jamie shut his eyes and smiled. What a change from last year. Last year, Jamie had been a virgin who never would have dreamed about having sex, let alone sex with a man who loved him. He had been firmly in the closet and avoided intimacy and it had taken Scott quite a long time to break through his defenses. They had endured a lot of ups and downs in their relationship, but lying here with his boyfriend in his arms, he knew that it was all worth it. Scott was worth everything.

"Are you ready for more, sweetie?" Scott whispered.

"Yeah," Jamie responded, twisting in Scott's arms so that he was on the bottom and Scott was on top. They were still facing each other, because Jamie liked to face Scott when they made love. They had tried other positions but enjoyed this the best, with Jamie on his back and Scott above him. Jamie brought his knees to his chest to give Scott better access and Scott reached for the nightstand where, sure enough, there was still some lube from before they had left. He poured it liberally on his hands and then touched Jamie.

Jamie gasped. His hands were so cold, but as they started stroking his opening they quickly caught fire and so did he, until he was moaning and ready for Scott to enter him. Scott chuckled and warned Jamie that he needed to prepare him properly to avoid injuring him. Jamie didn't care, he just wanted Scott, but he allowed Scott to continue stroking his opening, gasping again as Scott slid one finger inside him, then another. When he felt he was stretched enough, he tossed his head.

"Please, Scott, now," he said.

Scott seemed lost for words and could only nod. He rubbed himself several times and then positioned himself at Jamie's entrance. There was the usual initial pain, followed by the pleasurable slide of Scott's cock into Jamie's body. Jamie cried out as Scott rubbed against his prostrate and the pleasure swamped his senses. Scott began thrusting immediately, as if he had been holding back for a long time. Jamie eased his body into a rhythm designed to catch each thrust and soon they were rocking together. The bed cushioned him beautifully and he luxuriated in the feeling of softness beneath him rather than the solid ground.

It was so much better being in a bed. The ground had its unique pleasures, but nothing could compare to a bed.

When they made love outside on the ground, Scott had always seemed to hold back for fear of hurting Jamie, but now he wasn't holding back at all and he and Jamie bounced on the bed, the hinges squealing but neither one of them caring. No one was nearby, and no one would care even if they heard. Sex was a welcome part of Tarragon society, especially for the Queen. Jamie cried out again and again, and then Scott shifted and suddenly their minds linked together.

Jamie became Scott and Scott became Jamie, and two became one. He thrust and received as one, penetrated and was penetrated together. They were united and Jamie could feel everything in Scott's mind just as he knew Scott could feel everything in his. Pleasure was the dominant force in both of them, but while usually both of them used this strange telepathy to seek out new ways to increase each other's pleasure, this time Jamie searched Scott's mind for his worries. He wanted to know what problems might arise during the semester that Scott might not tell him about, but all he found was a face and a name: Derek.

Jamie winced and knew that Scott immediately picked up on his pain, though Scott didn't seem to recognize the cause yet. Jamie forced Derek out of his mind and tried to focus on pleasure. It wasn't hard to do with Scott inside of him, but Derek kept haunting him. Scott had made love to Derek, had seduced the boy and taken his virginity. What if Scott was thinking about Derek every time they made love? What if that was why Derek's face was in Scott's mind?

Scott could probably tell that he was losing Jamie's attention because he grunted and thrust hard against Jamie's prostrate. Jamie gasped and was immediately back in sync with Scott as Scott neared his completion. Scott thrust a few more times, then Jamie felt an explosion within him. Scott went limp above him, but the man took Jamie's cock in his hand.

"Let me finish you," he offered.

"No," Jamie said, pulling away.

The connection between them snapped apart as Scott's cock left his body. It was unusual that they didn't cum at least close to each other; normally they had good timing. And it was even more unusual that Jamie didn't want to finish at all, but thoughts of Derek had put a damper on everything and he didn't want to experience pleasure right now. He wanted to think.

"What's wrong?" Scott asked.

Jamie rolled on his side. His cock was still hard, but rapidly losing its rigidity as Jamie's body reacted to its sudden loss of interest in sex.

"I just thought of all the problems we're facing," he said. It wasn't a lie, exactly, but he didn't want to bring up Derek specifically.

Scott spooned him and drew him close against his chest.

"I know, sweetie, but we'll take care of them all. We'll get through this together."

Together, Jamie thought. Would Derek be in that together? Did Scott still have feelings for the boy? Why had Scott been thinking about Derek at all during sex? There were too many questions, and Jamie knew that the hardest part of going back to school might be the fact that Derek was going to be a student, and there would be no escaping him. No matter what he or Scott did, Derek would be in their lives and they would have to deal with him. Jamie didn't know what had gone on between Scott and Derek besides the sex because he had never asked – been too scared to ask – but what if Derek had the power to rip Scott away from his side?

Jamie sighed and snuggled close to his boyfriend. Whatever threat Derek posed, he and Scott would get through it together, as Scott said. Until then, he just had to have confidence that Scott loved him despite his flaws, and that the love they had for each other couldn't be faked. Jamie shut his eyes and tried to mentally steel himself for the first day of classes to follow.

CHAPTER FOUR

First Day

Mike awoke to Ashton's hand caressing his hair and for a moment he luxuriated in the older man's loving embrace. It was so easy at times like this to forget what Ashton had done to him, what Ashton was capable of doing to them all. It was easy to forget that Ashton had broken something inside of him that could never be fixed. He snuggled closer and inhaled the musky scent of Ashton's body, wishing they could be together like this forever: Ashton stroking his hair, him lying beside his lover without a care.

Then Ashton leaned over him and he flinched involuntarily, his mind immediately going back to the night when Ashton had beaten him for something he hadn't done. Ashton made a tutting noise at his movement and kissed his head.

"You know I'm not going to hurt you, don't you, pet?"

"I know," Mike said.

He did know, too. Ashton had made it clear that the beating was a one-time thing, a mistake. Ashton had falsely accused him of something and hadn't bothered to check his facts, and Ashton had promised never to harm him again. He would keep his word, but Mike couldn't help but be afraid of Ashton ever since then. The fear mingled with the hate in his heart for the man and it poisoned moments like these that should have been full of pleasure, but were instead full of fear.

Ashton sighed and patted Mike's head. "It's time to get up. We have a long day ahead of us."

Mike untangled himself from Ashton and sat up. It was the first day of classes and it was his responsibility to oversee the freshmen. This was his second time doing it; last year had gone flawlessly but the council members warned him not to get too cocky. There had been enough near-mishaps last year that he knew even a perfect year would require his full attention, and he worried that he wouldn't be as good a teacher this year because of his relationship with Ashton. Ashton was an all-consuming force in his life and he found himself thinking of Ashton all the time, but he needed to be able to focus on his students. He worried that he wouldn't be able to build a wall between his personal and his public lives, and that the students wouldn't be his top priority. Or rather, that Ashton wouldn't let the students be his top priority.

As Mike dressed, he looked around Ashton's room. He practically lived here now, he spent so much time here. He had a drawer to himself, and a corner of the bathroom. Even when he went back to his apartment, it was usually because he had forgotten something, not to spend any real time. But if he wanted to be a good teacher, he would need time alone to focus on his students. He needed time to grade papers, if nothing else, since he couldn't imagine grading papers with Ashton nearby. The man would be far too alluring; the papers couldn't compete. Ashton would understand, wouldn't he? Mike worried that Ashton would view him requesting time alone as an insult, or a way of pulling away from him, and punish the action the way he had punished Mike before. He did not want to endure that again.

But he would wait until it became an issue. For the first few days, after all, there would be no papers, no assignments, only learning students' names and attempting to be friendly to everyone and get everyone settled in. He had to stay in constant contact with the RAs to make sure the freshmen were settling into their dorms and college life, and also keep in contact with the other teachers to identify potential problems that could be fixed immediately. Exactly one hundred students were accepted into each class, but by the time of the first year exam, only about ninety remained; the others had been sent home or expelled because they weren't adapting properly to life in Tarragon Academy. Mike was the arbitrator of who stayed and who left, and it was a harder job than he had imagined when he first took the job. There were many unpleasant surprises about his job, but there were many rewards as well, and seeing almost all of his students emerge with properly bonded dragons was one of the proudest moments of his life.

Mike said goodbye to Ashton and headed to his office to prepare for his first class of the day. The actual class would be a breeze – they simply went over the syllabus and then played a name game to start learning everyone's names. The name game was partially so that the students in the class could start bonding with each other and forming a strong class mentality, but mostly it was to help Mike remember each of his hundred students. He had met many of them at the prospective student weekends in the spring and he had taken pictures and memorized names with the pictures, but students frequently changed their appearance drastically when entering college and the pictures were of limited usefulness. He grabbed his syllabi from the office and went to his first class.

He was about five minutes early, the perfect time. It was early enough to establish that students were expected and encouraged to show up early, but not so early that it became awkward standing at the front of the room waiting for class to start. Most of the class was already present and he recognized several faces from the prospective student weekends. One face in particular stood out and he had no trouble associating the name with the face: Derek. Ashton's son. Mike couldn't help but feel a little sorry for him, coming into the academy with that kind of renown. He wondered if Ashton even cared for the boy, or even really knew he existed. Ashton was not the fatherly type and while it was almost certain that Ashton had fathered children since he took part in so many mating flights, Ashton had never once mentioned his partners or if they had given birth afterwards.

He mentally ran through the other names and when he was sure that he knew them, he called out the students' names and saw their relief and surprise that he remembered them. Mike smiled welcomingly and continued through roll call to the students he didn't know. A few students came in late, having gotten lost on their way to class, and he welcomed them to the class as he had everyone else. Arriving late on the first day was not an issue, after all, even though arriving late any other day would be. He went over the syllabus and they moved to the name game, attempting to memorize everyone's names. Mike had no problems memorizing everyone's names and the class applauded when he whipped off all of their names without hesitation. It was the first class of the day; this was easy. When he got to the third class of the day, however, he would start having issues.

He dismissed class and most of them wandered away. Derek, however, stayed to talk to him and he tried to look as kind and welcoming as possible. Derek smiled and shook his hand.

"Hi, I'm Derek, as you know, I guess," Derek said. "I just wondered where all the upperclassmen are. I was looking for someone, a senior, but the only people I've seen on campus are freshmen."

Mike nodded. So Derek was looking for Scott already. Jamie wouldn't like that. Scott had been assigned to seduce Derek and the two had somehow become friends, it seemed, despite what Mike imagined was Jamie's disapproval.

"The upperclassmen are on the far side of campus. Their classes are separate from the freshmen, and there is very little mixing between freshmen and upperclassmen. If you're looking for someone, I can pass a message for you."

"No, that's okay," Derek said. "I didn't realize the freshmen would be so isolated."

"It's an odd tradition, I agree," Mike said. Derek didn't know, but it was a necessary tradition. The freshmen were the only people on campus who didn't know about dragons, and it was vital for them to be isolated so that they didn't accidentally find out. One year, a long time ago, a freshmen had accidentally run into a dragon on campus and the shock of the encounter had warped his mind. The boy had killed himself because he was unprepared to handle the truth. Freshmen had to be warned very carefully about the dragons through the first year exam in order to save their lives, and the rest of the time they needed to be protected.

"Thanks, Mr. Ferrin," Derek said, waving as he left the class.

Mike waved back, then gathered his materials and headed to his next class. He had back-to-back classes in the morning, then a break, then another class in the afternoon. It was a pleasant enough schedule. He enjoyed teaching back-to-back and getting things over with, even though he constantly felt like he was saying the same things over and over again – probably because he was. He made the same jokes twice in a row, refining them based on his previous class's response, and repeated the same information, tweaking it if his previous class had seemed bored or unresponsive. Sometimes it was boring and he dreaded going into his second class in a row, but usually it helped him to teach twice. He just wished he had gotten the same classroom and didn't have to hike to another building for his second class.

There was very little crowd as he headed to his next class. He hadn't been exaggerating when he said that the freshmen were isolated; the only people wandering around this area of campus were freshmen, and there were only a hundred of them so the campus seemed almost empty. In the spring, upperclassmen would share these buildings with the freshmen and the campus would come alive, but fall semester was always a little unusual. Upper campus, where the rest of the college lay, was packed with people, though since there were only about three hundred students there it still wasn't the type of bustle most people thought of when they pictured a college campus. Tarragon Academy was extraordinarily small, and extraordinarily hard to get into.

Mike often thought of the families around the world who belonged to the Tarragon society, each of whom assumed that their children would go to Tarragon Academy and be paired with a dragon. Yet many of those children didn't get in, and had to try year after year until they were finally granted admittance or until they perished due to the Tarragon curse, whichever came first. Parents were deeply resentful of people like Jamie, whose parents weren't graduates yet who was admitted on his first try. The fact that he had partnered with a Queen made some people even angrier, as they believed that their child, who had been denied entrance, could have done the same if given a chance. Mike knew that Jamie was raising an army, but he wondered if Jamie knew the resentments his presence caused in the hearts of certain people. Ashton would find some staunch supporters, even though Ashton was the one who denied their children access in the first place.

It wasn't that there weren't enough dragon eggs. Back in the days where there were multiple Queens, numerous hatching grounds had been built and it was estimated that there were thousands of unhatched eggs, if not tens of thousands. Ashton liked to limit admission because it gave him power over the society. He could choose the families that pleased him best and incite the others to strive to serve him better. Mike wondered if Jamie would open admission to the college if he had his way and got rid of Ashton. If he did, he would gain a lot of supporters, even the people who resented his admission. But would he even know that this was an issue? He was so new to Tarragon society, and Scott was too, neither of them really understood the issues facing most people and it was a weakness in their recruitment efforts. Mike longed to help them and he longed to get rid of Ashton, but Ashton held his leash and there was nothing he could do about it. As much as he hated and feared Ashton, he was Ashton's pet. If he tried to leave, Ashton would only find someone else.

Mike took a deep breath and shook the thoughts from his mind. He entered his next classroom with a smile fixed on his face and looked at the hopeful faces before him. They were always so hopeful on the first day, and so fearful. He hoped that his easy manner and kind nature lessened the fear, because he wanted his classes to be safe environments for learning. He glanced at his watch. Five minutes early again. Perfect.

CHAPTER FIVE

Upper Campus

Derek trudged through the muddy path towards the upper campus where he could just make out a bustle of people that looked like students from the backpacks slung over their shoulders. What a weird tradition, he thought, keeping the upperclassmen away from the freshmen. But he was determined to see Scott on the first day, and he didn't have another class for three hours, so what else did he have to do? As he walked, it began to lightly sprinkle – not enough to call rain, just a thick mist that enveloped him in moisture. It became almost difficult to see where he was going, but he kept heading forward, not letting the mist confuse his feet.

The mist cleared after several minutes and he was at the edge of a walking path leading to the campus buildings. Several students were also on the path and they stared at him strangely, as if they knew he didn't belong. Well, the campus only had four hundred students total, so they probably did know he didn't belong. He realized that he had no way of knowing where Scott was.

Derek ran up to one of the students.

"Excuse me," he said.

The student turned to him, looking at him like one looks at a viper.

"You're not supposed to be here," the student said.

"I'm looking for someone named Scott," he said, ignoring the rude comment. He'd gotten worse comments, and worse glares. At Scott's name, the students exchanged looks and the venomous glares stopped.

"Oh," the student said. "He's in chemistry right now. Flowers Hall, to your right. He doesn't get out for an hour, though, and you shouldn't hang around here."

"Thanks," Derek said, glancing to his right and seeing the sign for Flowers Hall.

The students wandered off. Even though they had warned Derek against staying, he decided to sit and read for the next hour while he waited. After all, that's all he would do if he returned to his dorm. Why not read here? He found a bench near Flowers Hall and sat down, getting out his book for Mr. Ferrin's class. He had been surprised that not everyone had the book yet, even though they were supposed to have all their books on the first day of class. Some students had ordered their books online, and some students didn't even know that books were required, or at least that's what they said. Derek found it hard to believe that someone could honestly believe there would be a college class without books. The first chapter was due on Wednesday, in two days, so he might as well get a start on it.

He was deep into the book when he heard a commotion and reluctantly tore himself away. At the other end of the knoll where he sat, several students were ganging up against someone. He stood up and dropped his book into his bag. He had been beaten up enough to know how important it was to have someone stand up for you, and now it was finally his chance to stand up for someone else. He drew closer slowly, though, to size up his competition. They were upperclassmen, after all, and likely to be larger and stronger than him. He didn't want to get beat up on his first day.

"Come on," one of the boys was saying as he grabbed the victim and pulled him close in a clearly sexual manner. "We all saw you, we know what you want."

"Leave me alone," the victim said, struggling to fight.

The victim was a boy much younger than the other boys, pretty close to Derek's age if he had to guess. He had beautiful auburn hair and a slim build and it was no wonder the older boys were hitting on him, but grabbing him in public like this was going too far. Derek approached and shoved one of the boys out of his way.

"What's going on?" he asked, hoping to draw their attention away from the victim so he could run away.

The boys turned to him with predatory looks in their eyes and Derek gulped. He glanced around. Where were all the teachers?

"Well, look here," the largest boy said, the one currently holding the victim. "A freshman wandered into our territory. You lost, freshman?"

"I'm waiting for someone. What are you doing?"

The boy smiled. "None of your business."

One of the other boys grabbed his arm and slid his arm around Derek's waist before he could react.

"Why don't we go somewhere more private, freshman?" the boy asked, pulling Derek away. Derek tried to step on his toes or knee him or slam his elbow into his face, but the boy was incredibly fast and blocked all of his movements. The boy laughed at his attempts to free himself.

"I'll make you forget whoever you're waiting for," the boy murmured, sliding his hand under Derek's waistband as Derek yelped in fear and surprise. The boy's hand rubbed against his bare ass as his hot breath steamed against his ear. Derek tried to struggle but everything he did brought him closer to the boy and further inside his control. He stopped fighting and the boy laughed.

"You see how this is going to go, don't you? Just relax."

The boy's hand slid between his cheeks and found his opening and Derek jumped, trying again to get away from him. But the boy stroked him, ignoring his struggles and his cries for help. The other boys surrounded them so no one outside could see what was going on. There must not have been anyone nearby to hear his cries, because no one came as the boy caressed his opening.

He could just make out the other victim getting similarly manhandled by the other boy, one hand up his shirt and the other down his pants as other boys held him in place. He didn't cry for help, though; he was trying to bite his attackers.

Derek thought of his first time with Scott and how gentle and loving it had been, compared to the fear and hatred he felt now as the boy circled his opened as if preparing to enter him with his finger. Derek tried to pull away and the boy laughed.

"You're not a virgin, are you?"

Derek blushed and struggled harder. His sexual history was none of their business but he felt exposed, revealed, and utterly helpless. He fought as hard as he could but other boys were holding his arms and legs now, and his pants were being undone. He was going to get raped in the center of the knoll, in front of the whole school, and no one was rescuing him. He screamed as loud as he could before one of the boys struck him in the head and everything went sideways for a few minutes. He was unable to talk or scream, unable to do anything because of the pain.

"You hit him too hard," one of the boys said. The noise was like a whip against his psyche.

"He's fine, keep going," the boy who had hit him said.

They must have decided he was fine, because soon the hands were back on his body and he winced as they returned to his opening with increased purpose.

A dark shadow fell across them and he flinched, expecting it to be the boy, ready to rape him.

"Stop right now," a deep voice said. Instantly the boys stiffened and Derek was released. Derek wobbled on his feet as he pulled up his pants and looked at the man who had stopped them. His heart soared. It was his father, Ashton.

The boys began making excuses and backing away, and Ashton let them. He checked the other victim first, then came to Derek and grasped his chin.

"Are you alright, Derek?"

"Yes, father," Derek said, trying to sound brave, as if he hadn't just been terrified.

Ashton nodded and turned to the other victim.

"Jamie, I'm going to have to insist that you have a guard with you at all times, for your own protection."

Jamie, Derek thought. The boy's name was Jamie. It rang a bell but he couldn't remember where he had heard it before. Jamie was staring at Derek with sheer disdain, Derek realized with a start. Did Jamie not realize that Derek had tried to help him? Sure, it hadn't turned out well, but Derek had at least tried to put an end to the bullying. And would Ashton had appeared if his son hadn't been the one getting bullied?

"I don't need a guard at all times," Jamie said, his attention still on Derek. "Maybe just between classes."

"As you wish," Ashton said, and Derek wondered if Jamie could tell that Ashton was only humoring him. Who was Jamie, though, that he required guards?

Suddenly the name snapped into place. Scott had mentioned the name, the name of his boyfriend. Jamie was Scott's boyfriend. And Jamie undoubtedly knew who Derek was, and the relationship between Scott and Derek, or else he wouldn't be glaring daggers at him. Derek reexamined the boy, seeking some reassurance that Scott would choose Derek over this boy.

Jamie was beautiful, there was no denying it. He had a certain androgynous beauty about him that was irresistible. He was slim, but Derek suspected he had enough muscle to look good with his shirt off. He glowed with a rich tan, and his auburn hair hung loosely over his forehead. His green eyes sparkled with jealousy and Derek knew he was being examined as well, and he hoped he stood up to the examination. Derek knew he was beautiful as well, people always told him that, and he knew he resembled Ashton, since people told him that too. He glanced at Ashton and was pleased by how handsome and strong Ashton looked. If Derek looked anything like that man, then he had a major step up on Jamie. But what would Scott prefer? That was the real question.

"Derek," Ashton said. "What are you doing in this part of campus?"

"I was looking for someone," Derek said, gesturing at his bookbag on the bench nearby. "I thought I'd get some homework done but I saw Jamie being bullied and decided to help."

Yes, he thought, remind Jamie that he had tried to help. He needed every advantage he could get.

"And this someone would be Scott, I assume?" Ashton said.

Derek nodded, and Jamie flushed a deep red, his eyes narrowing. Ashton just shrugged.

"I will let Scott know that you asked after him, but you do not belong on this part of campus. I have to insist that you return to the other freshmen now."

Jamie smiled as if he had scored a victory.

"Scott will come and visit you later today," Ashton continued. Jamie's smile slipped. "I'll make sure of it."

Jamie stared at Ashton in shock, as if he wanted to protest but couldn't. Derek grinned. He had what he wanted. Ashton approved of him and Scott together and with Ashton on his side, it seemed likely to happen. He felt a passing remorse for Jamie, especially when he thought of what Jamie had just been through, getting attacked by upperclassmen, but thoughts of Scott wiped that remorse away. He was going to get what he wanted, finally, after a lifetime of regret and want, and his father was going to help him.

CHAPTER SIX

Unexpected Kindness

J amie shivered as Derek left the upper campus. He was in a state of shock from everything that had happened. First, the jocks who had terrorized him during his freshman year had cornered him on the knoll and grabbed him, feeling him up like they had every right in the world to do so. They were all in his class, but they were several years older than him and, being on the football team, were considerably larger and stronger. There used to be six in the gang, before the first year exam, but one of them hadn't been able to bond with his dragon properly and had died during the exam. Now there were only five, and they seemed especially angry as they cornered Jamie. Jamie had tried to fight, but it had gotten him nowhere except grabbed like a kitten by the back of his shirt while the ringleader stuck his hand down his shirt and inside his pants.

Jamie tried to forget the feel of the man's hand sliding against his skin, sliding against his ass towards his opening. It was horrifying. Only Scott was allowed to touch him like that, but Scott was in class and no matter how terrified Jamie was, he wasn't going to interrupt Scott's first day. Jamie needed to learn to stand up for himself. When Derek had first tried to interrupt the jocks, Jamie had been relieved, if a little worried that his savior would end up getting the same treatment, which was exactly what had happened. And when Jamie recognized the face of his savior as the face from Scott's mind last night, the face labeled Derek, then Jamie had felt only a slightly vicious satisfaction that Derek was getting bullied as well. He had instantly been ashamed of that thought, but he couldn't help it. He despised Derek and if Jamie was going to get abused, Derek might as well get abused too.

And then, out of nowhere, Ashton had appeared and stopped the whole chaotic scene. The jocks had fled, Derek had been sent back to the freshmen campus, and now Ashton and Jamie were alone together. Normally that would have been a frightening prospect, but all Jamie felt right now was relief that the ordeal had ended and gratitude that Ashton had saved him. He was angry that Ashton had promised Derek he would send Scott to see him, but it was a small price to pay for getting rescued from being raped in the middle of the knoll.

Jamie shivered again, and Ashton unclasped his cloak and wrapped it around Jamie's shoulders. Jamie wondered at the generous gesture, but then again, Ashton was often kind. In fact, Jamie had been convinced that Ashton was a kind person until fairly recently when he finally discovered Ashton's true nature. So it wasn't out of character for Ashton to display such a thoughtful gesture.

"Are you sure you're alright?" Ashton asked, rubbing Jamie's back. Normally the touch would have creeped him out, but now it felt comforting, not like a come on at all.

"I guess I'm okay. Why did they do it? Am I going to get attacked like that everywhere I go?"

He remembered what the jocks had said about seeing him during the mating flight. Everyone with a dragon had seen him naked and desperate to be touched and it shamed him to his core. Everyone he had met had held some residual lust for him, including all of the representatives Scott had been bringing. Most were quite capable of tuning it out, since he hadn't mated with them, but a few still seemed to hold out hope that they could be his mates.

"There was a mating flight this morning, and all of them lost," Ashton explained. "They must have been looking for a replacement and you just wandered by."

Jamie hugged the cloak closer. The females in his class were starting to have their mating flights and the men who were bonded with male dragons had been acting differently. The second year was nearly as challenging as the first, according to the teachers, because they had to learn how to live in Tarragon society. Mike was in charge of the first year, but another man, Thomas, was in charge of the second year and Jamie didn't like him. He was on the council, for one, and Jamie instinctively distrusted anyone on the council. He also seemed to be one of the people who found it hard to let go of his lust for Jamie. According to Marisol, Thomas had been one of the approved pairs to mate with her during their mating flight, so Thomas had every right to expect to be in the running for the next mating flight, but Jamie knew that the only person who would ever fly with Marisol would be Narné, Scott's dragon. He wouldn't allow anyone else.

The sophomores on the men's campus were especially having a hard time getting used to the mating flights, which could happen at any time. A female dragon would send out a signal to nearby males, and they would begin flying above the mountain in a chase that ended with the winner mating with the female and the other dragons unsatisfied. Most other dragons simply went to the hot springs to soak their lust away, but their human partners had no easy solution and it was a fairly regular occasion to see fights breaking out after a mating fight as the aggression and testosterone worked its way out of the men. But Jamie had never been attacked before, and certainly he had never heard of anyone trying to rape another man before. But it did make sense: the jocks were full of lust, and still had lust for Jamie thanks to his mating flight, so when they saw him, they saw their chance to act out their fantasies. He grabbed the cloak as tight as he could and was grateful that Ashton had suggested a guard. He didn't want someone following him all the time, but perhaps the campus wasn't as safe a place as he had thought.

"Is this going to happen a lot?" Jamie asked.

"No," Ashton said. "I'll make sure of it. I noticed these boys were causing trouble earlier today and I've been keeping tabs on them, though apparently I wasn't watching closely enough. But I will make sure that you are protected from any males after the mating flights. This will not happen again."

"What's going to happen to the guys who attacked me?"

"Arion is dealing with their dragons. I've found it's more effective to deal with the dragons than the humans."

A vision of Arion biting through another dragon's throat filled Jamie's mind and he shuddered.

"What is he doing to them?"

"Talking, mostly," Ashton said, glancing down at Jamie as if he knew what Jamie was worried about. "Arion would never harm another dragon. No dragon would."

Jamie felt the jagged edge of a lie in Ashton's voice as he spoke, but he didn't pursue it. His ability to tell the truth was growing stronger, but he hadn't shared that ability with anyone yet. And in this case, he didn't want to know the answer and find out that Arion had harmed other dragons. He would rather believe the lie. Although, he thought to himself, Arion had already harmed Marisol by feeding her drugged food, so Ashton knew this was a lie and was lying straight to Jamie's face. Yet he seemed sincere. Perhaps he really had thought he was helping Marisol by feeding her the drug, as he insisted. Jamie shook his head. No. Ashton was pure evil, and he couldn't be trusted no matter how pleasant and sincere his surface was. Jamie had already learned that lesson the hard way, and he wouldn't learn it again.

"So now I have to have a guard everywhere?" Jamie asked.

"Only if you like," Ashton said. "It's for your protection."

"Who will it be? It can't be my representative; Eric teaches. And Mike teaches too."

Those were the only two people Jamie really felt comfortable around aside from Scott, and he was wary to let someone new into his circle. But he recognized that he did probably need protection, and it couldn't be one of them.

"There's a graduate living in dragon canyon that I believe might be willing," Ashton said. "He's a bit, well, unruly, but I believe he might be up to the task. His name is Alan. You two can meet, and then decide if you want him or not."

Jamie pondered for a moment. Ashton was suggesting the man, which was a mark against him, but Ashton thought he was unruly, which was in his favor. He would have to meet the man to size him up, and he would have to read his dragon's mind to see whether or not the man served Ashton.

"That might work," Jamie said hesitantly. "Maybe we can meet later tonight, after my classes."

"I'll set it up," Ashton said. "Now, then, what are you doing on this part of campus? You don't have class for several hours."

"It's not really your business, but I was going to wait for Scott to get out of his class and have lunch with him."

"I see," Ashton said with a smile that almost looked genuine. "That sounds romantic. Well, I'll leave you to it. Watch your back, and if someone does attack you, don't hesitate to have Marisol summon Arion. I know you can talk to all the dragons and just because Marisol can't come to your rescue doesn't mean another dragon can't."

Jamie flushed. He hadn't even thought to call for a dragon to save him. He had considered summoning Scott, true, but he had never thought that just summoning Narné would be enough. However, if he had summoned Narné then Derek would have seen it, and Derek's memories would have to be erased. As much as Jamie hated the boy, he didn't want to be responsible for erasing the boy's memories. Jamie loosened his death grip on the cloak and handed it back to Ashton.

"Thank you, Ashton," he said sincerely. Although he hated Ashton, the man had truly done him a favor and he had been kind on top of it.

"You're welcome, my Queen," Ashton said, taking Jamie's hand and kissing it.

Jamie blushed, but the gesture wasn't sexual in any way as it sometimes was when people did it to him. Instead, it seemed a sincere sign of respect, something he hadn't expected from Ashton. Ashton wrapped the cloak back around his own shoulders and headed toward dragon canyon. Jamie went to the bench where Derek had been sitting and his smile slipped. Derek was still a problem. Ashton had promised that Scott would see Derek today, and Jamie needed to make sure there weren't any lingering feelings between the two. Obviously Derek still had feelings for Scott, but did Scott have feelings for Derek? Jamie didn't know. He knew that he came first in Scott's heart, but he wanted to be the first and only, not the first of many.

Scott's class was released early and Jamie sprang up from the bench the moment people started streaming out of the building. Sure enough, Scott's dark head appeared and Jamie pushed through the crowd to reach him and envelop him in a hug. Scott seemed surprised to see him, but hugged him back with abandon. The other kids in the class stared, some with jealousy, and Jamie knew they were still thinking of him as he had been the night of the mating flight. He wished he could go back and undo the vision, but by sending out that vision, he had sent the mating flight into such confusion and chaos that Scott and Narné were able to slip in and win the flight. Without that vision, Scott would not be at his side today. It was humiliating having the entire campus know what he looked like naked and in need, but it was worth it to have Scott.

"Is something wrong?" Scott asked, and for a second Jamie wondered if he was out of order somehow after the wrestling the jocks had given him. But no, he had fixed his hair and straightened his shirt and he knew he looked impeccable. Scott was just asking because Jamie had never met him after class before, but Jamie intended it to be a daily thing.

"I thought we could have lunch together before class."

Scott smiled. "That sounds great. Where do you want to go? Cafeteria or dragon canyon?"

"Cafeteria is fine," Jamie said. Only students were allowed in the cafeteria, so there would be fewer people and less people meant less staring at him. He hadn't expected that coming back to campus would put him at the center of attention so much, and he didn't like it at all. Tarragon Academy felt like a trap: everyone was constantly watching everything that he said and did, and there was no freedom at all. He was just grateful that the German representative had gotten rid of the listening devices. It would be a few days before the council replaced them, and now Scott and Jamie knew where in the room to look.

Scott and Jamie flashed their student IDs and entered the cafeteria. Jamie automatically started to head towards the room reserved for freshmen, but Scott grabbed his arm and steered him to the upperclassmen room. Jamie smiled weakly in thanks. Who knew what might have happened, especially if Derek were in there? He had already faced Derek once today and didn't have it in him to face him again. It would be hard enough knowing that Scott was going to see Derek later in the day; they didn't need to see him at lunch as well. They sat down and Scott began telling Jamie about his classes, and Jamie smiled and nodded, listening to his beautiful boyfriend and trying to ignore the stares.

He had already decided not to tell Scott about the attack earlier because it would only upset his boyfriend. He would explain the guard by saying that he wanted protection in case anything happened, not because something had already happened. Scott didn't seem to notice anything out of the ordinary, and Jamie was relieved. He hated keeping secrets from Scott but he didn't want Scott to worry, not when he was already taking steps to make sure it would never happen again. But as Scott talked and held his hand, Jamie couldn't help but feel the jock's hands sliding along his body and he shivered. Though he might never tell Scott, he knew it was scarred into his memory forever.

CHAPTER SEVEN

More Than Friends

Scott kissed Jamie goodbye and headed towards the freshmen dorms. Arion had instructed him to go see Derek as soon as possible and Jamie had reluctantly agreed. He was going to have to straighten out this relationship with Derek, because he could tell it was putting a strain on Jamie. He wanted to reassure Jamie that there was nothing between him and Derek, that Jamie would always come first, but Jamie didn't seem to believe him. And maybe for good reason, Scott thought. After all, he felt friendship for the boy, and he wanted to have some sort of relationship with him. And if Derek did partner with a Queen dragon as Narné had predicted, then Derek needed to be on their side, not Ashton's side, and only friendship would get him there.

But nothing more than friendship, no matter what Derek wanted. Scott wasn't prepared to cheat on Jamie and he wasn't interested in extending the sexual nature of their relationship any further. He remembered their first time together and how gentle it had been, but he also remembered the next morning when Derek had pinned him and sucked him off, giving him no chance to fight or refuse. Derek had been ruthless, just like his father, and Scott knew he would do anything to get Scott back, even if it meant fighting dirty. Scott just needed to be prepared for any of his tactics.

He arrived at the freshmen dorms and went to the second floor where Derek was roomed. He knocked, and the door opened immediately. Derek must have been waiting for him. Derek was on the other side of the door with a wide smile and he pulled Scott into a hug before Scott could react, but it was a friendly hug so Scott allowed it. The boy looked good, he thought. He was wearing a deep green shirt and jeans, and his hair fell in loose curls around his eyes as he brushed it back with one hand and gestured Scott inside with the other.

The room was well-furnished and Scott was willing to bet most of it was Derek's, not his roommate's, because it all matched and it fit Derek's personality. Strong lines, bold, modern furniture, and a complex interplay of light and dark colors. Occasionally there was a piece with a more traditional bend, and Scott suspected that it was his roommate's influence. Derek had come prepared and Scott wondered if Ashton had purchased any of the furniture for his son. Probably not; he couldn't imagine Ashton giving Derek any special treatment. Even at the prospective student weekend he had barely seemed to notice Derek except as a weapon to use against Scott.

"What a beautiful room," he said. In reality it was a suite of rooms nearly as big as the apartments the freshmen would move into for the spring semester. The large dorms were supposedly a selling point for the campus, although the academy didn't need any selling points since getting in and bonding with a dragon was the only way to survive past young adulthood in the Tarragon society.

Derek smiled and gave him a brief tour of the bedrooms before they returned to the main room. Derek sat on the couch and gestured for Scott to join him. Scott carefully sat at the opposite end of the couch, with a large cushion between them.

"Where's your roommate?"

"He's at a friend's dorm. I asked him to leave for the night."

"You don't want to alienate your roommate so quickly," Scott warned.

"We already don't get along," Derek admitted. "I know him

from high school. He was pretty upset to find out that I was his roommate. We've already requested a change."

Scott nodded. Normally they roomed people from the same high school together because they were friends, but whoever was in charge of roommate assignments had screwed up this one. It was fairly rare that mistakes like this were made, but it happened. It was unlikely that another room would want to switch, so Derek would likely end up in the dorm by himself and his roommate would get another separate dorm. It would be lonely going through the first semester alone, but better than having a roommate you hated.

"How was your first day?"

Derek flushed and hung his head. "I suppose Jamie told you, didn't he?"

"Told me what?"

"About those upperclassmen in the knoll."

Scott racked his mind, but Jamie hadn't said anything about the knoll. He had been waiting in the knoll for Scott at lunch, but hadn't mentioned that something had happened.

"No, he didn't say anything. Did something happen? Were you on the upper campus?"

"Yeah," Derek said. "I went to see you. Only I saw some upper-classmen ganging up on someone instead. I tried to stop them, but they grabbed me and tried to- tried to touch me."

His lips twisted back in a grimace and Scott reached out to take his hand. He was shocked that something like that had happened on campus, especially to a freshman on the first day of school.

"Ashton came and scared them away, though. He was looking out for me," Derek said. "He made sure me and Jamie were all right, then sent me back to the lower campus."

"Wait, Jamie? Jamie was the other boy getting attacked?"

Scott's mind spun. Jamie had been especially quiet today, but

Scott had chalked it up to the stress of the first day of school and the request to see Derek. Had he actually encountered Derek earlier in the day and, much worse, been attacked by his classmates?

"Yeah," Derek said with a shiver. "Luckily Ashton stopped it before anything happened. They were so- They asked if I was a virgin and I was scared they were going to do something to me, right there in the middle of the knoll."

Scott's lips tightened. If they thought Derek was a virgin, then their actions would be somewhat excusable in the eyes of the council. Rape wasn't as big a crime if it led to a student being prepared for the first year exam, after all. It was one of the reasons Scott hated the council and was fighting against Ashton. But surely Ashton wouldn't let anyone rape his own son, especially when Derek wasn't actually a virgin. There would be severe consequences for those upperclassmen and Scott shuddered to think what would happen to them for threatening not only Ashton's son but the Queen as well.

Scott was still holding Derek's hand and he squeezed it.

"Are you all right? That must have been terrifying."

Scott remembered his own encounter with Mike, when he had been taken in the hallway. He had refused at first, but at some point his resistance had faded and he had said yes to Mike. He knew that Mike didn't consider it rape because he had said yes, but Scott considered it rape because he had said no so many times before saying yes. It felt like rape, and according to everything he knew and read, it was rape. And the council had done nothing. It had happened at their request, even, right in the middle of the school with teachers all around, none of them caring what happened to him. And something similar had almost happened to Derek. Raped in the middle of the knoll. It was unthinkable.

"I guess I'm okay," Derek said slowly. "I can't stop thinking about what almost happened. I kept screaming, but no one answered. No one looked. No one came to help until Ashton did."

Scott winced. Derek had done everything right, but the students and teachers at Tarragon Academy were trained to ignore such signals. Screams could be from animals being eaten by dragons, after all, or they could be from a sanctioned sex act or a mating flight. Dragons sometimes screamed for no purpose at all and students had to get used to it. It was no wonder no one had responded, but Derek couldn't know any of that. All he knew was that he had called for help and no one had responded.

"I'm sorry, Derek," he said, realizing that he had been in one of the nearby buildings and had probably heard the screams but dismissed them without thinking, the same way everyone else did. "Upper campus isn't a good place for freshmen. If you want to see me, send a message and I'll come visit you."

"You promise?" he asked, eyes lighting up.

"Well, if I can make it," Scott amended, already seeing the flaw in his offer. He couldn't have Derek asking for him every day, or even every other day. They needed some distance so Jamie wouldn't grow jealous even though there was nothing between them. Although Scott had to admit that part of his anger at the thought of the upperclassmen touching Derek was jealousy that someone else was touching what belonged to him. Scott was the first person to be with Derek, and he felt like he should get some say in who else touched the boy.

He wondered why Jamie hadn't said anything about the attack and decided that Jamie hadn't wanted to worry him, but it still didn't explain everything. He trusted Jamie with everything and he didn't like the idea of Jamie keeping secrets from him, especially big secrets like this. Jamie had been sexually assaulted in public, after all. That was a major ordeal in his life, and Scott wanted him to feel comfortable telling him about it. He didn't want there to be awkwardness or secrets between them. Derek was able to tell him about it, so why couldn't Jamie?

"How did the rest of your day go?" Scott asked awkwardly, not knowing how else to change the conversation.

Derek took Scott's hand in both of his and smiled. "Great. I like my teachers and my schedule. The history class Mr. Ferrin teaches seems really interesting."

"It is," Scott said. "That's the required class, right? I've heard Mr. Ferrin is a great teacher."

It felt strange to call Mike Mr. Ferrin, and even stranger to compliment him, but all of the freshmen had been in agreement that he was great. And he had successfully led the freshmen through their first year with a minimal number of casualties, a feat that would hopefully repeat itself this year. Scott longed for a time when there would be no casualties and wondered if having recently laid eggs would make the difference. Most of the problems with the hatching came because the eggs had lain still for so long and the dragons inside became aggressive and attacked the person who freed them without thinking. The new eggs, Marisol's eggs, would be fresh, and the dragons inside wouldn't be aggressive. No one really knew how they would react. Mike would prepare the students for a fight, but everyone was hoping that the dragons would be more docile and willing to talk with their partners before attacking them.

Derek and Scott chatted about Derek's classes for a while longer, with Scott giving advice on Derek's other classes and teachers. Whenever Derek asked about Scott's classes, he gave vague, generic answers and switched the subject. All of his classes involved dragons and Tarragon society and weren't suitable conversation for a freshman. While most seniors took classes in the areas that they wanted to work in, Scott was required to take additional classes in dragon care, dragon breeding, and Tarragon society as part of his role as the Queen's mate. On the one hand he was flattered, because it showed that Ashton was accepting him in the position, but on the other hand it was severely limiting his options once he left the academy. The other students were receiving top of the line education in business, science, planning, writing, and all sorts of other fields that would lead directly to grad school or jobs; he was being groomed to stay at the academy the rest of his life. If he ever stopped being Marisol's mate, he would have nothing to fall back on. But he wouldn't stop being her mate. He would be the only one to fly with her. He was committed.

They chatted for over an hour before Scott looked at his watch and realized it was past time to go. He had only meant to stay for twenty minutes or so, enough time to say hi but not enough time to make Jamie jealous. Jamie might be jealous of an hour, but he would be able to tell that nothing happened between them other than conversation. As Scott stood to leave, Derek seemed to hesitate. Scott turned towards him just as Derek took his shoulders and leaned in for a kiss. Their lips locked and Scott gasped in surprise. Derek's tongue slid into his open mouth and tried to dance with his tongue but even though it felt incredible, he resisted the urge to kiss back. Derek's eyes were closed and there was an expression of bliss on his face that reminded Scott of Jamie. Scott pulled away and the bliss turned to hurt.

"I'm sorry, Derek," Scott said. "I just can't have this type of relationship with you. I have a boyfriend."

"I know," Derek said, keeping his hands on Scott's shoulders. "I'm sorry. You just looked so beautiful. I hope you'll come and see me again."

Scott took a deep breath. "Derek, if you think something is going to happen between us, then I don't think it's wise for me to come back."

Derek nodded. "I'm sorry," he repeated. "It won't happen again, I promise. But I do want to see you again. Friends?"

"Friends," Scott said, and something loosened in his heart. He was glad to be able to call Derek a friend and not have to worry about seduction or sex. Now he just needed to explain the situation to Jamie and hope that Jamie understood.

CHAPTER EIGHT

Bodyguard

J amie was a little skeptical when Scott arrived home and explained that he and Derek had agreed to be just friends, but he had other, more pressing worries. The man that Ashton had recommended as his guard, Alan, was coming over to meet him and he wasn't sure whether he should greet the man as a potential friend or foe.

"You're sure Marisol can't give you more information?" Scott asked, reclining on the couch with his feet up on the ottoman as Jamie paced back and forth.

"There's something odd with him and his dragon. Marisol can't read him the same way she can read everyone else. He's like that other dragon, you remember the one who was sent to guard me last year? The one who could make his human almost completely invisible to the senses unless he wanted to be seen?"

Scott's lips twisted and Jamie knew he remembered. The man had been stationed outside Jamie's room after they had had a fight, and he had prevented Scott from coming and apologizing. Jamie had assumed that Scott didn't want a relationship anymore because Scott wasn't coming to see him, but in reality there had been a guard posted outside his door that Jamie wasn't even aware of. Alan and his dragon were different, but similar in their abilities. Jamie could pinpoint their location but he couldn't read the dragon's mind. It was like the dragon's mind was buried in mist, and Jamie wondered if that mist operated like the rest of the mist at Tarragon Academy and could be penetrated under the right circumstances. After all, even though the mist served to protect the mountain, it also tended to guide people along its paths as though it had a mind of its own.

But Jamie would reserve judgment until he actually met Alan, which should be any minute. He paced some more and envied Scott's calm. Scott had handled his confrontation for the day; Jamie's was still coming up. He noticed that Scott looked on edge about something and wondered if Derek had told Scott about the assault they had endured. Probably, and now Scott thought Jamie was hiding it from him when in reality Jamie had just wanted to wait until after Scott and Derek dealt with their relationship to tell Scott. Oh well, he thought. Scott had kept secrets from him, and as soon as Scott had returned, Jamie had told him the truth about his day and explained why they were meeting Alan.

A knock at the door, and Jamie opened it. The man on the other side was older than Jamie expected, perhaps in his forties, though he had the ageless look Jamie was starting to associate with everyone in Tarragon Academy. He had auburn hair like Jamie and a small nose, but large brown eyes that dominated his face. His skin was tan, but it was clear that he spent most of the year pale as there was an edge of red around the tan and looked as though the tan were new; perhaps he had just returned from a vacation somewhere tropical. He stretched out a hand and Jamie was impressed by the gentle strength in the handshake. Alan looked slightly shaken to see Jamie, and stared at him a great deal more than Jamie felt comfortable with, but he knew everyone who met him had to balance his reality against the image in their heads from the mating flight so he tried not to be offended.

"You look just like your mother," Alan said.

Jamie's heart stuttered. "What?"

"Your mother," Alan repeated. "You have her eyes, and her hair."

Jamie numbly pulled his hand back and stepped backwards into the room. People who knew his mother often said he looked like her, but no one at the academy ought to know her, especially not this stranger. Scott came up behind him and placed a hand possessively on the small of his back as if to give him some sort of stability.

"My name is Scott," he said, shaking the man's hand. "The Queen's mate. I don't believe we've met."

"My apologies," the man said. "My name is Alan. Ashton thought I would be a good guard for Jamie."

"How do you know Jamie's mother?"

"Perhaps I could come in?" he asked, gesturing to the hallway in which he still stood.

Jamie snapped out of his shock and invited Alan inside, seating him on the couch and getting him a drink. Jamie and Scott settled together on the loveseat opposite him with drinks of their own. For the first time in a while, Jamie wished his drink were alcoholic, but not only was he underage, no one wanted his drinking to affect Marisol in her hatching so he was doubly forbidden from alcohol. Alcohol had also been involved in his mother's death, and he had never really been interested in experimenting with it. Alan took a sip of his drink and sighed before returning to Scott's question.

"I was a friend of Miranda from childhood. She lived in Tarragon society with us, though her parents weren't members and died young as a result. But she was raised with us, and when we went off to the academy she moved to Portland to be closer to us. We didn't know at the time the secrets of the academy, or how separate from her we would end up being. But she loved it here in Portland. She met her husband, had a child, and seemed to be happy before she died."

"Did she have a dragon?" Jamie asked, remembering the deformed creature from his dreams.

"Of course not," Alan said, but he said it so quickly Jamie

could almost hear the lie even though he couldn't feel the lie with his gift. "She didn't attend the academy and only those in the academy are granted access to the eggs."

"What about my dad?"

Alan was silent for a moment, his hands clenched into fists. "Your... father was a good man. He treated you and your mother well. I just wish I could have done more for you after they died."

"Why would you do anything?"

Alan looked up at him and for a second Jamie caught a glimpse of himself in those eyes.

"I was her friend, Jamie, and I should have protected you as she would have protected my kids if anything happened to me."

"You have kids?"

"Yes, two. One of them was granted admittance to this academy. The other one died because he wasn't allowed to come here. I was so relieved to hear that you had been accepted, and even more when I heard you had survived the first year exam. But I never would have imagined you would partner with a Queen dragon. It's rare that someone with a parent who isn't a member of Tarragon society partners with a dragon from an older nesting ground."

"So you're saying my father isn't from Tarragon society? He's just an ordinary person?"

"Yes. But your mother loved him, and since she knew nothing about the truth of Tarragon society there were no rules broken when she married him."

"Wait, there are rules about marrying someone who isn't in Tarragon society?"

"Yes," Alan said. "Once you know about dragons, you can only marry someone who also knows about dragons. Occasionally exceptions are made, but only rarely and usually only if the people are relatives of council members."

"What happens to the others, who are in Tarragon society but don't have dragons? Do they even know what Tarragon society means?"

"No, they think it's a religion, or a cult, or a way of life. But they all die young unless they attend Tarragon Academy."

Jamie's mind felt like it was whirling with too much new information. His mother had Tarragon blood but she supposedly didn't know about dragons, so no rules were broken when she married his dad. But if she did know about dragons, then a rule would have been broken and perhaps his father had paid the price of that rule with his life. The question remained, however: did his mother have a dragon? Alan didn't seem like he was willing to talk about it and Jamie couldn't read Alan's dragon's mind, so the answer was likely to elude him once again. But if his mother had a dragon, then the council would surely know. And if the council knew, then it was possible that they had sent a dragon to kill his father to prevent their secret from getting out. It was a chilling thought, but one he had to take seriously. After all, the council was capable of it, he knew. But had they actually done it?

"How did my father die?" he asked.

"I don't know, Jamie," Alan said, and again Jamie felt the slightest hint of a lie, but he was unable to follow it and ferret out the truth. It was frustrating.

"So why are you here? To taunt me with memories of my parents? If you really care about me, why bring up my past? Is this why Ashton sent you?"

Alan sighed. "No, and I'm sorry for mentioning it. Ashton told me you were in trouble and I decided that it was finally time that I start honoring your mother and start protecting you. If you don't want that protection, I don't blame you."

Jamie thought about it. If he was honoring a commitment to Jamie's mother and not obeying Ashton, then he might be a valuable ally. But there was no way to tell. He would have to assume that Alan was working for Ashton and keep on his toes the entire time. That was probably why Ashton had chosen him; Jamie would be unable to tell his true allegiance no matter which side he was on. But he would make a better bodyguard than anyone else, Jamie figured. But he just couldn't bring himself to commit.

"Look, I know Ashton's recommendation isn't the best thing I have going for me, Jamie, but know that after what happened to your parents, I would do anything to protect you."

Jamie's heart stilled for a moment and he felt Scott stiffen behind him.

"What do you mean, what happened to my parents?"

Alan cursed. "I didn't mean to say that."

"But you did. What happened?"

"I can't tell you," Alan said. "I've been sworn to secrecy. But I can tell you a story, from Tarragon lore, that may answer your questions."

Jamie scowled. His classes were full of myths and tales and he didn't need another one now. But he was desperate to know what happened to his parents, and if a story were to help him, so be it. He nodded.

"Once upon a time, as they say," Alan began, then he hesitated and laughed. "I never thought I would be telling you a story, Jamie."

Jamie waved his hand impatiently and the man cleared his throat. "Sorry. Once upon a time, a Tarragon princess lived at the foot of a magical mountain where the dragons ruled. She was destined for great things and her belly was swollen with the promise of new life. But then her heart led her astray and she fell in love with a commoner who had no Tarragon blood at all. She was cast out of Tarragon society and doomed to live on the outskirts of the mountain forever. But she fought back. When the hatching began, she hid in the mountain and made her way to the eggs. As she formed the bond with her dragon, her belly reached its peak and the child was born on the hatching grounds, surrounded by the eggs and the mist, part of them from his first breath. And so the first Queen was born, conceived in forbidden love, sensitive to the mountain as no other human could be, destined to return to the hatching grounds and find the elusive Queen egg."

"That's the story of Tilda, the outcast, and her son Heron who hatched the first Queen dragon," Scott said. "I remember that from junior year."

"So that actually happened?" Jamie asked.

"It has, in many variations," Alan said.

Jamie thought about the story and shivered. He had never asked about his birth; he assumed he was born in a hospital like everyone else. What if he had been born on the mountain, and that's why he seemed to be so sensitive to the dragons? After all, he had seen Narné before the first year exam, which was not supposed to happen. Scott had been shocked by it. And he could communicate with all of the dragons, but he didn't think that was Marisol's special ability – it was *his* special ability and humans weren't supposed to have special abilities. What if his mother had found her way to the hatching ground when she was pregnant and Jamie had been partially bonded to the deformed creature when he was born? After all, in all of his dreams the creature had been with him, not with his mother, and he had felt a connection to it even if that connection was fear.

But in the story Alan had told, the princess – his mother, and he was pleased she was a princess in this story – had already been pregnant when she fell in love with the outsider. He wasn't surprised that his father was an outsider, since he had never seen the deformed dragon after his mother's death, but had the council then killed his father to cover up the secret of dragons?

He studied Alan. The man had no doubt sworn to the council that he wouldn't talk about what happened to Jamie's parents, and it was unlikely that Jamie would learn any more from him. But he had learned a lot, and Alan seemed genuinely concerned about his welfare. Guilt was a good motivator, after all. But he couldn't help but notice that in the story, no mention was made of the man's fate and he wondered why Alan seemed especially reticent to talk about that. Had he been involved in Jamie's father's death? Surely not. Surely a man like Alan, who was loyal to Jamie's mother, wouldn't attack or harm his father.

"You can guard me," Jame finally said.

Alan smiled and extended his hand, and Jamie shook it firmly. He still wasn't sure this was the best idea, but it was better than being attacked on campus. Alan left him, promising to return first thing in the morning to escort Jamie to classes. He already had a schedule of Jamie's classes and Jamie filled him in on when he left and where he went aside from his classes. Alan would only be with him during the day, luckily, and Scott would watch out for him at night. It seemed like a good enough deal, and soon Alan was leaving and it was just Scott and Jamie.

Jamie flung himself back on the couch with a sigh, but Scott watched him like a hawk.

"Don't you have something to tell me?" Scott asked. "About what happened to you today?"

Jamie winced. "Yes," he said. "I was waiting to tell you until this all got sorted out."

"I had to hear it from Derek," Scott said, perching on the couch next to Jamie. "You don't know how it feels to hear about an attack on my boyfriend from someone else. I didn't know anything had happened to you today. You have to tell me these things. I know you don't want to worry me, but you have to tell me."

"I know, Scott, I know I made a mistake," Jamie said. "Can we just move past this?"

Scott let out a little sigh and kissed his forehead. "Tell me what happened, and then I'll consider just moving past it."

CHAPTER NINE

Spaghetti Dinner

J amie had plenty on his mind with Alan and Scott and Derek competing for his attention, not to mention his duties as Queen and his attempts to build an army, plus the never-ending homework and essays, and he barely had time to think about anything as everything started slowly working itself out. As the weeks passed by and nothing seemed to be building between Scott and Derek, he began to relax. And even though he hated having someone follow him everywhere, he was now used to having Alan trail him between classes and it prevented any other incidents from happening. He didn't altogether trust Alan, since he could tell that Alan was at least somewhat loyal to Ashton, but he appreciated Alan's presence whenever he had to walk past large groups of upperclassmen who eyed him like a dragon eyes a tasty piece of meat. He hadn't had a chance to talk to Alan about his parents again, partially because he was always rushing off to class and there just wasn't any privacy or time, and partially because he was afraid what answers he might get.

For weeks, everything ran like clockwork. Alan would meet him in the morning and escort him to his classes, and in the evenings he would be with Scott. Scott went to visit Derek every week to make sure the freshman was doing all right and Jamie heard that he was adjusting well, although the other students were giving him a hard time. Jamie felt bad about that, and even felt a little sympathy for Derek, but not too much. After all, Derek was still a threat to his relationship with Scott even if Scott didn't admit it. Jamie knew that Derek was just waiting for the right moment. Both Jamie and Derek were watching Scott like hawks, Jamie to make sure he didn't falter and Derek to make sure he did. Jamie felt especially bad for Scott to be trapped in such an unpleasant situation, but Scott seemed oblivious and seemed to think that it was possible to be just friends with Derek.

Scott also handled all of the recruiting, and Jamie hadn't realized how much he had been doing over the summer. While Jamie had been lazing away his days at the hatching ground, Scott had been creating a huge support system and learning the ropes of Tarragon society in order to start building Jamie's army. Already many people on campus were aware of the impending war, and most of the visitors could sense the potential for violence. Ashton must have sensed it, but he made no move to stop Jamie or Scott from talking to foreign leaders, even encouraging them at times. Well, encouraging Jamie. He continued to try to distance Scott from anything to do with ruling unless he had no other choice. But Jamie was invited to meetings with foreign dignitaries and introduced to all of the important people on campus, as befit his role as Queen, and he was starting to feel overwhelmed with his new responsibilities and with school.

All of his classes were focused on becoming a Queen; he was mostly being privately tutored by various council members and only shared two classes with other students. They wanted to make sure he understood his position immediately, and they also seemed to think that there was no time for him to explore other areas of interest. He would remain at Tarragon Academy for the rest of his life, so there was no need for him to learn about anything else. He resented it a little, since he had other interests, especially in the other tribes that worshipped mystical creatures, but he understood the council's reasoning. They wanted to have a Queen who understood what it meant to be Queen. His own interests would have to come later.

As the end of the semester neared, Jamie invited Amar and his girlfriend over for dinner. He shared a class with Amar, luckily, so the two saw each other at least twice a week, but Jamie had gotten so busy with his new responsibilities that he had barely had time for his friend. And Amar had been dating Nikki for almost a year, which was pretty serious, especially for Amar. He felt like he should get to know her better, since the few times they had gotten together had always seemed to be interrupted by dragon affairs. She had been one of the few people to talk to him openly about the mating flight and he appreciated her honesty, and her kindness during the previous winter when he and Scott had been separated. Now that everything was finally going well, he wanted a chance to hang out with them.

Both of them had classes that ended at five, so they planned to head over to Jamie's apartment in dragon canyon afterwards. Jamie didn't have late classes on Thursdays so he was busy preparing the meal: spaghetti with vegan sauce for Nikki. Spaghetti was about the limit of his cooking abilities. Scott was an excellent cook and frequently whipped up incredible delicacies for them during the week and especially on the weekend, but he had a class as well and then a meeting with a representative, so it would be a while until he came home.

Home. Jamie smiled. This little apartment was his home, and would be for as long as he lived. He loved it. It was spacious and luxurious, far larger than anything he could have ever imagined, and equipped with the finest furniture and appliances money could buy. No expense was spared for the Queen. Marisol's chamber opened off the main hallway and she could walk into the bathroom and Jamie and Scott's bedroom as she pleased, though she wasn't here right now. Now, Narné was the only dragon to occupy the massive dragon chamber that was built for two dragons, and he looked dwarfed in the enormous chamber without his Queen at his side. But soon enough Amar and Nikki's dragons joined him and the chamber was filled with the sounds of chortling dragon laughter as they began their party.

Amar arrived first, just a few minutes after his dragon. He and

Jamie embraced and Jamie welcomed him inside. Amar let out a whistle.

"No matter how many times I see this place, I still can't get over it," he said, gesturing to the nice furniture and the large window that looked out over the entire dragon canyon. Jamie's room was at the highest level of the canyon overlooking everything else, and the view was the best in the canyon. Today a faint mist lay in the canyon, but the view was still breathtaking.

Nikki showed up several minutes later and kissed Jamie's cheek in greeting. She then went up to Amar and kissed him on the lips playfully.

"So where's Scott?" Amar asked.

Jamie knew that Amar still didn't fully approve of Scott, but he was making an effort to befriend the man. Amar hadn't forgiven Scott for being assigned to seduce Jamie, nor for being so friendly with Derek at the prospective student weekend. Jamie didn't blame him for the latter one; he had doubts himself on Scott's real feelings towards Derek even though he knew Scott loved Jamie with all his heart.

"Scott has some business to attend to. You wouldn't believe how much work goes into being Queen. I'm so glad Scott's sharing the responsibility with me."

Jamie explained some of what he was doing, leaving out everything about the war and trying to overthrow Ashton. There weren't any listening devices in the room, but he hadn't ever told Amar or Nikki about his plan, and he wasn't sure how they would react. He had considered telling them tonight, but he would let things play out and see where the evening led. They weren't exactly loyal to Ashton, but like all students, they just assumed he was a good person, just like Jamie had assumed. It would take some convincing to get them to believe that he was the monster he truly was.

The conversation turned to classes, a subject Nikki could finally share with them now that they were sophomores and had their dragons. Before the first year exam, she had always managed to change the subject when it came to classes and now they knew why: she couldn't talk about her classes without mentioning dragons and dragons were the academy's deeply held secret.

Jamie wondered what would happen if freshmen were told about dragons earlier, if it would cut down on casualties. One of the reasons he had been injured was because he was stunned by the presence of a real, live dragon, after all. But then again, his experience wasn't normal. He had been the first in his group to shatter an egg, and he had gone out with no preparation or warning. Amar had known that he would be facing a dragon when he went into the woods. He was more prepared. But still, perhaps telling students farther in advance would help.

"Tephis has been giving his teachers a run for their money," Amar said proudly. His dragon was extremely wild, no doubt a reflection of his partner in many ways, and he was always outsmarting his teachers. "He's already learned how to fire."

"Fire?"

"You know, when they breathe fire. It's called firing."

Jamie shivered. Both of his parents had been killed in fires and there was strong evidence that dragons had been involved in both deaths. Marisol had shown no signs of breathing fire until she laid her eggs, and the sight of her breathing fire had filled him with terror. Now Tephis was doing it too?

"Marisol did that when she laid her eggs," Jamie said.

"Ah, I knew Tephis couldn't be the first," Amar said in a slightly dejected voice. "Marisol is ahead of everyone."

"It's because she's the Queen," Nikki said. "Tephis is still the first of the ordinary dragons. Not that he's ordinary at all."

"Right," Amar said, perking up. "Eric says we'll start learning how to control his fire immediately. I can't wait. A real fire-breathing dragon. How exciting."

Jamie tried to push his parents' deaths to the back of his mind, but it was hard. His mother had died in a house fire that he suspected was caused by a deformed dragon that had hatched outside of the proper hatching season. And his father had died in a fiery car crash, only the cause of the fire was unknown. It was possible that another dragon had started the fire, but there was no way to prove it aside from asking Ashton or the council and they would only deny it even though Jamie knew for a fact that dragons were used in war to kill people. He was hoping that Alan would know about his father's death, but he hadn't asked yet.

But Amar didn't know any of this, and he wasn't trying to upset Jamie with talk of fire. So Jamie smiled and sounded impressed, and tried to change the subject as quickly as possible. Nikki seemed to sense something wrong, because she helped change the subject back to classes as Jamie went to the kitchen to serve the spaghetti. With his back turned to them, he let his face show his distress for one moment and shut his eyes. He felt Marisol comforting him and reached out to her, luxuriating in her touch. Then he opened her eyes, fixed a smile on his face, and carried the spaghetti to the table.

They ate in relative silence, with the only conversation being compliments on the cooking and the odd comment here and there. When dinner was over, Jamie picked up the plates and put them in the sink, then invited everyone into the living room. He checked his watch. Scott should be home soon. They chatted about nothing for a while, and then Amar said something that made Jamie's skin crawl.

"You'll never believe it," Amar said, "But Ashton, the head of the council, came to visit me today. He wants to give me private lessons about Tarragon society. I guess since I'm your friend, he wants to make sure I know your role and stuff."

Jamie stiffened. Ashton was trying to intrude into his friendship? What was Ashton's game? Was he trying to drive a wedge between Jamie and Amar or, worse, was he trying to turn Amar into his pawn and use the man to spy on Jamie? Whatever his game was, Jamie wouldn't let it happen.

"You can't do it," Jamie said, slamming his fist into the chair arm.

Nikki and Amar both seemed shocked at his adamant statement and Jamie blushed.

"I mean, you shouldn't do it. I'll tell you what you need to know, but don't get any closer to him than you have to."

"Why? He's a nice guy. He did my interview to get in, and I'm sure he's the reason I got in. I don't know what my parents would have done if I didn't get in," Amar added. "This was the only place I applied."

"He's not what he appears," Jamie said. It seemed that he would be telling Amar and Nikki about Ashton after all. He took a deep breath, and then began telling them what he had learned about Ashton over the past year, and all the things Ashton had done to him, from trying to rig the mating flight to separating Jamie and Scott to drugging Marisol to attempting to seduce Jamie when he was ill. All of Ashton's crimes, laid out before Amar and Nikki. They were aghast.

"Jamie, have you really been going through all of this?" Nikki asked.

"Yes," Jamie said. "But I will fight back. And I need your help."

"Anything," Amar said, and Nikki nodded.

Jamie sighed. He glanced around the room and sent a question to Narné as to whether anyone had been in the rooms since the listening devices had been destroyed. So far, only Jamie, Scott, Amar and Nikki had been in the room, Narné replied. He reached out to Marisol and had her check Amar and Nikki's dragons just to make sure neither of them secretly sympathized with Ashton. They were both clean.

"This has to stay absolutely secret," Jamie said. "Talking about it could have dire consequences for me and for you. Are you sure you want to know?"

"I want to know how to help you, Jamie," Nikki said, and Amar nodded.

Jamie carefully placed his hands on his thighs and began to tell them about the war. He was careful not to tell too much. He didn't share the visions Narné had seen about him and Derek leading armies, or even the fact that they were recruiting the foreign representatives. He just told them that a war was coming and they would have to pick sides. He told them as much as he could without revealing vital information about his plans, because he knew that if Ashton was already interested in Amar, then he might pressure Amar into revealing this information. He knew Amar would keep it a secret, but Ashton could be ruthless. The less Amar knew, the better for Amar and for Jamie.

Amar and Nikki were stunned at first, then Nikki nodded.

"A war is inevitable, I think," she said. "The girl's campus has similar problems. Our leader Margot is a lot better than Ashton, but we still have problems with corruption and especially with the first year students being hurt and raped. But the council would never dream of going against Ashton's will and change the laws on that. Only by getting rid of Ashton can we change, and Ashton's not likely to go without a fight. But are you sure you can do this?"

"I have to try," Jamie said.

He had his doubts – thousands of doubts – and they swarmed through his mind every night when he tried to sleep, but he was determined as well. When the time came, he would be ready. He just hoped the time wouldn't come too soon.

CHAPTER TEN

Warning

Scott finished his last exam and put his pencil down with a sigh. He brought the paper to the front of the class and was dismissed. The test had been on social hierarchy in Tarragon society, and he knew he had nailed it. He knew more about social hierarchy than most, because he lived it every day. Ever since becoming the Queen's mate, he had learned the hard way how to distinguish between the important and less important people and split his time accordingly. Social rank was not just based on the humans, however; it was mostly based on the strength of the dragon. While his teachers never actually mentioned anything about the ranking system of dragons because the dragons held that secret dear, it was implied: there were ranking dragons and non-ranking dragons. And at the top of the ranking dragons were their male leader and their female leader.

Right now the male leader of the dragons was Arion, without question. He had strength, abilities, and – perhaps most importantly – time on his side. He had not only been in the shell for a long time, he had been out of the shell for over a century at least, gathering experience and loyalty among the other dragons. They were extremely unlikely to turn against him. However, according to the laws of dragon and Tarragon society alike, the male leader ought to be the Queen's mate. Normally the Queen's mate would be the same as the strongest, oldest dragon, because in a fair flight such a dragon ought to be able to win. However, Marisol's flight had been so chaotic and Jamie had such a strong preference for Scott that the flight had resulted in Narné being the Queen's mate.

Some dragons were willing to consider a young dragon as their leader, because Narné was a ranking dragon with a lot of strength and abilities. The only thing Narné lacked was time out of the shell, and that would eventually take care of itself. Most dragons believed that if Narné wanted to turn against Arion, he had every right to do so, but they would stay out of the way. It was the humans who would do the fighting, not the dragons. Or at least that's how Jamie summarized the dragons' thoughts when they discussed battle plans. The dragons would fight to protect their human partners, but it was unlikely there would be any dragon casualties because they wouldn't be trying to kill each other. Unless, Jamie said, there was some way to prove that Arion had overstepped his bounds and tried to kill another dragon. That was the one law all dragons held dear, and no dragon was above that law, not even Arion. Jamie and Scott didn't have any plans to use that loophole, but it was nice knowing there were some things dragons refused to tolerate.

On the human side of the hierarchy, things got a lot more complicated. There was a male and female head as well, and then the council, but the council was made up of ranking and non-ranking dragon partners. In older days, only ranking dragon partners could get on the council, but Ashton had twisted it so that anyone he liked could get on. As a result, the council didn't always have the best interests of the academy in mind and had become corrupt. Of course, none of this was on the test, but Scott had learned it all from his time working with council members and representatives. The test was easy in comparison: it just asked who the current heads were and what the general structure of the society was like. It had none of the nuance and subtlety of the actual council.

Scott glanced at his watch. Jamie was having dinner with Amar and Nikki and while he wanted to hurry home and join them, he had to meet with a representative on the women's campus first. He headed towards the path when a car honked. He was so startled he jumped, and everyone around him turned with him to stare at the limo parked by the building. Cars were forbidden from campus and it had been months since Scott had even seen one, and the other students wore similar looks of awe. The front window rolled down and a woman gestured towards Scott. He looked around to make sure she was pointing at him, then approached the car.

"We're here to take you to the women's campus," the woman in the front seat said. "Please get in."

He opened the back door of the limo. He hadn't been in a limo since he was a child doing ads for television and his parents spent the money on frivolities like limo rides to the studio and closets full of shoes. He blushed at the memory and was grateful that Jamie still seemed oblivious to his past as a child actor. It was one secret he hoped Jamie never found out about.

As he slid in the limo, he realized there was a woman sitting across from him. She had severely spiked short grey hair and dark-rimmed square glasses and he instantly recognized her as Margot, head of the women's college and female head of the university. Until Marisol was born, her dragon had been the female head of the dragons as well, but the appearance of a Queen pushed her dragon out of the running despite Marisol's youth. Scott had never thought about how Margot would feel having her dragon suddenly demoted, but now his mouth went dry and he realized she might be furious and take her anger out on him. She knew about his war with Ashton and had even warned him about it in the past, and seemed to be a good person, but why was she in the car?

"You have no reason to fear, little one," she said, waving one hand as if to calm him. "I only wish to speak to you somewhere we won't be monitored. How goes your efforts?"

Scott swallowed. He had no way of knowing whether the car was bugged, and he wasn't completely sure he could trust her.

"Fine," he said guardedly.

She laughed. "Relax. Ask your dragon about my intentions if you have questions, I know that's how you're judging people."

"What makes you think that?" he asked as he sent a message to Narné to get Marisol to evaluate Margot and her dragon. The response came quickly: she could be trusted, but he should be on guard. She was hiding something.

"Marisol is able to read other dragons," Margot said. "Ashton may not have figured out the potential uses for that ability but I have."

"So why are you here right now?"

The limo was driving through the woods and Scott realized they were between both campuses – if she wanted to hurt him, no one would hear him.

"I wanted to warn you. Ashton is planning something. I don't know what, but it will have grave implications for you and your cause."

"What do you mean? How do you know this?"

"He has been too agreeable in the council lately, a sure sign that he is planning something. And I have my own ways of learning information. I may rely on people rather than dragons, but my results are just as effective."

Scott rubbed his chin. He had gotten comfortable this school year, going to classes and recruiting in his spare time. He had forgotten that he was recruiting for something that would actually happen. He didn't know what he was thinking, but for some reason he supposed everything would continue as it was going, peaceful and safe, until he and Jamie were ready to take the first step. But of course Ashton would try to strike first. After all, so many people on campus now knew or had gleaned the conflict that it was highly unlikely Ashton didn't know what they were doing, and it was only a matter of time before he acted.

"When?" Scott asked. "When is he going to act?"

"Soon," Margot said. "I don't know how, or when exactly, but it will be soon. You need to plan your next step. What will you do when the campus is no longer safe for you?"

"Return to the hatching ground," Scott said. "Fight from there."

"Perhaps that will work," Margot said with a shrug. "Narné has finished all of his training and is an adult now, so perhaps the dragons will follow him. But you will need more than that to stand against Ashton."

"What do you suggest?"

"You need something to get the dragons on your side, some proof that Arion has violated the laws that all dragons must follow."

"You mean proof that Arion has killed another dragon."

Margot's eyes widened in surprise for a moment as if she hadn't expected him to know that, then she nodded.

"How am I supposed to get that information? I mean, he hasn't ever done that, has he?"

"You might want to ask your friend about the collar around his neck," Margot said, waving one hand towards her own neck. "Your friend at the hatching ground, that is."

Scott stiffened. She knew about Kale? He had the same gold necklace that Mike had but Scott had never paid it any attention. It must mean something, though, and it must be the proof they needed to get the dragons on their side.

"Thank you, Margot," he said. "I'll ask him."

The car came to a stop and she gestured for him to get out. He did, bowing slightly to her as his books recommended he do for the head of the women's academy, and the limo drove off towards the apartments. He looked around, slightly stunned from the conversation, mind whirling. He needed to get back to the hatching grounds and talk to Kale, but first he had to talk to the South Korean representative and see if Korea would be on his side. He took a deep breath. There would be plenty of time to talk to Kale. Ashton might be acting soon, but there would still be time.

The South Korean representative was a beautiful woman who bowed to him as he approached, and he bowed in response. They sat down to talk and she began quizzing him on the Queen, as most of the representatives did. They had to return to their home countries with detailed accounts of the Queen's hatching, her egg laying, and especially her mating flight. The mating flight was especially important because everyone in her home country – everyone in the world – had been a part of the mating flight thanks to Jamie's global cry of need. Everyone needed reassurance that it wouldn't happen again, because it had thrown every single dragon into a state of instant lust and disrupted all sorts of plans and activities. All around the world, everyone in Tarragon society had become creatures of lust and the sudden switch had nearly given away their secret in many places. All of the representatives wanted reassurance that Jamie would never, ever do it again and Scott was happy to provide that reassurance, even though he gave it with a heavy heart. That move was what had enabled Narné to win the mating flight; without it, Arion almost certainly would have won. He didn't know what would happen in the next mating flight when it would be a fair flight.

He inquired about the dragons in South Korea and how they fit into society. Most lived in a mountainous area near a town called Jecheon in the center of the country. It was a beautiful city, she said, and there was even a movie set nearby where they had ancient buildings set up for movies and it was beautiful to see the dragons flying above the set looking as they must have looked in ages past. The mist protected them from outside eyes, just as the mist did everywhere else Scott had asked about. There was definitely something magical about the mist; it seemed to emanate from Mount Tarragon but follow dragons wherever they went, and it seemed to have universally grown thin over the past few years but grow thicker since spring. Jamie had shared his opinion that Kale's blood had been a sacrifice that thickened the mist and as much as the idea disgusted Scott, he had to admit it seemed likely.

The South Korean representative presented him with a gift of soju, an alcoholic drink made in South Korea, and thanked him for his time. Since he was with two council members who were loyal to Ashton, he couldn't bring up the war or recruiting, but he asked Narné to ask Marisol to scan the South Korean's dragon just in case. He had developed a rapport with her and if she was friendly, perhaps he could approach her in the future. Narné was silent for a while, and Scott was forced to smile, accept the gift, and say goodbye without knowing Narné's answer. He watched the woman walk off and wondered what was taking Narné so much time. Occasionally Marisol was napping and had to be woken up to scan a dragon's mind, but it never took this long.

Something is wrong with Marisol, Narné finally said.

Ice ran through Scott's veins and he remembered Margot's warning. Was Ashton acting already? The soju nearly slipped through his hands but one of the council members caught it.

"Careful, Scott," he scolded. "Jamie will want his gift in one piece, even if he is too young to drink it."

Scott smiled weakly and nodded, waiting for more information from Narné. The other council members each took one of Scott's arms as they escorted him towards the path to the men's campus. He wondered at their positions. They were loyal to Ashton, so if Ashton were acting, were they perhaps here to prevent him from interfering? But what was happening? What was wrong with Marisol?

Marisol is fine, Narné said in a slow voice, *but she cannot reach Jamie. Their bond is blocked.*

Arion, Scott thought. It had to be Arion. Arion was the only one who could block a dragon's bond with his partner, and if Arion was blocking that bond then it meant Jamie was in trouble. He pulled away from the council members but they held him still.

"You're not going anywhere yet," one of them said.

"What's happening to Jamie?" Scott demanded.

"Jamie is safe," the council member said. "He's with Ashton, where he belongs."

"He belongs with me," Scott said, dread washing over him. "Let me go!"

"Let him go," the other council member said after glancing at his watch. "It's too late now."

They released him and Scott began sprinting down the path towards the men's campus. Too late now. The words echoed through his mind. Was it too late? What had happened to Jamie? He dashed at full speed and prayed he would get there in time.

CHAPTER ELEVEN

Kidnapping

Minutes after Amar and Nikki left, someone knocked on the door. Jamie went to open it, a little surprised. The only person he was expecting was Scott, and Scott would just come in, not knock. Unless Scott had brought the representative with him, in which case Scott was going to get an earful later. The apartment was clean enough, but there were dishes in the sink and glasses still out, and Jamie liked things to be perfect when he had guests over. He opened the door and was floored to see Ashton on the other side.

"Good evening, Jamie. May I come in?"

Jamie almost said no and slammed the door in his face, but Ashton had been on his best behavior lately and was unlikely to try anything with Scott due to arrive home any minute. So he invited the man in, clearing the glasses away and gesturing for Ashton to take a seat. Ashton stood instead and helped clear the glasses. Once the apartment was clean, they both stood in the kitchen only a foot apart and Jamie shifted uneasily from one foot to the other. He still remembered when Ashton had kissed him, and how good it had felt. He had been ill, and on a drug that made him extremely sensitive sexually, but he knew that Ashton was also very skilled and it made him nervous.

Ashton placed a finger on Jamie's chin and tilted his face up until their eyes met.

"There's no reason to be afraid, child. I'm just here to talk."

"What about?"

Jamie pulled his head away and turned to one side. There was a glint of silver and then without warning, a sharp pain in his arm that began spreading. He stared at his arm in shock and saw a syringe filled with a strange yellow liquid that Ashton was pumping into him. The pain was excruciating and he screamed and tried to rip his arm away, but Ashton held onto him until all of the liquid was inside him. The liquid burned through his arm and his body went limp. Ashton caught him as he fell to the ground.

He reached out to Marisol and hit a blank wall in his mind. Truly terrified, he tried again and again, always hitting a blank wall. He tried Narné and found the same. Every dragon he tried had the same result: nothingness. He was utterly cut off from all of dragonkind and he had never felt so helpless or lonely. Ashton lifted him like he weighed nothing and carried him out of the room, shutting the door behind him. Then he headed down the corridor and through a series of endless tunnels until they were at Ashton's chambers. Jamie tensed, or would have if his body was responding to his brain. Was Ashton going to rape him? The fear that had enveloped him when the jocks attacked him at the knoll returned in full force and a tear ran down his cheek.

"Hush, Jamie," Ashton whispered. "I won't hurt you."

You lied to me and drugged me, he wanted to shout. But he couldn't, because his body was completely unresponsive. Ashton carried him through several rooms that looked like ordinary enough rooms until he reached what looked like a solid wall. Ashton pressed a knob in a bookshelf and the bookshelf swung on a hinge to reveal a hidden room behind it. Jamie flinched. There was a bed in the hidden room, with chains on it, and a small toilet. Was Ashton going to keep him in here? Ashton lay him on the bed and sure enough, manacled his hands and feet to the bed. There was plenty of chain, so he would have leeway to walk around the small room, but he saw a wheel that could get rid of that leeway if Ashton wanted him pinned. What was going on? Was he really being kidnapped?

Ashton kissed his forehead and heat stirred through Jamie's body, an unwelcome heat. He did not want to be aroused by anything Ashton did, but like before when he had grown hard when Ashton kissed him, he felt like he had no control over his body or his actions. Ashton kissed his cheeks, then his nose, then finally his lips. Jamie felt his lips parting to allow Ashton inside of him and the heat increased exponentially within him. Just like before, Ashton's hand crept down his body and cradled between his legs as he began to get hard, and Ashton skillfully rubbed against him until he was panting into the kiss, desperate for Ashton's touch.

It must be the same drug, Jamie thought. He was sedated but sexually sensitive, just like before. He prayed that Marisol was all right, because he had no way of knowing. He kept instinctively reaching out to her for help and finding nothingness. It was terrifying, almost as terrifying as Ashton's hands evoking such intense pleasure. Not even Scott could bring him to this point so quickly. His back arched involuntarily to press him against Ashton's hand and the man began removing Jamie's pants. Another tear slid down Jamie's cheek but Ashton ignored it. He unchained Jamie's feet long enough to pull off his pants, then chained him again. He did the same to his hands to get his shirt off, and then Jamie was chained naked to the bed, terrified and more aroused than at any time other than the mating flight. He was a little grateful that Marisol wasn't able to share his emotions because otherwise he was sure this would trigger a mating flight, and with Ashton so close he knew Ashton would win.

Ashton continued to stroke his cock and kiss his body for several more minutes, then stood up. He placed a thin blanket over Jamie that tented in the most embarrassing fashion over Jamie's arousal.

"I'll be back to finish this," Ashton promised, then he slipped out of the room. Jamie couldn't see how he opened the door to get out, but it was good to know that there was a way out of the room.

He heard shouting in the other room and hoped it was Scott, here to save him. He tried to calm his body down, but the blanket was rubbing against his cock and his nipples and sending him into a state of bliss and it was humiliating. It had to be the same drug. He remembered the vision he had picked up from Mike's dragon's mind of the doctor listing the side effects. Hypersexuality. This was definitely hypersexuality. He would never act this way on his own. His body was usually under his control. He heard a dragon's roar from outside, then another. Would Scott start the war right now? His heart thudded with more than pleasure now. Worry and panic filled him. They weren't ready. The reinforcements from other nations wouldn't arrive for weeks in some cases. They couldn't fight the war yet. Scott had to keep his head and not attack immediately. Attacking Ashton would accomplish nothing but Scott's death.

The shouting in the other room grew louder but Jamie still couldn't make out who it was. It had to be Scott, and Jamie was just glad it was shouting and not fighting. Would Scott survive a fight to the death with Ashton? Would anyone? Ashton was ruthless; he had proved as much with this move. He had been kind to Jamie, lulling Jamie these past weeks into forgetting how ruthless Ashton really was. Here Jamie had just finished telling Amar and Nikki how horrible Ashton was, and then he allowed Ashton into his apartment. What a fool he was. He shifted uncomfortably against the blanket. His arousal was finally starting to wear off and now the blanket was merely a heavy weight against his sensitive skin.

The shouting grew dim again, and then the door opened and a shadow appeared. Jamie's heart thudded in hope, but then the shadow stepped into the light. It was Ashton again, looking annoyed. When he saw that Jamie was no longer aroused, he looked even more annoyed.

"That boy has ruined our evening, I see," Ashton said, stroking one hand down the center of Jamie's chest under the blanket.

Jamie shivered, but the touch didn't fill him with heat as it had before. "Well, no worries. There is plenty of time for you to see what I have to offer."

Jamie longed to lunge at him and attack him, maybe bite him or head butt him or something, but he was limp and couldn't move.

"You will be my guest here until you come to your senses about your next mating flight and realize that I will be your partner," he said.

Jamie was a little surprised. He had been terrified that Ashton would win the mating flight because of Arion's strength and speed, not to mention experience, and had never imagined that Ashton felt threatened by Narné. But this made it seem that Narné was a real threat to Arion, which gave Jamie hope. He just had to hold on until the mating flight, and perhaps all of this would be over. He would certainly try to escape along the way, of course, but this gave him hope. Because once Scott won the mating flight twice, many more people would be willing to support him, at least according to Scott. They viewed his first mating flight as a fluke, which it was, to some extent, and said they would wait until a proper mating flight to make their decision. Several representatives held that position and if Ashton was so worried about the mating flight that he had kidnapped Jamie, then Narné had a better than expected chance of winning. Jamie just had to hold on.

Ashton kissed his forehead and stroked his cheek, then left the room. Again, Jamie was unable to see how Ashton left. He hoped the switch was in the room but since he hadn't seen anything, he was starting to worry that it was a remote and Ashton kept it on his body. That would make sense, since Ashton would know that Jamie would try to escape and leaving the means for escape in the room was asking for trouble. Jamie shivered under his blanket and was grateful now for the cloth. It was cold in this little room and there were no windows. The light was on above him and Jamie suspected Ashton would always leave it on to mess with Jamie's sense of time. Days could pass but perhaps they would feel like weeks because Jamie would have no idea how much time was really passing. He would have to keep careful track of the meals he was given and the sleep he had. And he would have to pray that Scott found him soon.

He reached out to Marisol again and was met with nothingness. The only good thing about that was that if Arion was using his power to cut Jamie off from the dragons, then he wasn't using his power on anyone else. But Jamie couldn't help but wonder if Arion had cut him off permanently or temporarily. He had to assume temporarily, because if it was permanent then the other dragons would surely rise up against him. The Queen was far too valuable to be cut off from her partner on a human's whim. The dragons made their own laws, but surely this would violate one of them. Then again, it would make sense that even a temporary block on his bond with Marisol would violate the dragon's laws.

After all, if he couldn't communicate with his Queen, then how would she be able to properly care for her eggs? No one knew how the Queen cared for her eggs, and what was to say that the bond with her human didn't play a major role in it? And giving Jamie a sedative that would also affect Marisol was extremely dangerous – what if Marisol went limp and crushed one of her eggs? Arion and Ashton were playing a dangerous game and the other dragons surely had to respond. If Scott knew anything, he would approach the council before starting an open war. Ashton's actions demanded censure and even though the council had failed to act in the past, surely they would have to act now.

He shut his eyes and prayed for sleep and rescue, in either order, knowing that both were likely a long way off.

CHAPTER TWELVE

Loyalty

Mike returned to Ashton's rooms after collecting his last paper of the semester, needing some love and support. Like his students, he was beginning to feel exhausted and worn out by the school year and the thought of the stacks of papers on his desk was disheartening, to say the least. The students might complain about having to write the papers, but he had to read all of them, giving good, thoughtful critiques for every single paper and trying not to feel like he failed when they all made the same mistakes and it appeared as if they had learned nothing at all from his class. There were always a few bright stars in the classes, of course, and that kept him going, but the majority of his paper grading was drudgery and he dreaded it.

Ashton had been good about giving him space to grade and be a teacher. He only spent one or two nights a week at Ashton's now, although he still had a drawer there and Ashton made it clear that he was always welcome. He mostly came for solace, even though he knew it was counterintuitive to come to a man he secretly hated for comfort and love. Still, Ashton was exactly what he needed at times like these. Mike wasn't ready to deal with his stacks of essays, and Ashton could provide just the right distraction. As he wandered slowly towards Ashton's quarters, he thought he saw Ashton carrying a limp Jamie quickly through the hallway. He frowned. He must have been mistaken. There was no way Jamie would let Ashton carry him like that.

His pace quickened and he reached Ashton's door in minutes. He knocked, but there was no answer so he let himself in. He was allowed to be in Ashton's room even when Ashton wasn't present; an honor only he was granted. He looked around. Everything seemed in order and Ashton and Jamie weren't anywhere. He must have imagined it. Then he heard movement from the library. But when he entered, there was no one there. He called out for Ashton, then shrugged and turned to go.

"Michael," Ashton said.

Mike jumped. Ashton was behind him, in the library, but Mike had no idea how he had gotten there. Had Mike just not seen him? Or was there an entrance in the library that he didn't know about? It was puzzling, and he was embarrassed that he hadn't seen Ashton when he had looked the first time.

"What are you doing here, Michael?" Ashton sounded annoyed, as if Mike were intruding on something. Perhaps he was, if Ashton had indeed been carrying Jamie.

"I thought I saw you and Jamie," Mike said. "Is Jamie here?"

Just then Eraxes, his dragon, blasted through his mind with a warning that Jamie was missing. Mike put his hands to his ears even though he knew it wouldn't help. Eraxes's voice was telepathic, not auditory, but the instinct to block out the noise was irresistible. Mike knew that every dragon across campus was getting a similar message and knew that things would be in a state of panic. He needed to get to his first year students to make sure they didn't notice anything unusual. Ashton placed his hand on Mike's back and the look on his face was half-sympathy, half-rage. A dangerous combination. Eraxes's message made little sense, but Mike made out that Marisol was not in contact with Jamie anymore. The only way that could happen was if Arion was blocking her.

"You're not blocking Jamie, are you? That'll start a war," Mike said. "The dragons will never stand for that."

"Jamie is being protected for his own good," Ashton said. "I've already explained this to the highest dragons."

Sure enough, moments after Eraxes's initial panicked blast of information, Eraxes sent out another, much calmer message that Jamie was safe and no one should worry. That would quiet the dragons; perhaps Mike didn't have to go to campus and check on his first year students. But Mike couldn't relax. He had seen Ashton carrying Jamie into these rooms. Jamie was somewhere in Ashton's chambers against his will most likely, if Arion was having to block his communication with Marisol.

"Where is Jamie?"

"He's safe," Ashton repeated. "You don't need to worry about it."

"Why can't he be in contact with Marisol? What have you done to him?"

"I'm taking care of him. Marisol will be fine."

"You don't know that," Mike said, his voice rising dangerously. A thought had entered his mind, a horrible thought, that Ashton had taken Jamie here to seduce him and he was blocking Marisol to prevent Marisol from entering her mating flight. But if Ashton was seducing Jamie before the mating flight, then Ashton had lied to Mike when he said that he would only have sex with Jamie during the mating flight. Mike couldn't handle the thought of Ashton having sex with anyone else. It had nearly broken him to watch Ashton and that girl have sex earlier in the year, and in some ways it had broken him. He would not let Ashton break his word.

"Michael," Ashton said in a calming voice. "What are you afraid of?"

"Are you going to have sex with Jamie?"

"Of course not," Ashton said, holding his arms out to show his sincerity. "I'm simply keeping him safe. Didn't you hear what happened to him on the first day of school? He was sexually assaulted."

"But he has a guard now, and nothing like that has happened

again. What have you done to him?"

"He needs to be kept somewhere safe until the mating flight," Ashton said.

Mike's eyes filled with tears. So Ashton was trying to ensure that he won the mating flight. Even if Ashton didn't have sex with Jamie – and Mike still had doubts about that despite Ashton's words to the contrary – he would gain a huge advantage if Ashton were the only person physically close to Jamie during the mating flight. Physical closeness played a huge role in the mating flight, and people who were touching the dragon in flight were the only people with a chance at winning. The only reason Scott had been able to win was because in the chaos of the flight, he had managed to get a hand on Jamie without anyone noticing. But for Ashton to go to such extremes was heart-wrenching for Mike. Ashton would never do anything like this for Mike. He would never risk a war for Mike, or go against the wishes of the dragons for Mike. Mike was his pet, nothing more, and Jamie was the Queen.

Tears began to stream down Mike's cheeks and Ashton sighed and embraced him. Mike buried his face in Ashton's cloak and inhaled his musky scent. He wanted Ashton for himself, but he had always known he might have to share him with Jamie during the mating flight. But never before. He had never suspected Ashton would kidnap Jamie to ensure his victory in the mating flight.

There was a commotion at the door, someone banging loudly and then the door opening. Mike wiped his eyes and Ashton pushed him aside. Scott entered the room with several council members flanking him. For a moment Mike thought the council members were here to bring Ashton to justice, but then he noticed that they were watching Scott, not Ashton. They were Ashton's men, here to make sure Scott didn't do anything rash. Mike tried to pull himself together and Scott looked at him curiously before his rage settled on Ashton.

"Where is Jamie?"

"He's safe, I assure you."

"Where is he?" Scott shouted.

"You are to have no more contact with him," Ashton said. "It has been decided that you are a dangerous influence. You have been seen consorting with known defectors."

"What are you talking about?"

"You spent time alone with the German representative," Ashton said. Mike remembered that meeting. Scott had been thrilled to be able to meet a representative on his own. Mike had never considered that it might be a set up and he was amazed at Ashton's forethought. He had been planning this for months. "The German representative is a known enemy of the council. Because of your apparent friendship, your loyalty has been called into question. You can either vow loyalty to me, here and now, or leave the campus forever."

Scott went white. "I'm not swearing loyalty to you, and I'm not leaving without Jamie."

"You don't have a choice," one of the council members said. "Either swear to obey our leader, or leave our society forever. Just be glad you get to keep your dragon."

Mike knew the real reason Narné wasn't being threatened was because Arion was busy blocking Jamie and couldn't also sever the link between Scott and Narné, but it would be a threat in the future if Scott tried to stay to find Jamie. He hoped that Scott would leave quietly, but he knew Scott was unlikely to go without Jamie at his side. He only hoped this wouldn't escalate into war. He knew Scott had been planning a war, but they weren't exactly ready for it. It would take weeks to gather their forces. If Scott tried to force things now, he would be defeated in a matter of days. Perhaps that was what Ashton wanted, Mike realized. He knew Scott had the potential to do major harm, so he was trying to provoke the boy into wasting his resources.

Scott looked around the room as if searching for Jamie, and then his face took on the vague look of someone talking to his dragon. Finally, he nodded.

"I will leave," he said. "But I won't stop looking for Jamie and when the dragons find out that this is against his will and not for his benefit, they will rise up against you."

"What will be, will be," Ashton said mildly. "Gentlemen, please escort Scott to his dragon and see that he leaves our skies."

The council members grabbed Scott's arms and dragged him out, and soon it was just Mike and Ashton again. And Jamie, somewhere, since he had to be in Ashton's quarters. Ashton ran a finger down Mike's cheek.

"There are many pieces in play, pet. Do not let your emotions get the better of you in this game, and you will be rewarded."

Mike nodded, but couldn't resist. "But you won't sleep with Jamie, will you? Not until the mating flight?"

"Why would I want anyone else when I have you, my pet?"

Mike relaxed and headed back to his chambers. He was half-way there when he realized Ashton's answer wasn't a yes or a no, and Mike still had no idea whether Ashton would sleep with Jamie. It was with a heavy heart that he sat down and looked at the stack of papers on his desk. He flipped through them until he came to the name of one of his better students. He needed something to remind him why he did what he did, and hopefully a good paper would do just that. He began reading, and felt a small smile work its way across his lips. If nothing else, his students learned something from him. It wasn't much, but it was something. He wrote an A on the paper and moved on to the next.

CHAPTER THIRTEEN

The Collar

A s soon as the council members and their dragons were out of sight, Scott turned Narné around and headed to the hatching grounds, singing the song that would take them to Marisol and her specific ground. When they arrived, Marisol was in a state of panic. She was lying limply around her Queen egg and seemed to be having trouble moving. Kale was standing next to her and his dragon was flying overhead as if trying to protect her from threats from the sky, even though there weren't any. Still, it was hard to protect her from herself. Narné dropped Scott off as close to the eggs as he could without endangering them, and then joined Vestis in his circles above. Kale was stroking Marisol's muzzle.

"She just went limp," he said as Scott approached. "I have no idea what happened. Then she announced to all the dragons that she couldn't contact Jamie, and then those council dragons responded that Jamie was safe. I don't know what to think or believe. Where is Jamie?"

"Ashton has him," Scott said, feeling the sting of those words. He had abandoned Jamie to Ashton, but there had been no way to get him. Narné had had a vision of what would happen if Scott had tried to rescue Jamie right then, and it led to all of their deaths. They would have to wait for the right moment to rescue Jamie or risk everything they had worked for, including their lives and their dragons' lives. He only hoped Jamie would be able to fight off Ashton's advances long enough for Scott to come and rescue him.

"You left him with Ashton?"

Scott scowled. "You don't understand. I couldn't get him or we all would have died. But I will rescue him. I just don't know where he is, or what happened. Ashton accused me of consorting with traitors. He's known what we were doing all along. We have to get our army together and strike."

"We should get our army together," Kale agreed. "But we need to strike on our terms, not Ashton's. Let's wait until it's right for us, not when we're reacting to something he did. Or don't you think he has a trap set up for us?"

Scott's scowl deepened. "You're right. He probably does. He's so damn sneaky. And how did he get Jamie? Jamie knows what he is. What did he do to Jamie? Did he hurt Jamie?"

Marisol shook her head. *It's the same drug we were on before,* she said in a weak voice. *Only he gave it to Jamie instead of me. I recognize it, though. It feels the same.*

Scott's hands tightened into fists. So Jamie had been poisoned. He thought of Amar and Nikki having dinner with Jamie and wondered if either of them had been in on it. But no, they were Jamie's best friends. They would never betray him like that. No, Ashton must have somehow snuck in and poisoned Jamie, then carried him away like a trophy when he was unable to fight from the sedative. Jamie had always been weak when he was on the sedative before, and that was when it was only through the bond between human and dragon. Scott shuddered to think how powerful it would be when given directly to Jamie. Did Ashton bother to measure it against Jamie's body weight? What if he gave Jamie an overdose? Ashton didn't seem like the type to care about things like that, he just did whatever he wanted and let other people worry about the details.

"Margot tried to warn me," he said, wishing he would have taken her warning more seriously and rushed home the minute she had mentioned danger. Then another thought came to him and he stared at Kale's necklace that she had called a collar. It did sort of look like a collar, now that he looked at it. Kale raised a hand to it nervously, as if he were embarrassed by it.

"Margot also told me to ask you about that," he said, gesturing to the collar. "She said it could help us."

"I don't see how," Kale said stiffly. "The council has never taken it seriously."

"What is it?"

"Every few decades, Ashton chooses someone to be his – well, his pet. He gives them his collar and showers them with attention and gifts. But the real purpose of the collar is to mark them as sacrifices."

"Sacrifices? Doesn't Mike have a collar like that, too?"

"Yes, he does, because I refused to sacrifice myself so Ashton had to find another."

"Jamie thinks the mist renewed itself because your blood was spilled. Is that the sacrifice you mean?"

"Partially. We are meant to sacrifice our lives, not just our blood. The person wearing the collar becomes bound to Mount Tarragon forever. I tried to run from it, go to the other side of the country, but I always felt its pull. But the mountain doesn't always demand a life. Some decades a blood sacrifice is enough."

"How do you know?"

"As soon as the mountain is satisfied, the collar falls off. Ashton or Margot retrieve it for the next sacrifice. There are no other ways of getting the collar off," he added. "It's like some sort of magic holds it together. But everyone who has worn a collar is bound to the mountain for life, collar or no. Even if we don't wear the collar currently, our lives can be sacrificed to appease the mountain."

"So why not just give the collar to a random stranger? Why give it to people with dragons?"

Kale sighed. "I've often wondered that. I've been studying it while I'm here, asking Vestis questions and learning more about the collar. Only dragons of a certain rank can be chosen, there must be genuine affection between the person who gives the collar and the person who receives it, and the person must put the collar on willingly. Most of the council has worn the collar and survived the sacrifice, you know, even Ashton. That's one reason they're on the council: they're bound to the mountain."

"Does any of this have to do with killing dragons?" Scott asked, trying to figure out how this related to Margot's advice. Kale went pale and looked down.

"When the human partner sacrifices his life, the dragon is slaughtered. The dragon would be killed anyway once the human is dead, but apparently part of the ritual is killing the dragon and letting the dragon's blood be part of the sacrifice. Arion is in charge of this. He's so big and strong the other dragons don't stand a chance. Ashton always chooses men who have just graduated to make sure that their dragons aren't too strong. That's one reason I refused to sacrifice myself. I wanted to say goodbye to my dragon, and when Vestis realized that Arion intended on killing him and he grabbed me and flew me to safety until I came to my senses."

Scott was stunned. If this were true, then Arion had killed many dragons before, but how to prove it? He couldn't ask anyone to sacrifice themselves and their dragon just to prove to the other dragons that Arion was a killer, but he couldn't think of any other way to get proof.

"Do the other dragons know about this?"

"No," Kale said. "They know about the human sacrifice, but they assume the dragons die afterwards from losing their human. They don't know the dragons are part of the sacrifice."

"And the dragons are fine with a human sacrifice?" Scott asked in shock.

"It's the only way the campus is protected," Kale said. "I know, it's barbaric. I wish there were some other way to keep the dragons safe, but the mist feeds off of sacrifice. And since my blood wasn't enough to unlock the collars, I think someone is going to have to die in order for the mountain to be satisfied this time."

"And you and Mike are the only two with collars, so it'll be one of you? No, I refuse to accept that," Scott said. As much as he hated Mike, he would never want the man sacrificed and his dragon killed. He wasn't even sure he hated Mike, exactly. He had mixed feelings for the man. Mike had raped him, but Mike did a lot of good as well. It was complicated.

"We're the only two with collars," Kale said, "but remember that anyone who has ever worn a collar could be sacrificed to appease the mountain. That includes most of the council."

"And Ashton," Scott murmured.

Kale nodded grimly. "Yes, but he's not likely to sacrifice himself. He would need a little help."

"Help I wouldn't mind giving."

"He would have to be at the top of the mountain," Kale said, "In the clearing where sacrifices take place. He would know what you were trying to do. He's no fool. I doubt you could pull it off. No, lay your sights on a council member if you really want to save me and Mike and expose Arion as a killer."

"You think Arion would kill a council member's dragon?"

"If it helped with the sacrifice, yes, I think he would."

Scott nodded. "All right, then, we need to plan our attack to draw the council members to the volcano. We need at least one of them to witness the attack, and at least one to be the sacrifice."

"Are you sure you're okay killing someone, Scott?"

Scott paused. All the talk of sacrifices had hidden the truth of the matter. When it came down to it, they would be killing another human. He stared at his hands.

"People are going to die in this war, aren't they? Why not make their deaths mean something?"

"You don't sound very convinced."

"Have you ever killed someone?" Scott asked, since Kale seemed so matter-of-fact about the whole situation.

Kale sighed. "I've made decisions that lead to people's deaths. It's not the same, really, but I have nightmares about it. I work with the President and I know that the people we kill are bad people, but they're still people. It's a hard thing to do. You need to steel yourself for it. I know you want to get rid of Ashton, but imagine killing him for a moment. When it comes down to the final moment, are you going to be able to strike the last blow and take his life?"

Scott was silent. He imagined Ashton on his knees begging for his life. He imagined lifting a sword to slice off the man's head. He imagined hesitating, because the man in front of him was a man, not a monster, and because he would be responsible for the death of a living, breathing human. Would he be able to do it? He didn't know, but he needed to figure it out before the final attack.

"Thanks, Kale," he said. "That may be the key we need to getting the dragons on our side, and where the dragons go, the humans follow."

Scott sighed. It was a big help, but it did nothing to get Jamie back. He wondered where Jamie was being hidden and knew that there was nothing he could do to help Jamie from here. It was infuriating knowing that Jamie was being held hostage and there was nothing he could do to help. He just had to sit back and wait for the right time, for when his armies gathered and he could attack on his terms, not Ashton's. He turned to Marisol.

"Marisol, will you let the others know that we need them, that the war is starting?"

She snuffled. *It is difficult to speak without Jamie,* she said woefully. *But I will do my best.*

Scott cursed under his breath. Ashton had managed to cripple one of their best weapons, Marisol. However, he had also given them a weapon, because as soon as people began to see how weak Marisol was due to Ashton's influence, they would be willing to fight even harder to protect her. And Jamie. After all, Jamie was their Queen too, so they would be fighting to find and protect Jamie as well. Scott just hoped it would be in time, but he tried to remember the vision Narné had seen of Jamie astride his Queen dragon leading dragons into war. In order for that vision to come true, Jamie had to be free and he and Marisol had to be in good health. Of course, Narné's visions were only scenes of possible futures, not the definite future, but it was still reassuring to Scott and gave him hope that Jamie would be rescued soon. How soon, he didn't know, but Ashton couldn't keep Jamie forever. There were plenty of people who were loyal to Jamie who would fight to find and free him and Ashton couldn't defend against all of them, no matter how strong Ashton thought he was.

Scott sighed and went to the big tent to organize the maps he had brought back on one of his summer trips. They would need the maps to plan out their attack strategy, and he wanted to get a head start before his army started arriving. Soon, the war would begin, and nothing at Tarragon Academy would ever be the same.

CHAPTER FOURTEEN

Seduction

J amie awoke to chains around his wrists and ankles and it took several minutes lying there before he remembered why. His memory was hazy and everything was in a fog. He tried moving his arms and was relieved when they obeyed. At least he wasn't paralyzed anymore. He sat up and the blanket slipped to his waist. He shivered. It was cold in this hidden room, and he pulled the blanket around his shoulders and took stock of his situation.

The room was small, with just enough space for a single bed and a toilet. He was grateful for the toilet and managed to get to his feet to relieve himself. The walls were stone, and felt thick. The room was probably soundproof, but he tried shouting for help anyway. There was no response and his voice seemed to melt into the stone without making an impact, so he stopped. With his bladder empty and his voice sore from shouting, he sat back on the bed and tried to find the door Ashton had entered from. The stone appeared to be completely solid, but he knew it swung open at some point and if he could find that point, perhaps he could figure out how the door worked. He got up and wrapped the blanket around him like a cloak as he ran his hands along the stone wall, hoping to feel some irregularity. There was none.

Tears of frustration leaked from his eyes and he studied the ceiling instead. That was when he noticed a glint of light from the corner, and saw the camera recording his movements. Damn that Ashton. He was probably watching Jamie's attempts and waiting for Jamie to tire out before he came in to gloat. Well, Jamie wouldn't waste his energy looking for a door he couldn't find. He would save it and then attack Ashton the moment he came in the room. He lay back on the bed and pulled the blanket over him, grateful for its protection as well as its warmth. He wouldn't want to lie here naked while Ashton watched through the camera.

He had lain still for several minutes when Ashton appeared beside him. He inwardly cursed because he hadn't been able to see the door. One moment the room was empty, the next Ashton was beside him and the wall was solid again. Ashton looked amused at Jamie's frustration as Jamie sat up and pulled the blanket tight around him. Ashton was carrying a syringe, he saw with fear.

Jamie leapt out of the bed and tried to knock the syringe from Ashton's hand but Ashton stepped out of his range and began spinning a large wheel in the corner, the wheel connected to his chains. The length on his chains shortened and his arms and legs were drawn back to the bed, and soon he had to lay in the bed the length was so short. When Jamie was pinned and couldn't move at all, Ashton stopped spinning the wheel and came closer. Jamie felt like a trapped animal and snarled, but Ashton ran a hand across his face lovingly. Jamie tried to bite him.

"Hush, Jamie. Not as much this time. I don't need you limp, but I do need you to calm down."

He placed the needle in Jamie's arm but try as Jamie might, he couldn't wiggle enough to dislodge Ashton's grip. More tears ran down his cheeks as he was completely helpless to the older man's will. Stinging pain filled his arm, followed by heat and relaxation. His body went limp and he stopped struggling. He still wanted to, but his body wasn't as responsive as it had been a minute ago. He was at Ashton's mercy. Ashton released the wheel and gave Jamie more slack on his chains and Jamie lowered his hands from above his head to cross over his belly protectively. He could move, but it felt like he was moving through water: everything was slow and heavy. He curled up into the fetal position on his side and Ashton stroked his head.

"That's better, isn't it?" he said, allowing his hand to travel to Jamie's bare back under the blanket. A stirring of heat swelled in Jamie's groin and he curled tighter to quell it. Ashton was trying to forcibly seduce him, but it wouldn't work. He would stay true to Scott no matter what.

Ashton sat on the bed beside him and arranged them so Jamie's head was on his lap as he continued to stroke Jamie's body under the blanket. One hand massaged his back while the other dipped down to his front, angling past Jamie's tightly crossed arms to linger on his nipples before attempting to make his way further down. Jamie was breathing heavily and quickly becoming aroused, though he hated to admit it. Every stroke of Ashton's hands was fire on his sensitive skin and he instinctively reached out to Marisol to see if she was reacting, but he still felt emptiness where their bond should be. He was a little grateful, because he didn't want her to feel what he was feeling.

"Marisol," he whispered. "Is she affected?"

"She'll share some of your symptoms, but because the drug was injected into you, not her, she'll barely notice it," Ashton said. Jamie tilted his head so he could see Ashton's face and try to figure out if he were telling the truth. Ashton was watching him with hawk eyes and a triumphant smile. "Or do you want Marisol to feel this? It would send her into a mating flight, wouldn't it, and with me so close the result is all but assured. Would you like that, Jamie? Would you like me to restore your connection to Marisol?"

As he spoke his hand made contact with Jamie's cock and Jamie cried out in pained pleasure, arching his back into Ashton.

"No," he whispered. Ashton was right; this would send Marisol into the mating flight and she had said that she couldn't have her mating flight until after the eggs hatched. If he pushed her into an early flight, the eggs might not hatch properly and he would be to blame. He couldn't do it. "I don't want Marisol to feel this."

"But you want to feel it, don't you?" Ashton cooed, running his hand up and down Jamie's length as he found himself stretching out of his fetal position to give Ashton better access to his body. He didn't want to, but it was happening without his will. He wanted Ashton's touch, wanted Ashton to feel him and touch him just like he was doing, he never wanted it to stop. He tossed his head and bit his lip as Ashton expertly flicked his wrist and the pleasure screamed inside Jamie's body. Even without the drug, this would be an incredible experience and with the drug, it was mind-blowing. And all Ashton was doing was touching him. What would it be like when Ashton was inside him?

Jamie opened his eyes wide at the thought. What was he doing? Was he seriously fantasizing about having Ashton inside of him? How could he? He tried to push away from Ashton but he had the strength of a kitten and Ashton had a firm grip on him now, stroking and massaging and sending blasts of pleasure through his body that were making him squirm with the need for more. He didn't know how long he could last. His balls were already aching with need and he could feel his body slowly clenching up in preparation for an orgasm. Ashton leaned down to kiss him and Jamie hungrily kissed back. He wanted Ashton. He didn't want Ashton. He needed Ashton. He didn't know what he needed. All he knew was that he was on the brink of something truly incredible and the slightest breeze would push him over.

Then Ashton tightened his grip and firmly jerked him, and everything exploded. Jamie screamed as his whole body ricocheted with the force of his orgasm and he spewed outward as if everything inside of him were being yanked out by Ashton's skillful hands. His body vibrated with pleasure so extreme it was almost agony and he screamed again as his body went tense with the force of it, and then everything went still and bliss overcame him. He went limp and his body seemed to dissolve into Ashton's lap. Ashton kissed him again and scooted out from under him.

"That's only the beginning, young Jamie," Ashton whispered. "I have so much in store for you."

Jamie turned his head to look at Ashton and at the sight of that hated, handsome face, a tear sprang to his eye. He had been so determined not to give Ashton what he wanted, but Ashton had taken it anyway. His body was a slave to Ashton now, and he had betrayed Scott. Ashton cleaned them both off and then laid the blanket back over Jamie. Jamie tried to watch as Ashton left but again it was like the man just disappeared; he was there one moment and gone the next, with no door swinging shut behind him, just the solid stone wall. Jamie gasped for breath, still having trouble breathing after the monumental orgasm he had experienced. He had never felt anything like it and while he knew the drug was the cause, he also felt like he had betrayed Scott by enjoying himself so much.

Sex with Scott was nothing like that orgasm, so tainted with fear and shame, but that orgasm had been incredible. Maybe he needed fear and shame to fully enjoy himself. Or maybe, he thought hopefully, he and Scott just hadn't found the right position yet and just hadn't gotten good enough together yet. After all, it took work to make sex good and they had been getting better and better at it. He remembered their first time back in the bed this semester and smiled. Maybe it wasn't as explosive as what he had just felt, but it was more sincere. At least until thoughts of Derek had ruined it.

Jamie's smile slipped. Scott had had sex while they were together. Had he felt more or less pleasure with Derek than he felt with Jamie? Jamie had never thought to ask – had never wanted to ask, really – but now he wanted to know. It would hurt if the answer was yes, but it would make him feel a little less guilty about his own pleasure at Ashton's hands. Anything was better than thinking that he was better suited sexually for Ashton than for Scott.

But even if Ashton turned him on fire, Scott still held his heart. That would never change. His sex with Scott was consensual, for one thing, and the moment when their minds met and combined was like nothing else in the world. He would take sex with Scott over an orgasm like he had just experienced any day of the week. Scott was safety, security, and love. Ashton was humiliation, fear, and fire. And love won out every time.

Jamie sat up in his bed and wandered the small room again, looking again for some sign of an exit. Scott would be looking for him, he knew, but he should do his part and try to escape on his own. He found nothing, and he decided that he needed to be more alert the next time Ashton came and left. He had seen the bookshelf swing out, so he knew there was a door somewhere in the wall, the only question was where and how it was hidden. As he felt his way around the room yet again, he thought of Scott and wondered what Scott was doing. He had heard raised voices outside before and it had to be Scott, but Scott undoubtedly didn't know Jamie was nearby. Jamie should have screamed then, but he had been limp from the drug. Maybe the room wasn't soundproof after all, he thought, and the next time he heard voices he would be strong enough to yell for help. He sat back on the bed and stared at the wall. There was nothing to do in this cell except for think, and he began plotting his escape after he got out of this room.

CHAPTER FIFTEEN

The Council Meeting

Mike could tell that Ashton was under a great deal of stress and he knew it had to do with Jamie. It had been three days since Jamie vanished, and the council had called a meeting to discuss the problem. The meeting was due to start in an hour and as Ashton paced, Mike knew there was little he could do to help but he felt he had to offer anyway.

"Ashton, you would tell me if I could help, wouldn't you?"

Ashton paused in his pacing and turned to face Mike. There was a gleam in his eye that frightened Mike a little.

"There is something you can do for me, pet, but you would have to obey me absolutely."

"Of course," Mike said, perking up. He hated seeing Ashton so aggravated.

"I need you to tell the council that you've seen Jamie and he's fine, that he's here of his own free will."

Mike's heart sank. Ashton wanted him to lie to the council.

"They'll know I'm lying," he said. "Eric will be able to tell."

"I've already dealt with Eric, and none of the other council members can read the truth."

Mike shivered at the way Ashton said he had dealt with Eric. He wondered what that meant. He knew Eric was in league with Kale, and therefore not in league with Ashton, but Ashton had always found him too useful to get rid of before. Had Ashton finally kicked him off the council? Mike hoped he hadn't done anything worse to the man, since Eric was a friend of his and they had grown closer over the summer as the only two people allowed to visit Jamie and Scott at the hatching grounds.

Mike let out a deep breath. "Ashton, you know I would do anything for you, but in order to be convincing I would have to actually see Jamie and know he's safe. Otherwise, I don't know if anyone would believe me."

"You just need to see him? You don't need to know that he's here of his own will?"

Mike scoffed. "I already know he's not, as do all of the council members. But I'll say that he is if you want me to. I just – I need to see him to know that he's all right."

Ashton tapped a finger against his lips, then nodded. He gestured for Mike to follow him and they went into the library where Ashton had seemed to appear from thin air the other day after Mike had seen him carrying Jamie. So Jamie was in the library somehow. Ashton pushed against a knob in the bookshelf – Mike was careful to observe which one – and a door slid open. Ashton yanked him inside just as the door slid shut.

They were in a brightly lit room with stone walls, but what held his attention was the single bed with Jamie chained to it. He looked disheveled and surprised to see them, and tears filled his eyes at the sight of Mike. He pressed his manacled hands together as if in prayer.

"Please help me, Mike," he said. "You have to help me get out of here."

Mike said nothing and tried to pretend that his heart was made of stone, but a plan was beginning to form in his mind as he observed the thin blanket that revealed more than it covered. Jamie was naked underneath. Ashton had lied to him. Ashton had been having sex with Jamie and lying to Mike about it.

Ashton waited a few more seconds, then pressed a button on a handheld pad and the door behind them opened. Again Ashton yanked him through and the door slid shut instantly. It was so fast that for poor Jamie it probably seemed like magic and he would be unable to find the doorway on his own. Ashton placed his hands on Mike's shoulders and stared deep into his eyes.

"You are not pleased, pet, but will you do what I asked?"

"Yes," Mike said. "I'll tell the council what you want them to hear. Jamie is safe and here of his own will."

Inwardly Mike was broiling with anger. He would lie for Ashton, but it would be the last time. This was the last straw. His loyalty to Ashton had been stretched thin ever since the beating Ashton had given him months ago for no reason, and now it was broken. He would do what Ashton wanted, but he would do it for his own purposes, not for Ashton. He needed to lull Ashton into thinking that he was still Ashton's obedient little pet when in reality he would become part of Jamie's army. Ashton would never suspect a thing.

Ashton kissed his forehead and Mike leaned into the kiss because he knew that was what he was supposed to do, what he would normally do in this situation, but Ashton's touches had no impact on him anymore. Ashton had lost his allure entirely now that he knew Ashton was keeping Jamie as a sexual prisoner. He cursed himself for being so foolish as to think that Ashton had ever loved him, was ever capable of loving him, but it was too late now. All he could do was try to make amends and help Jamie overthrow the man.

Ashton and Mike left the rooms to head to the council meeting and Mike noticed Alan, Jamie's bodyguard, entering the rooms. He was probably assigned to make sure no one tried to free the boy while Ashton was away. Ashton didn't want anyone stealing his precious Queen. He was surprised, since Alan had apparently known Jamie's parents and should have been the last person to help with Jamie's imprisonment, but it confirmed what Mike had suspected ever since Alan was assigned to Jamie: Alan was one of Ashton's enforcers. Perhaps he was even the one who killed Jamie's father, since that was undoubtedly a command from Ashton. He shook his head. Justice would come to Alan, just as it would come to Ashton.

The council meeting began as usual with just the men, since it was a busy time on campus, but as people were just starting to quiet down for the start of the meeting, a flurry of activity along the back of the room caught everyone's attention and a stream of new council members entered the room: the women. Margot was at the head and she looked angry. Instead of taking her usual place among the council members, she went up to the dais where Ashton stood and faced him down as the rest of the council – the full council – sat down.

"Were you going to start without us?" she asked as the last people settled down.

"I didn't expect you to come at all, what with the final exam approaching," Ashton said.

Mike shifted awkwardly. He was standing to one side of the dais, not authorized to sit with the council and not important enough to be on the dais. A few council members looked at him curiously, as if wondering why he were there, and more than a few looked at him with sneers as if they knew exactly why he was there.

"The Queen is in danger, and you dare instruct your dragons to diminish the concern," Margot said. "You have cut the human Queen from his dragon when his dragon is preparing for the hatching. Do you have any idea how that will impact the hatching or the eggs?"

"Do you?" Ashton asked. "I asked the boy directly if he wanted me to connect him with Marisol again and he said no. Eric will vouch that that is the truth," he added, looking directly at one of the council members.

Eric flinched, but nodded. "That is the truth," he said. Then he shrank back in his chair. Mike wondered if it actually was the truth or if Ashton had threatened him into saying it. He knew the other council members were wondering the same thing.

"The Queen must stay in contact with the dragon," Margot said. "And not only have you separated them, you've harmed Jamie."

Mike blinked in surprise. It was the first time he'd heard a council member besides Eric and Ashton say Jamie's name before. Normally they referred to him as the Queen or the Queen's partner, but calling him Jamie meant that they viewed him as an individual and not just a role. That was a vast improvement and it boded well for Jamie.

"Mike here has seen Jamie and can vouch that Jamie is staying with me of his own free will."

Mike prepared to step forward and speak, but Margot slashed her hand through the air.

"I don't need to hear more from your sycophants, Ashton. You have been drugging the boy with the same sedative you used earlier on the Queen dragon, and as a result Marisol is unable to properly care for her eggs. I don't care whether Jamie is here of his will or not, you cannot be allowed to damage our first batch of eggs in a century."

Ice ran down Mike's spine. Ashton was drugging Jamie again? No wonder the boy was so desperate to leave. But he hadn't seemed drugged when Mike had seen him. Still, if that accusation was true, then Marisol would be in danger and so would the eggs. Why on earth would Ashton risk it?

"I don't know who you're getting your information from, Margot, but they are clearly misinformed. Perhaps they are attempting to divide us at a time when we need to be united more than ever."

"My source has an agenda, true," Margot acknowledged. "But I personally verified the truth of his statements. Marisol spoke to me individually, and she can speak to any of you who doubt the truth of my statements."

"No dragon can speak to a human besides its partner," Ashton said, but he sounded less than certain. Mike knew that Marisol and Jamie had worked hard to keep their special abilities under wraps, but it looked like this secret was being revealed in a big way. He reached out to Marisol to see if she was getting communication from other council members and he got an annoyed huff that yes, they were all trying to contact her at once and it was very confusing, but she was telling them the truth.

Even Ashton got the vague look on his face that meant he was communicating with a dragon and his skin went white as he must have made contact with Marisol. The council members were beginning to talk amongst themselves, and there was anger in their voices. Maybe this would finally be the moment. Maybe a war wouldn't have to be fought. Maybe Ashton would be dethroned right here, right now.

Ashton lifted his arms. "Council members, please. I did use a drug to calm Jamie down, at his request, but it shouldn't have affected Marisol as well. Jamie wished to keep this a secret, but since you insist on knowing the details of this event, I can tell you that he is suffering from severe anxiety brought on by his new role as Queen. He requested a drug that would help him calm down. Now that I know that it does affect her, I will obviously not use it again. I will consult with doctors to make sure Jamie has treatment for his anxiety that does not affect Marisol or her hatching."

"And what will become of Jamie?" Margot asked.

"He remains with me, again, at his request. The pressures of being Queen are enormous and he needed a break. You all remember that he needed to take the entire summer off, and he needs another break now."

"Why isn't he at the hatching grounds with his dragon, then?" Margot challenged. "And why is he cut off from his dragon?"

"She is one of the things he needed a break from," Ashton said. "Their bond is strong enough to survive a little time apart, and he needs rest away from the stresses of being Queen. Soon enough he'll be ready to face the world and he will be able to tell all of you that this break was his idea and done entirely with his permission."

The anger in the council members was nearly gone. A few still seemed unconvinced, but Ashton had woven a clever lie. Margot didn't seem inclined to push Ashton any further. She shrugged.

"It might have been better to inform Marisol of this break before it happened to prevent panic on her part, but if this is true, then the council will not interfere."

"And the rest of the council? Does Margot speak for all of you?"

The council nodded as one and Ashton smiled. Mike couldn't believe that they fell for Ashton's lies, but perhaps some of them were only pretending to fall for Ashton's lies. After all, Ashton could be very convincing but the council members were good liars as well. He knew for a fact that several of them had been to the hatching grounds, and Jamie only allowed people who hated Ashton to visit the hatching grounds. So some of these people were allies in the war against Ashton, but it was impossible to tell who. As they filed out of the room, Ashton came up to Mike and stroked his head.

"You did well, pet."

"I didn't do anything," he said.

"You supported me by being here, ready to speak on my behalf. They all know you are one of Jamie's friends and your support made a difference even if you didn't speak."

Mike smiled weakly. He hadn't thought of it like that. What if people actually believed that he was here to support Ashton and he sincerely believed that Jamie was with Ashton of his own free will? He half-hoped the council could see through to his true motives, even while he didn't want Ashton to find out about them. It was a complicated situation, and one he knew couldn't last. But Jamie couldn't last, either. After all, how long could Ashton possibly keep the boy a prisoner before someone rescued him or he escaped? Mike didn't know, but he knew it couldn't be long. Jamie had too many allies for them to leave him rotting in a cell at Ashton's mercy for long.

As they walked back to Ashton's rooms, Ashton twisted his fingers through Mike's. Normally the touch would make him shiver in anticipation, because it was a promise of the night to come, but tonight it left him cold. He knew that Ashton had another lover, and that thought was more than Mike could stand.

CHAPTER SIXTEEN

Hatching

J amie paced his little cell. He had been trapped here for a week now, if his sense of time was still correct and Ashton were feeding him three times a day as he suspected. Ashton had stopped using the drug on him after the first couple of days and he didn't know why, except that Ashton must be worried about the effects on Marisol. He doubted Ashton cared about him, especially since the drug had such an intense reaction in him. Without the drug, Ashton was still able to pin him to the bed and get a rise out of him, but it was more difficult and the pleasure he felt from the man's touches was far less extreme.

Jamie was grateful; if he had continued with the drug, he could easily see himself growing addicted to Ashton's touch and craving that explosive fire, but without it Ashton's touches were nowhere near as arousing as even the thought of Scott. He was ashamed that his body betrayed him every day when Ashton came to visit, but Ashton had not yet gone further than touching him and jerking him off. It was as if Ashton really believed Jamie would invite him to do more. Jamie shuddered. If the drug had been involved, he could see himself desperate for more, but now that he had control of himself, Ashton's visits had become something he tolerated, not something he enjoyed. Or enjoyed too much, at least. He couldn't pretend that he didn't enjoy them a little bit, and it shamed him to the core.

His presumably third meal of the day had already been

brought to him by Alan, who refused to say a word or even look at him. It was as if he didn't exist in Alan's eyes, and Jamie felt betrayed beyond words that Alan was participating in his captivity. Alan had known Jamie's parents, surely he would want to stand up for Jamie and against Ashton. But instead the man brought him his food and must be guarding the entrance to the door to his cell. He felt equally betrayed by Mike, who had come to see him several days ago, before the drugs had stopped. He sometimes wondered if Mike was the reason the drug had stopped, and he felt better thinking like that. At least Mike had insisted that something about his captivity change, even if he didn't – or couldn't – rescue Jamie.

Jamie reached out to Marisol to see if he could reach her yet and as usual there was silence. As was usual after his third meal, he tried reaching out to every dragon, trying desperate to find someone he was connected with, but with no luck. He was utterly cut off from all communication. Ashton would be in soon, if his schedule held true. It was another reason Jamie was able to count days, since he assumed Ashton stopped by every day to molest him. Persuade him, Ashton would say. Jamie snarled to himself and flung himself on the bed.

Something felt different today. It felt like he was supposed to be doing something, or going somewhere, and instead he was trapped. He had experienced this before, of course, but never to this extent. Something was happening that he was supposed to be a part of, and he wasn't there. He wondered if it was the war that he was sensing, and if he was missing out on being the head of the army. But no, that didn't quite feel right. He laid down and stretched his hands over his head in the same position Ashton pinned him in when Ashton touched him, leaving his belly vulnerable and exposed. Something was wrong, something he was missing.

He stood up again and began pacing, then stopped and faced one of the walls. That was where it was coming from. That direction. He stared at the blank wall for a long time, trying to figure out what was going on. He shut his eyes and caught a glimpse of Marisol, and he bit his lip in anger. He needed to be in contact with Marisol, he knew it, but he couldn't. Unless, he thought, unless he reached out to the one dragon he had never tried reaching out to: Arion.

Arion, he thought. *Let me speak to Marisol now.*

He could feel the dragon's surprise, and his reticence. Arion was no doubt under orders to keep them separated, but he hadn't expected a direct order from his Queen. All of the dragons were supposed to value their Queen more highly than even the head of the council and their partners, so he ought to obey. But would he?

I must ask Ashton, Arion replied in a very humble voice.

Let me speak to her now, or the eggs will be in grave danger, Jamie said, not knowing if it were true or not but knowing it would spur Arion's action. He felt a panicked grumbling from the dragon and within seconds came the dragon's response.

He is not pleased but I must allow you to speak to her. The channel is open.

Immediately, Jamie felt Marisol fill his mind and his world became brighter. Then he entered her mind and gasped at the image there. She was being attacked by a human, and fighting back as best she knew how. She was in no real danger, as the human was armed only with a stick, but no one ought to be attacking the Queen. He jumped into her mind entirely and felt his own body disappear. He became Marisol and felt her surprise and relief at his presence.

The eggs were hatching, he realized, and this boy was here to steal one of them. And not just any egg, Jamie sensed. He was here to steal Marisol's most prized egg. Jamie peered through Marisol's eyes and recognized Derek, and rage filled him for a moment. Marisol clawed at him and ripped his legs with her sharp claws. The boy cried out and Marisol was on him in an instant, ready to kill him, but Jamie hesitated and so did Marisol.

Derek was destined to have the egg. He wasn't going to harm it, as Marisol seemed to fear. He coaxed Marisol into releasing the boy, and he could feel her panic as she sensed more boys and girls approaching down the path towards her children, her eggs. She wasn't prepared to let them go even though the eggs were beginning to rock with their readiness.

Jamie took a firm line and forced Marisol to fly away. She reluctantly obeyed, snarling all the while, and soon had flown to the beach where Narné and the others were. Jamie's heart melted when he saw Narné and Scott, and in response to his outpouring of love, Marisol headbutted Scott and nearly knocked him to the ground. Then, without warning, the contact with Marisol was cut.

I am sorry, Arion said. *But your contact is no longer needed.*

Jamie cursed and opened his eyes. Ashton was looming over him and he realized he had fallen onto the bed. Jamie swore at him and tried to attack him, but Ashton had tightened the length on the chains to prevent such a move.

"Why did you cut me off? Marisol nearly killed the freshmen and only I saved them! How did you know the danger was passed?"

"You were speaking your thoughts aloud," Ashton said. "When you mentioned seeing Scott, I knew the danger had passed and the freshmen were safe."

"Unless Marisol changes her mind and decides to go after them after all," Jamie said, furious and embarrassed that he had been verbalizing the entire time he was in Marisol's mind. "What gives you the right to keep me from Marisol?"

"You gave me permission, before."

"For the moment," Jamie said, but the wind had been knocked out of him as he remembered begging Ashton not to share his emotions with Marisol for fear of sending her into a mating flight. Now that the eggs were hatched he would have to be especially careful. "I didn't mean permanently."

"And it won't be permanent. Just until your mating flight. Which I'm guessing by your changed tone is now a possibility, is it not? Marisol was waiting for her eggs to hatch before her second flight?"

"She's waiting for a lot of things," Jamie said.

"Yes, well, she won't get all of them," Ashton said dryly, no doubt inferring that Jamie's freedom was among those things. "Is it safe to assume she won't attack the other freshmen?"

"No, she won't attack."

Jamie said it heavily, dully. It was good that Marisol wouldn't attack, but he hated feeling like he had been manipulated into it. Still, he didn't want the freshmen hurt. He couldn't even imagine what it must be like to find a dragon egg with an angry mother dragon protecting it. He knew the freshmen were given swords, but those would stand little chance against Marisol. He frowned. Derek hadn't had a sword, but rather a stick. Maybe Derek, like Jamie, had triggered the first year exam for everyone and that was why Marisol had reacted so aggressively: not only was Derek coming after her precious Queen egg, he was also the first student she had seen and she didn't know whether she could trust them or not.

He hoped all of the students who found their way onto Marisol's hatching grounds were worthy of the eggs. After all, they were Jamie's children as well, though the thought was strange. They were the result of his and Scott's love, proof that he and Scott loved each other absolutely. As long as these dragons survived, there would always be evidence that Scott was the Queen's mate. And as much as he knew Ashton wanted to erase that evidence, he knew Ashton was just pleased to have new dragons on campus. At least, he assumed so. It would be horrible if Ashton started discriminating against Marisol's children just because they shared Narné's blood, but now that the idea had occurred to Jamie he couldn't shake it. The best thing to do would be to end the war quickly so they wouldn't face unjust discrimination, but how could they fight the war when Jamie was a prisoner?

Ashton's breath ghosted across his face and Jamie shoved him away forcefully.

"Not today," he said firmly. "I need to focus on Marisol today. Even if I can't be in contact with her, she still needs my thoughts for the hatching to go well."

To his great surprise, Ashton nodded. "I understand. I will leave you to your own devices, then. But do not try to challenge Arion's loyalties again. He obeys me, not you."

Jamie nodded and watched as Ashton left. He wondered about Arion's loyalties. It had seemed earlier as if Arion had talked Ashton into letting him communicate, so even if Arion was loyal to Ashton, Arion was still a good ally to have. The dragons generally kept out of human affairs, as far as he knew, so perhaps Arion was only mostly loyal to Ashton, as was true for so many dragons. He had all day and all night to think about it, he thought as he lay down in the bed, because despite his brief communication with Marisol he knew he wasn't going anywhere soon.

Looking back to his brief time in Marisol's mind, he realized that he had seen no plans to rescue him, not even a trace. If Scott and the others had a plan, surely they would have told Marisol about it. Which meant that they had no idea how to rescue him, and he had no idea how to rescue himself. They were trapped in a sort of limbo, with no one able to act or break the stalemate. Scott couldn't save him, Jamie couldn't save himself, and it would be up to one of Jamie's other allies to save him, but Jamie's allies were all forbidden from being on campus after Ashton's crackdown with Scott. Jamie sniffed and realized he was on the brink of tears. Being in contact with Marisol had been overwhelming and while it had been welcome, it had brought as much pain as pleasure and he felt doubly helpless now. He stared at the wall where he knew the door was, even though he had found no trace of it, and prayed that a savior would come and rescue him.

CHAPTER SEVENTEEN

The Queen Egg

D erek jogged around the track and kept an eye out for anyone who looked likely to assault him. He had been left alone since the first day of classes when he was attacked by the upperclassmen, but the fear of that attack kept him on his toes. He had heard that Jamie was given a bodyguard and he sometimes wondered why Jamie got such special treatment when he wasn't given a guard at all. In fact, Jamie seemed to get a lot of special treatment. Everyone at the college was practically obsessed with him, at least all of the teachers and upperclassmen. Even the freshmen were curious about him and whenever Jamie wandered by the lower campus, all the freshmen rushed to see him like he was some sort of celebrity.

The weird part was that Jamie seemed to expect it, as if he had done something great that everyone should praise and be in awe of. But all he had done, as far as Derek could tell, was get the handsomest man on campus to be his boyfriend. It irritated Derek to no end that Scott was so hopelessly in love with Jamie. He kept thinking that there had to be a chink in their armor, but the two had such a strong love it was impossible to break through. He wished that someday, someone would love him as much as they loved each other, and he wished that that someone would be Scott.

Not that he had anything against Jamie, especially. Derek, like the other freshmen, heard all the gossip about Jamie. Jamie was an orphan; both of his parents had died in fires before he was thirteen. Jamie had lived a hard life before coming to the academy and Derek did feel some sympathy for him. But not a lot. Derek himself didn't come from an easy background. While he and his mother had always had enough money because Ashton was good about child support, it had been hard growing up without a father – or rather, with a father who was too busy to come and visit you. Ashton was always in his life, but as an absence that could never be filled. Now, though, he finally had his chance to get to know his father, but Ashton was as elusive as ever. Derek hadn't given up yet, though. He had four years to prove himself a worthy son, and he was going to catch Ashton's attention. He just didn't know how yet.

As he jogged around the track, he noticed the mist rolling in. It rarely behaved like this and he marveled at how thick it was before he realized he was trapped with almost no visibility. Then a path opened before him and he followed it, not having many options and intrigued at the intelligence the mist seemed to be displaying. It was as if the mist were leading him somewhere, and he was eager to see where. He could just make out the edge of the forest as he passed into it, and see the branches from trees along the edges of the thick mist, but the path before him was clear so he continued to follow it. He walked for nearly twenty minutes before he came to a fork in the road and suddenly the mist vanished. He was alone in the woods and as he looked around, he grew dizzy and disoriented. He couldn't tell which direction he came from or where he should go. There was a fire pit nearby and he considered trying to make a fire to warm up in the suddenly cold winter weather, but perhaps it would better to just try to get home.

He closed his eyes and turned in a circle, trying to sense which direction felt most like home. He wished he had more practical knowledge about the woods or shadows, although the sun was sinking and hidden behind clouds and wouldn't be of any use in finding his direction. He didn't know where the campus was in relation to the woods, either, so he would have to trust his gut instinct on this. One direction just felt right, so he opened his eyes and headed down the path.

Before long he came to the coast of a large lake. There was a canoe docked at the shore and even though he hadn't crossed a lake to get to this point, he knew without question that he needed to cross the lake to get home. This was his destiny. Excitement began to build in his belly as he hopped in the small canoe and began paddling towards an island in the middle of the lake. He saw movement on the island, but soon it stopped and was covered in mist. He steered the boat away from the mist to a clear beach that looked easy to land on. The canoe slid easily up onto the shore and he leapt out, trying not to get his shoes wet and failing as the water from the lake lapped against him. His shoes would survive, however. He looked around. To his left was a forest, and to the right, along the beach, the mist formed an impenetrable shield. He was already obeying the mist, so he decided to go into the forest.

There was a path in the forest that looked regularly used and he went quickly down it until he reached a large clearing. At the closest end of the clearing were a large number of enormous, perfectly round boulders. At the far end, though, his eyes were drawn to a larger boulder being protected by something out of a legend and his heart stopped as he realized what it was. A dragon.

He looked around for a weapon and found a sharp branch that was adequately like a sword. He already knew it wouldn't be a good weapon, but he needed something. That boulder the dragon was guarding was calling to him and he knew he needed it, needed to touch it, and in order to do that he needed to fight off the monster above it. He stepped forward and the dragon turned her head to him as if aware of him for the first time. She bared her teeth and lowered her head in a defensive posture, raising her body to circle the boulder protectively. He took another step forward and raised his stick. She growled.

He continued to walk forward, reassured when she didn't attack but allowed the advance. When he got close enough, however, she swiped at him with her claws and he leapt backwards, falling hard on the ground and clutching at the stick as his only defense. She had cut the material of his shirt but done no damage, yet. She shifted easily around the boulder until she was between him and it, and he scrambled to his feet just as her claws speared the air where he had been lying. She wasn't playing games anymore and adrenaline was pumping through his system.

He lunged and attacked with his stick, but it bounced off against her diamond-hard scales easily and she let out a huff of air as if amused by his attempts. She lowered her head and snapped her jaws at him, then lashed out with her claws again. This time she made contact and her claws ripped through his legs and sent him reeling to the ground face first. She pounced and her great mouth was poised over him as if she were going to eat him. He sobbed in terror, unable to even crawl away due to the pain in his legs. He wasn't even sure that his legs were working properly; they were numb from shock and he prayed that she hadn't severed any important muscles.

Then she hesitated and removed her jaws from his body. She removed them slowly, letting her teeth drag along his skin and leave deep marks that drew blood and would likely leave scars. But she did withdraw without eating him and he cried out in relief. Her wings extended and she took to the air, circling around twice before landing somewhere in the mist. He didn't care where she went; she was gone and wouldn't be attacking him anymore. He stared at the boulder. It was still calling him, but he wasn't sure he could reach it now. He tried to stand and his legs didn't work. Instead, he dragged himself to the boulder.

When he reached the boulder, he placed one hand against it. There was a tinkling sound, almost of bells, and then the boulder began to crack. Red liquid oozed out and Derek took his hand away in disgust, but then he realized that the boulder was an egg and whatever was inside was hatching. He lay on the ground and watched in shock as a tiny creature emerged, just like the larger one he had just fought. The little creature fell out of the shell and landed on him, squawking and flailing its limbs to attempt to right itself. Its claws dug further into Derek's body and he wailed and covered himself as best he could. Then a buzzing sound filled his head, and he heard a strange voice.

Thank you for freeing me, the voice said and he knew without question that it was the dragon.

Derek stared at the little dragon.

"Who are you?" he asked.

I am your partner now, and forever. My name is Jettie.

A wide smile crossed Derek's features as he felt something shove against his mind and suddenly a whole world of experiences opened up to him. The dragon was sharing her life with him, and reading his life at the same time. They were bonded together and would always be together. He would never be alone again.

CHAPTER EIGHTEEN

Persuasion

Scott watched the freshmen cross the lake to the island one after another. No matter how many crossed, the canoe seemed to magically appear for them and then disappear once they had finished crossing. A thick mist had enveloped the path to the eggs and the students had to fight their way through the dense forest before arriving at the clearing at the top of the hill. Marisol hissed every time a new student arrived, and watched their progress like a hawk until they headed down a different path that led them straight through the encampment where Scott, Kale, and about two dozen other men, women, and dragons preparing to fight Ashton were stationed. The other two dozen dragons had taken to the air as soon as the hatching started, but Marisol, Narné and Vestis remained.

Derek was the first to emerge into their camp, and when he caught sight of Scott his entire face lit up even more than it already was. He stumbled to Scott and enveloped him in a hug, for a moment outrunning his little Queen who hopped behind him and whined when she was abandoned. Derek quickly rushed back to her and approached a second time at her speed.

"Scott, you'll never believe what happened!"

Then he caught sight of a petulant Marisol wrapped around Narné at one side of the camp and went pale.

"Don't worry," Scott assured him. "She's just nervous about her eggs."

Derek looked to be in one piece, although he had the usual injuries from a hatching. His legs and torso bore deep scars that he would carry with him for the rest of his life, most likely. Oddly, his torso looked as if he had been bitten, but his little Queen was far too small to have fit him in her mouth. He stared at Marisol and realized that Marisol must have attacked Derek. She hid her head behind Narné's furled wing when he looked at her accusingly.

"Are you all right?" he asked Derek. "Sit by the fire and let me bandage you up a little."

Derek looked relieved and he sat, his little Queen sitting next to him and watching all of them with cool eyes. She glowed, however, when she looked at Narné and Marisol, as if she knew they were her parents.

"Oh," Derek said. "I'm sorry, you probably can't hear her. This is Jettie," he said proudly. "She's my partner."

Scott smiled. He sounded incredibly happy about Jettie, as a new freshman should about his little dragon.

"A pleasure to meet you, Jettie," Scott said, bowing slightly to the dragon. "She's a Queen dragon, like her mother," Scott continued, gesturing to Marisol, who was no longer hiding and instead displaying her brilliance for Derek to admire. Scott guessed that Marisol was talking to Derek, because he wore that vacant look of talking to a dragon and he didn't know why else Marisol would have put herself front and center as she was doing.

"I don't blame you," Derek said, apparently in response to what Marisol was saying. "You were just trying to protect your children."

Marisol rumbled happily as Scott wrapped bandages around Derek's legs. He wondered if all the freshmen would come through camp and need to be healed, and just as he thought this, another freshman stumbled into the camp, looking dazed. He was completely uninjured and had a green dragon hopping along beside him. Scott and Kale exchanged a look and Kale went up to the student and asked him to sit and stay for a while. This was a perfect opportunity to recruit the young students. Perhaps, Scott thought, he could persuade them not to go back to campus at all and to stay here. They would need a teacher, but what student wouldn't like the idea of running away from school to join a rebellion?

"What are you doing here, Scott?" Derek asked, as if he could read Scott's thoughts and knew Scott was thinking of ways to keep him here.

"Ashton forbid me from campus," Scott said. Derek's eyes grew wide. "He didn't want me stirring up trouble."

"What sort of trouble?"

Scott hesitated. This was a delicate situation because Derek worshipped Ashton; Ashton was his father, after all. But perhaps Derek could see beyond that to what Ashton really was.

"There are things about the academy that need to change. Rules that hurt people rather than helping them. And the only way to change is to fight back."

"You mean Ashton, don't you?"

Derek's voice was an odd blend of mature cynicism and youthful hope. Scott nodded.

"Ashton has to go," Scott said simply. "If there were an easier way, we would do it, but we've tried every other way. We need to stand up to him once and for all."

"You say we. You mean you and Jamie?"

"Yes, Derek," Scott said, knowing he was once again on slippery ground. "Marisol is Jamie's dragon."

"No wonder she attacked me," Derek said. But Jettie head butted him and must have said something to cheer him up, because he smiled and nodded. "You're right, Jettie."

Having people communicate to dragons telepathically in your presence was annoying, Scott thought, but it was part of life in Tarragon society. And most people learned how to do it more subtly as they grew more adept at talking to their dragons. Derek, on the other hand, was brand new to the dragon world and probably didn't even know how to talk to Jettie without speaking out loud. Scott wondered what Jettie's gift was. Derek couldn't talk to other dragons and Jettie couldn't talk to other humans, that was clear, but she was undoubtedly gifted with an equally valuable talent. Finding it might be a challenge, since some dragons didn't show their talent for years.

Derek was bandaged completely and he stood up.

"Well, I'd better get back," he said.

Scott stood as well. "You could stay here. We would be honored to have you."

"I don't think Jamie would approve."

"You might be surprised," Scott said, his heart aching for Jamie, wherever he was. Yet even after Jamie returned, he knew Jamie would value having Derek on their side rather than opposing them.

"No," Derek said firmly. "I need to go back, and Jettie does too. I need to show my father what I've accomplished. You say she's a Queen. Is that rare?"

"Extremely," Scott said. "Your father ought to be very proud. If he isn't, you can always come back here where you will be valued."

Derek smiled a lopsided smile. "Thank you, Scott. I'm sure I'll see you again."

He headed towards the beach with Jettie at his heels, and by the time he arrived at the water's edge a canoe was waiting for him. Scott shook his head. He did not understand how this place operated, with vanishing and reappearing canoes and a mist that guided the students along the proper path. But then another student was coming out of the mist with a blue dragon, and Scott knew he had another chance to persuade a freshman to stay here rather than return to Tarragon Academy. He needed to be more persuasive than he had been with Derek, but he hadn't wanted to railroad Derek into doing something he regretted. Better to let Derek go home and see that he wasn't wanted and then return than force him to stay and have Derek always wonder what would have happened.

The other two dozen men and women living at the camp were carefully keeping out of sight, but as more freshman began pouring out of the woods Scott called for them to help. They were all on the same side, and had all been new members of Tarragon society at some point in time, after all, so they were at least somewhat qualified to talk to the freshmen and in no time it seemed like the camp was crawling with newborn dragons and excited freshmen. Some of the freshmen decided to leave, some felt they had to leave but wanted to return when their dragons were older, and some, nearly a third, decided to stay. Scott was ecstatic. Ten new dragons to add to his cause. They wouldn't fight in the war, obviously, but they would show that his cause had backing from the newest generation as well as the older generations.

Their training would be an issue, but Kale, surprisingly, offered to teach the students. He said he had been considered as a teacher before the incident with Ashton made him run away to Washington DC, and he knew most of the material they taught to students after the first year exam. He immediately began teaching the students how to distance themselves from their dragons, since all of the dragons could speak telepathically and several students were already having trouble losing themselves in the minds of the dragons. While he focused on the new students, Scott climbed the mountain to the clearing.

Every single egg had hatched, and there were no bodies on the ground of either student or dragon. No casualties, at least from this hatching ground. In fact, aside from Derek there had been no injuries, either. And Derek hadn't been attacked by his dragon but by Marisol. So there was some truth in the commonly held belief that the longer a dragon stayed in his or her shell, the more aggressive they became. Scott wondered how the new students would fit into Tarragon society, where fighting and scars were a way of life and even his dragon, Narné, celebrated the fact that they had fought before bonding. Would the bonds of the new students be as strong without battle to cement it? Would the older students accept the newer students without scars as proof of their mettle?

So many questions remained unanswered, but as Scott looked out on the broken eggshells that looked like slabs of marble lying on the ground, he felt pride fill his heart. After all, these were his children, his and Jamie's. He and Jamie were now inextricably bound to Tarragon society and no matter what happened next mating flight, even if the worst happened and Ashton won, there would be no erasing Scott's impact. His dragons were out in the world, living their lives, happily partnered to some of the best students the world had to offer. He beamed as he looked around, and then he heard heavy wingflaps overhead as Narné and Marisol both landed. Narné had never landed at the clearing before for fear of disturbing the eggs and he sniffed around curiously, inhaling the scent of his progeny. Marisol took up her position curled around the shards of the Queen egg and looked at the shattered eggshells mournfully.

They are in the world now, she said to Scott and Narné. *I can protect them no longer.*

"You can still protect them, Marisol," Scott said. "By being the best Queen you can, and by taking out Ashton. Both of those things will lead to a safer world for our children."

Marisol rolled over onto her side and Scott instinctively rubbed her belly.

I miss Jamie, she said mournfully.

"We will get him back," Scott vowed.

He missed Jamie too. It had been ten days since Jamie had been taken and Scott couldn't imagine what horrors Jamie must be facing, but every attempt they had made to rescue him fell flat. Scott had tried contacting people, Marisol had tried persuading friendly dragons to get their humans to act, but all to no avail: Ashton's will was too strong. They needed a miracle for Jamie to escape, but perhaps the hatching would afford them that miracle. After all, Ashton would be busy plotting things for his new Queen, Jettie and Derek, and perhaps he would slip up his guard of Jamie. Scott and the others would have to be extra careful to make sure to pounce on any opportunity that arose after Derek and his new Queen returned to campus.

CHAPTER NINETEEN

Father's Pride

Derek felt Jettie pressing up against his mind and for a moment he became disoriented and had the insane impulse to hop rather than walk, because his wings were in the way of his feet and he couldn't manage a gainly walk like a human. Then he remembered he was a human and the impulse passed; he was back in his own mind and nearly back at the fork in the road where Mr. Ferrin waited with several other people, some of them women. He had never been to the women's campus and he studied them curiously, but they looked normal enough. They were, however, staring at him in slack-jawed amazement. Or rather, they were staring at Jettie.

He and Jettie entered the light of the firepit that he had passed on the way to the island. Mr. Ferrin was the only one who didn't look shocked to see Jettie, and he wondered if Mr. Ferrin was the only one who knew about dragons. But no, the other boys on the island had emerged with dragons, and Scott and the other people in the camp hadn't batted an eye, so it couldn't be a secret. He then remembered what Scott had said about Queens being rare and figured that's why everyone was staring at Jettie. They must be able to tell she was a Queen. He puffed up his chest in pride and felt the little dragon at his side do the same.

It was strange having a dragon bonded to him. She felt like an extension of himself, but he knew she was an independent creature. They had complementary personalities, he knew, and it was probably the reason they had been able to bond together, but she was separate at the same time. Very bizarre.

He went up to Mr. Ferrin, since he was the only person Derek knew, and gestured to Jettie proudly.

"This is Jettie," he said. "We're partners now."

Mr. Ferrin smiled. "Pleasure to meet you, Jettie. And congratulations, Derek, you've passed the first year exam."

Derek blinked. So that was the fabled first year exam? It hadn't been so hard, and it hadn't involved almost anything that he had learned over the semester. Sure, it had sort of used the fencing skills he had learned, and it helped that he knew about dragon-worshipping clans so the sight of Marisol wasn't as shocking, but it wasn't much of an exam. He had basically found an egg, gotten chewed up by the mom, and then bonded with the baby.

"Who bandaged you?"

"Scott," Derek said. "I ended up at his camp after finding Jettie."

"That was lucky," Mr. Ferrin said, examining the blood seeping through some of the bandages. "Often we'll get students who have severe blood loss, but you should be fine in a day or two, aside from the scars."

Derek winced. He hated the idea of scars on his body, even though he knew Scott had scars and didn't seem to care about them. He wondered suddenly if Scott had gotten scars from the mother of his dragon. It would make sense; they had looked like claw marks when Derek had seen Scott undressed. But he knew that most of the students didn't have scars, at least the students who came after Marisol flew away. He half-wished he were one of those students, but then someone else might have stolen his egg and he knew he was destined to have Jettie for his own. She nudged him and agreed.

"Well, Derek, normally we wait here for all the boys to come back, but since you've bonded with a Queen we need to get word back as soon as possible. I'm going to send you with one of the upperclassmen here back to campus, where you'll be examined by a doctor. We can't take any chances with you."

Derek flinched at the mention of an upperclassmen, remembering the attack on the first day of school, but the man Mr. Ferrin gestured to seemed nice enough, and was looking at Jettie in awe.

If he tries to hurt you, I will kill him, Jettie said confidently.

Derek laughed and rubbed her head. "All right," he said to Mr. Ferrin. "I'll head back to campus then. Will my – I know Queens are rare, Scott told me. Will my father be there?"

Mr. Ferrin looked at him with what might have been pity in his eyes. "Yes," he said. "I imagine your father won't want to miss this. He'll be very proud of you."

Derek smiled. Scott had said the same thing. Somehow, bonding with Jettie was something to be proud of. He felt her nudging him and telling him that being bonded with her was obviously a great reward and he stifled a laugh, knowing the upperclassman walking with him couldn't hear Jettie and wouldn't understand his laughter. The upperclassman smiled at him.

"You can talk to her," he said. "When I first got my dragon, I talked to her all the time. No one else ever knew what I was saying. You'll learn to talk to her in your head eventually, but no one expects a newbie to do that."

"Thanks," Derek said.

They were walking slowly so Jettie could hop along beside them. She wasn't able to walk properly because of her disproportionately shaped body: she was all hands and feet and wings, with very short legs and arms. He knew from seeing Marisol that she would even out and grow into something truly beautiful, but for right now she was simply adorable as she hopped along behind them. He was tempted to offer to carry her, but he remembered vividly how she had fallen out of her shell and cut him with her claws and he didn't want her accidentally injuring him more. Already his legs ached and he was worried about his leg muscles, and his torso was a mass of pain. He was mostly in shock, he figured, because the pain came and went in waves and he was pretty well able to ignore it, but it was still there.

When they finally reached campus, the upperclassman led him to the gymnasium where a bunch of doctors were wandering around. He heard a vast intake of breath as everyone saw Jettie and must have realized she was a Queen, and then one of the women doctors was leading Derek to an examining table that had been set up with curtains around it in the corner of the gym. She ordered him to strip and he did, grateful for the curtains. Jettie had to wait outside the curtains, but he could feel her presence. He could tell that several people were approaching her and introducing themselves almost as if they expected her to reply, and he longed to be out there to introduce her since she couldn't introduce herself.

"Jettie," he told the doctor waiting on them. "Tell them her name is Jettie."

The doctor nodded and went out of the curtain for a moment to tell the observers. He could hear them oohing and aahing over his little Queen and it made him happy. Perhaps Ashton would be equally impressed. The doctor returned and examined his marks, asking for a complete description of what had happened. He explained everything, from Marisol's attack to what Marisol had said afterwards about fearing for her eggs' safety and having Scott offer to let him stay on the island. The doctor nodded with pursed lips, then began applying ointment to his still-bleeding cuts and bandaging him again, tighter this time until he could barely bend his torso or flex his legs. She looked angry, for some reason.

"Is there something I did wrong?" he asked. "Mr. Ferrin seemed to think I did everything right."

"You did," she said. "But Marisol should not have attacked you."

"Oh," he said. "She did explain it. She was worried about her eggs and frightened that I was trying to steal or harm one of them."

The doctor shook her head. "That's not it. If she had been in contact with her partner, she wouldn't have touched you."

"What do you mean?"

The doctor sighed. "It's not something you would understand now, but perhaps in time you'll know."

Derek frowned. Of course Jamie was in contact with Marisol, and he had assumed that was precisely the reason Marisol had attacked. Jamie saw him as a threat, so Marisol had jumped to the conclusion that he was a threat as well and had attacked him. He still didn't know why she had stopped attacking him, but what did any of it have to do with Jamie?

Inwardly he was scowling. Of course Jamie would be the person with the other Queen. Now they really were in direct competition for Scott's affection. Both of them had the rare Queen dragon and both were in love with Scott. Before, Derek could now see that Scott would love Jamie not just for who he was but for his dragon. But now that the playing field had been evened and Derek had a Queen as well, perhaps he could bring Scott around to his side. It would take time and a great deal of guile, but he was determined. He felt Jettie's agreement, but also a hesitation. Narné was her father, and she hesitated to become involved with him. Derek tried to convince her that he could be with Scott even if Jettie wasn't with Narné, but she seemed to think otherwise. He was trying to figure out her concern when he heard a familiar voice outside the curtains. Ashton.

"And who does this lovely creature belong to?" Ashton was asking one of the nurses.

Derek leapt up, wobbling slightly on his stiffly wrapped legs, made sure his medical gown covered him completely, and then flung the curtain open. Ashton's eyes zeroed in on him and they opened wide first with surprise, then pleasure, then – finally! –

pride. A wide smile crossed Ashton's face and Derek knew he was beaming to have made his father so happy.

"Are you the partner of this Queen dragon, Derek?" Ashton asked in a voice that said he already knew the answer and was eagerly awaiting its confirmation.

"Yes," Derek said proudly. "This is my partner, Jettie."

Ashton squatted so he was on eye level with Jettie. "It is truly a pleasure to meet you, Jettie. You have no idea how pleased I am."

He stood again and embraced Derek. Derek went stiff with surprise, then hugged Ashton back with the ferocity of eighteen years without a father figure all condensed into a single moment of loving forgiveness. The hug seemed to last forever and Derek buried his head into Ashton's shoulder as tears formed in his eyes. This was everything he had ever wanted. Everything he had ever dreamed. His father was hugging him out of love and pride. He had pleased his father and earned his father's love. Everything was at peace in the world. Then Ashton backed away, but still kept his hands on Derek's arms, squeezing him gently.

"Tell me what happened, and how you found your Queen," he said.

Derek told him everything, from the mist parting and leading him to the island to Marisol attacking to Scott and the others on the island to returning to the gym. Ashton looked troubled at the mention of Scott, but let it slide. Derek remembered that Scott had said that Ashton was the one to kick him off campus and wondered what exactly had happened between the two. It was difficult having a conflict between the man he loved and his father, and he hoped he could help reconcile them. Ashton fingered the bandage on his chest.

"I am sorry you were injured, son," he said, and Derek's heart sung at being called his son. "I should have done more to prevent it."

The doctor appeared just then, looking angry. "You should

have let Jamie talk to Marisol, and this injury never would have happened. What if she attacks the other students?"

"Be calm, Emma," Ashton said. "Jamie was in contact with Marisol when he realized what was happening, or else Derek would not have survived. And Jamie assured me that Marisol would not hurt the others. Derek even reported that Marisol had left the actual hatching grounds, so the others are not in danger."

Derek shivered. So Jamie had been the one to call off Marisol's attack. If that were true, then he owed Jamie his life and he didn't like that. He didn't want to owe the boy anything, because it would make it harder to steal Scott from him.

The doctor, Emma, sighed and held out her hands. "I just don't like seeing the freshmen harmed. You know that, Ashton."

"I do know, but you should watch yourself."

Derek looked at Ashton quizzically. As far as he could tell, Emma hadn't said anything out of line but Ashton was acting as if she had. He remembered what Scott had said about Ashton needing to be gotten rid of and wondered if this was what Scott meant. He hadn't told Ashton about the content of his talk with Scott, only that he and Scott had talked, and suddenly he was glad he hadn't shared the specifics. He didn't want Ashton to ever look at him with the disgust he was showing Emma. He wanted to forever be Ashton's prized son. Jettie bumped her head into Derek's bandaged leg and he couldn't hold back a smile. She wanted to impress Ashton too, and the strange undercurrents of hatred were not to her liking. She wanted to be the center of attention, and her movement succeeded. Emma reluctantly smiled at the little creature, and Ashton reached out to scratch her eye ridges, which had her cooing in delight.

"As soon as Mr. Ferrin returns, he'll instruct you and the other freshmen on how to care for your little ones," Ashton said. "Until then, take very good care of our little Queen. She has a great destiny ahead of her."

Ashton gave Derek's shoulder a final squeeze before leaving the gymnasium, but Derek's smile lasted far longer than his figure vanished out the door. He had done it. He had impressed his father. He remembered all the baseball games he had played as a child, always hoping against hope that his father would somehow show up and watch him as he scored home run after home run, and always being disappointed until he gave up the sport altogether despite being offered a place on the varsity team his freshman year in high school. He remembered sending a card to Ashton every Father's Day, giving it to his mom to mail, and then finding a box full of his cards one day when he was eleven – she hadn't mailed a single one. He remembered all the times Ashton had been absent from his life, but now he sensed Ashton would want a place in his life, all because of Jettie. She was more than a pleasant presence and a partner, she was his key to making his father love him and he loved her all the more for it.

Derek and Jettie scooted to an abandoned corner of the gym and cuddled together, Derek very careful to avoid her claws. She was the best thing to ever happen to him, and he would never let her go.

CHAPTER TWENTY

Redemption

Mike brought bolt cutters in a large black duffel back to Ashton's rooms as soon as the first year students had been sent to bed. All but eleven of them, that was. One boy had died, and ten had chosen to remain with the rebels, according to the students who returned. It was amazing how calm the first year students from Marisol's hatching ground were, and they were uninjured as well, aside from Derek.

Derek. He posed a major problem. Mike's mind ran with all the possibilities of having a second Queen on the campus. Jamie's influence would be lessened, for one thing, and his war against Ashton might stall, since it seemed Derek was firmly on Ashton's side. However, Jamie was the senior Queen and all tradition said that Jamie was the one people should follow, not Derek. Plus, Jamie and Scott had done a brilliant job of undermining Ashton's power on campus, not that it needed much undermining in many places. Ashton's lust for power and his recent kidnapping of Jamie had revealed just how thin support for Ashton was, and Mike was determined to take advantage of that. He just hoped Ashton didn't take any significant steps, like eliminating Jamie. With Jamie gone and Derek to take Jamie's place, Ashton would have a Queen as his pawn to do with as he may. He might not be able to become the Queen's mate, as incest was strictly forbidden among humans and Derek was his son, but he could still dominate Derek in other ways and ensure that power in the academy remained with him.

Jamie was in a precarious situation, and Mike couldn't wait any longer. Tonight was the night he would act against Ashton. He took a deep breath and stowed his duffel bag against the wall as he entered the bedroom, where Ashton already lay in bed, awake and grinning. The day had gone unbelievably well for him, because he had never imagined another Queen would be born, let alone bonded to his son. Mike had suspected that there was a Queen egg in Marisol's batch, since every time he flew into the island over the summer she seemed to be protecting one egg in particular, and he had also suspected that Derek would win her given Amar's predictions last spring about which prospective students would end up with dragons. That boy had been a godsend; thanks to Amar, there was only one casualty this year. One. Mike prided himself on being part of the reason for the high survival rate, but he knew part of it was because they had weeded out the weak students before the year even started. Perhaps next year there would be no casualties at all.

Mike climbed into bed fully dressed, and Ashton embraced him. This was the tricky part. Mike didn't exactly have a plan other than somehow knocking Ashton unconscious. Ashton, however, was bigger and stronger than him. He was planning on using sex to get close to Ashton, to wait until Ashton was enthralled in pleasure, and then striking. So he cuddled against Ashton and tried to kiss him, but Ashton pulled away from the kiss after only a moment.

"You have done a fine job with the first year exam, pet," Ashton said.

Normally Mike loved talking to Ashton, because it made him feel like Ashton valued him as a person and not just a sexual partner. But tonight he didn't have time for chitchat. Still, he didn't want Ashton to think anything was wrong so he smiled and replied.

"Amar was a large part of it, as were Marisol's eggs. None of the boys and girls who ended up at her hatching were injured aside from Derek."

"Derek said it was Marisol who attacked him in an attempt to protect her eggs," Ashton said.

Mike's eyes widened. That made sense, in a way. Marisol had been fiercely protective of the eggs over the summer, and Derek was the first student to stumble into a hatching ground, setting off the first year exam for everyone else. Marisol must have been surprised and a little frightened at having her eggs suddenly taken away from her.

"He has forgiven her," Ashton continued, "But it shows poor judgment on the Queen's part."

"Perhaps it was because she wasn't in contact with Jamie," Mike said without thinking. "I'm sure Jamie would have been able to control her instincts."

Ashton slapped his shoulder lightly as if reminding him which side he was supposed to be on, and Mike blushed. He couldn't give up the game yet, not when he was so close. But Ashton didn't seem to think anything of his comment, as he was still staring into space, deep in thought.

"The Queen is still a child," he continued. "She acts like a child, attacking anyone who gets near what she considers hers. That is hardly behavior fit for a Queen. Derek's Queen, on the other hand, has already shown a great deal of maturity. She has adapted easily into living on campus and is quite polite to those around her."

Mike nodded, already seeing how Ashton was going to spin this into making Jettie the dominant Queen on campus. The humans might be persuaded, but would the dragons listen? They followed their own laws, for better or worse, and they weren't swayed by things like maturity – they valued age and time. It was one of the reasons Ashton was still in power, because he was the oldest dragon on campus and no one could really challenge him. Technically Narné was as mature as Arion, but Arion was older, therefore Arion, despite not being the Queen's mate, was in charge of the dragons. So even if Jettie were more mature –

which Mike doubted, since she was fresh out of the shell – it wouldn't matter, because Marisol had more time living among them.

"It may not matter, however," Ashton continued. "I wanted to warn you, pet."

He stroked Mike's hair. "The mating flight may be taking place soon. Perhaps even tonight, now that the hatching is over."

Mike tensed involuntarily and stared at Ashton in horror. Then his eye caught the gleam of a syringe on the bedstand. It was filled with a yellow liquid just like the syringe he had once seen injected into a cow for Marisol. It was the sedative given to knock out Jamie and Marisol and make them sexually sensitive. It probably didn't contain much of the drug, since Marisol would still need to fly, but enough to keep Jamie from struggling. Ashton didn't notice where his gaze went, instead focusing on massaging Mike's tense body.

"I know you're not pleased about this, pet, but you've had plenty of time to prepare."

"Will I be in the flight?" Mike asked, gritting his teeth.

What if he couldn't stop Ashton in time? Would he at least have the chance to compete against Ashton in a fair flight?

"If you must," Ashton said. "If that would ease some of your jealousy."

Mike met Ashton's eyes then. So Ashton thought he was tense with jealousy, not anger. Well, it was true. He didn't want Ashton sleeping with anyone but him. But most of all he didn't want Ashton sleeping with Jamie against Jamie's will, especially when the fate of the flight was all but decided. Marisol might start the flight closest to Narné, but with Ashton being the only human able to touch Jamie, the result was nearly sealed. Ashton would be able to read the boy's movements and predict Marisol's, and he would be able to trick the Queen into his arms.

Without thinking, Mike grabbed the syringe and stabbed it into Ashton's chest, pushing the contents out as quickly as he could. Ashton's eyes went wide with shock and he cried out in pain, but then he went limp and his eyes closed drowsily. With one hand, he reached up to caress Mike's cheek. His hand wavered and then fell to the bed. Mike gasped, realizing that he had attacked Ashton.

It wasn't the end, he thought. He could say that jealousy drove him to it, that he wanted Ashton for himself and didn't want to share him. But he could tell by the angry glint in Ashton's half-closed eyes that the punishment for this would make his previous punishments look like nothing. No, he had taken the first step in his betrayal and he had to go through with it.

He searched through Ashton's pockets for the pad with a single button that would release the door lock in Jamie's room. He found it on a chain around Ashton's neck and had to lift Ashton's head to remove it. He couldn't resist a quick peck on Ashton's lips as he took it. The man was so beautiful. There was a key attached to the pad and Mike let out a sigh of relief. He wouldn't need the bolt cutters. A key was infinitely easier. He reached out to Eraxes to come wait for them outside, then went to the library and pressed against the knob. The door swung open and he darted inside, knowing how quickly it closed. Jamie was lying on his belly on the bed, sound asleep.

Mike shook him away and while Jamie struggled to come to his senses, Mike unlocked the manacles on his hands and feet. Jamie rubbed his wrists and ankles and looked at Mike in confusion.

"What are you doing?" he asked. "Is this some trick of Ashton's?"

"No," Mike said, hurt for a moment that Jamie didn't trust him. Then again, Mike had refused to help him the last time he was in here, so Jamie had no reason to expect anything more on this trip. "I'm here to rescue you."

Mike grabbed Jamie close, then pushed the button to open the door. Nothing happened. Mike cursed. Was the button triggered to react only to Ashton's fingerprint? Was all of this in vain, and now they were both prisoners? Ashton was going to kill him for this; there was no other solution. He pushed the button again, slowly and as hard as he could. The door swung open. Mike leapt through and dragged Jamie behind him just as the door shut.

Jamie was attempting to cover his nudity but Mike didn't have time for modesty. He didn't know how long the drug would last in Ashton and he didn't want Arion to attack Eraxes. He yanked Jamie down the hall to the chamber that opened up on the dragon canyon, the dragon chamber. Arion watched them curiously but made no move to stop them, interestingly enough. Ashton must not be able to communicate with him, or else the drug had paralyzed Arion as well. Looking closer, he realized Arion was completely limp but his claws were flexing as if he longed to get up and chase them.

Eraxes appeared in the opening and Mike climbed on his neck, pulling Jamie up behind him. Jamie clutched him tightly as Eraxes leapt out into the cold winter air. He could feel Jamie shivering and wished he had thought to bring a cloak or clothes or something. Probably a cloak, since there was no time for clothes. As they flew away towards the hatching grounds, he heard Arion let out a roar. Yes, Arion was definitely paralyzed and not just letting them go without a fight. The next time he tried to visit campus, Arion would rip him to shreds. He shivered, not from the cold but from his actions. He had be- trayed Ashton. He had turned against his master. There was no going back.

Jamie had better be worth it, he thought.

Eraxes sung the song to get them into the hatching ground and at first he felt pressure against them, as if he were being kept out. Then the pressure faded and he felt a welcoming voice envelop him. Marisol had initially thought he was a spy, but then she had noticed Jamie with him and was inviting him into her domain. He hated to think that she doubted him like that, but he knew his actions were hardly those of an ally. After all, he had been sleeping with and aiding Marisol's enemy for months, why would she be able to read his true intentions and realize he was really a friend? He landed on the beach and immediately was swarmed by Scott and Kale.

Scott helped Jamie down and enveloped him in a large hug. Kale made sure that Jamie was all right, then helped Mike down and gave him a hug. He kept an arm slung around Mike's shoulders even after the hug, and Mike leaned into him. Here was a man who fully understood the sacrifice he had just made, and the love he had just lost. He felt like Kale understood him better than anyone else in the world, and he was grateful for Kale's presence.

"You did it, Mike," Kale said. "And I know it couldn't have been easy. You and Eraxes will be safe here."

"Thank you," he whispered, feeling tears fill his eyes. Then he caught sight of the students starting to wake up and see what the commotion was about, and his teacher instincts kicked in. These were, after all, the same students he had just spent a semester teaching. He couldn't be seen crying in front of them.

When they realized who he was, they swarmed him with stories of their dragons and the nagging question they all seemed to have: was it okay that they had stayed behind and not returned to campus? Mike assured them that they had made the right choice, but inwardly he was wondering how they were going to get food for all the growing dragons. This war would not be over in a day, and the young dragons needed meat, and lots of it. The blue dragons could eat fish and the green dragons could eat some vegetation, but meat was the cornerstone of a growing dragon's diet and there was none on this island. They would have to raid the campus, which would lead to skirmishes and potentially no food at all for the students. A tricky situation indeed. But at least they were here, and safe, Mike thought. He could work the rest out in time.

He looked to see how Jamie was doing and saw that Scott had escorted Jamie into one of the tents, no doubt to change into some clothes and talk in private. It had been over a week since the two had talked, and they undoubtedly had a lot to catch up on, especially since it seemed the war was starting. There were over two dozen dragons on the beach, and it seemed as if the island had grown to accommodate them. Marisol had said that the hatching grounds could be as large as needed, but he hadn't really believed it. Scott probably didn't notice because the change was gradual, but for Mike, coming here after a semester away, the change was noticeable.

Kale stayed at his side as he talked to the freshmen and when their questions were answered, he sent them to bed with their dragons. All of them were exhausted from the first year exam and the thrill of meeting their new dragon partners, and the dragons were exhausted from being outside of their shell for the first time. Mike smiled as he watched them leave, then his smile slipped as he thought of Ashton and what Ashton must be doing as the drug wore off. At the very least, Mike could expect his bond with Eraxes to be cut off forever, and he could expect Ashton to come after him personally. The thought terrified him, but he knew he had done the right thing.

He reached out to Kale and took the man's hand. Kale understood. Kale knew what it was like to betray Ashton and then have to live with the consequences. Kale took his hand and drew him close in a hug, and Mike rested his forehead against Kale's neck and inhaled the scent of the man, so different from Ashton's musk and so welcome and inviting. Perhaps not everything about this new life he had chosen would be bad, he thought as he tightened his grip on Kale and felt Kale tighten his grip in return. Perhaps he could find a home here with the rebels.

CHAPTER TWENTY-ONE

Divided Council

"**I** have to go back, and quickly," Jamie said as he threw on the fanciest clothes he could find in the chest they had brought to the island over the summer. There wasn't much selection and none of it was designed for cold weather, so he found himself layering clothes and hoped he still looked imposing.

"No way in hell I'm letting you go back," Scott said. "What if Ashton kidnaps you again?"

"He's knocked out right now, and I have to talk to the council before he wakes up and twists this to his advantage. I'm telling you, Scott, this is the only solution."

Jamie knew he was right. The plan had formed in his mind even as he and Mike flew and Mike had brokenly told him what he had done to Ashton to aid in his rescue attempt. As soon as Jamie heard about the sedative, he knew he would have to return. This was his moment to shine, and it needed to happen quickly or he would never be free from Ashton's control. He hadn't counted on Scott being such an obstacle, however.

As he raced towards Marisol, barely giving her a wave of greeting and ignoring the others on the beach, Scott raced alongside him trying to talk sense into him. Or what Scott thought of as sense. And it was sense, in a way. Ashton had tried to harm him so of course he shouldn't return to the campus. But Ashton was going to be knocked out, and this would be Jamie's only time to talk to the council freely. No matter what Scott said, he was going through with this.

"Marisol," he said, regretting that he had to speak aloud. Arion was still blocking his bond. "I need you to convene an emergency council meeting. Everyone, both campuses, as soon as possible. Immediately. No delays. Don't let them ask any questions, just tell them to arrive. Scott, I need you to let me do this, and let me do this alone. You aren't allowed on campus and I can't have you risking your life or harming my chances of success."

"Jamie, I would never-"

But Jamie didn't care what Scott would never do; he slashed his hand through the air to cut Scott off.

"If I don't come back, then at least I went down fighting. But I will come back, and there will be others with me. A lot of others, if my plan goes well. Be prepared to greet them and try to look as prepared and impressive as possible."

"Of course, Jamie, but-"

Jamie leapt on Marisol's back and they took off before Jamie could hear Scott's objection. It cut him to the bone to ignore Scott like this after being reunited for such a short period of time, but time was of the essence and he couldn't afford a long, sappy farewell as much as he craved one. He would get time with Scott soon enough, after he returned. He didn't like to think what would happen if he didn't return, if Ashton kidnapped him a second time. There would be no escape a second time. It was a miracle Mike had gotten the courage to stand against Ashton in the first place, and no one would dare repeat such an action.

Jamie and Marisol landed inside the council chambers. The chambers were designed to be open to the air and were technically big enough to hold a dragon, even though Jamie had never seen a dragon at the meetings. But today, he needed Marisol at his back as proof that he was Queen and because he couldn't talk to her telepathically. She was his weapon, and he needed her close at hand. Council members from the men's campus were already arriving and some from the women's campus were arriving on dragonback, getting dropped off outside. He watched them come in and they all seemed surprised to see Jamie and Marisol on the dais, even though Marisol had been the one to call the meeting. He waited until Margot arrived on her dragon, then looked around. Surely they had enough people. Not everyone was present, but he couldn't afford to wait for the stragglers.

"Are there enough here for a meeting?" he asked in what he hoped was a confident tone.

"Ashton is not here," a voice answered.

"Ashton is not required to be present," Margot answered. "This is a council meeting called by the Queen, not by the head. Yes, Jamie, there are enough people here for quorum."

Jamie nodded, and for an instant his body locked in panic. Some of these people would like nothing more than to bundle him up and take him back to Ashton. He looked at Margot and relaxed. She might not be on his side, but at least she thought what Ashton was doing was wrong, or so he assumed.

"For the past ten days," Jamie began in a strong voice, "Ashton has been holding me against my will and drugging me and Marisol. You all know the truth of the drugging; Marisol has already communicated with you about this. During tonight's first year exam, one of the students was almost killed because Ashton was preventing me from being in contact with Marisol."

There was a stir at his words. He knew the drugging wasn't new, but being held against his will and the first year exam ought to be.

"Ashton assured us that you agreed to let him cut off your communication with Marisol," Margot said.

Jamie flushed. "I asked him to cut off contact on a single occasion in order to prevent Marisol from entering her mating flight, because if she went into her mating flight before the eggs hatched, then the eggs would suffer. Immediately afterwards I asked for contact with Marisol again."

There was another stir, and then a voice rose up.

"So Ashton was trying to provoke you into a mating flight before the eggs hatched?"

"Yes," Jamie said. "That is one reason he used the drug on me and Marisol."

He didn't know who had spoken, but he was heartened by the fact that it was someone he didn't know because it meant other people were outraged, not just Margot.

"What would you have us do, Jamie?" Margot asked. "Ashton is head of the council and it is unlikely he will be voted off regardless of how he has treated you or mistreated the eggs."

"If you believe that what he has done is wrong, then I would have you leave this place and join me in my fight," Jamie said, letting all of his confidence shine through. "Ashton cannot be allowed to stand unopposed and if you believe in justice and want to fight this corruption, then come with me. Join me."

"Where exactly would we go?" a voice asked. "Ashton controls everything."

"The mountain itself is on our side, because the mountain has provided us a safe harbor," Jamie said. "And it is there that we will make our stand."

He didn't want to specify that it was the hatching grounds but he suspected that most of them guessed it. There were murmurs of interest and dissent, and soon the room began dividing with most of the people sounding angry and standing on the right side of the room, and a minority sounding hopeful and standing on the left. The left were his people, he knew, and they had finally identified themselves. Margot alone stood in the middle, and she didn't look likely to take sides.

"You intend to leave tonight?" she asked.

"Yes," Jamie said, again in the strongest, most confident voice he could must. "I have already had Marisol get in touch with friendly dragons across campus. Everyone loyal to me is leaving this campus, but we will need the leadership of a council. I am asking you to consider what you really believe in, and act accordingly."

"Don't act too soon," a new voice said, and Jamie flinched. It was Ashton. His steps dragged a little as he entered the room and walked through the aisle in the middle of the two groups of council members, so the drug must still be affecting him slightly, but he was fighting it well. Inwardly Jamie cursed. Having Ashton present would make the council members less likely to stand against him. But the ones on the left side were looking at him defiantly and didn't seem likely to change their minds.

Marisol growled low in her throat as Ashton stepped onto the dais with Jamie.

"This boy is delusional," Ashton said. "I told you before he was suffering from anxiety, and it seems he has finally snapped. You shouldn't listen to a word he says."

"He seems perfectly logical to me, Ashton," Margot said.

Jamie wondered why she was still in the middle of the room when she was so clearly on his side, and wondered if her status as head of the women's college prevented her from taking sides. The other council members, even the ones loyal to Ashton, nodded their heads in agreement with Margot's statement.

"This boy attacked me," Ashton said. "He drugged me and left me for dead."

"That's a lie," a voice said, and Jamie was surprised to see Eric separate himself from the crowd on the left. "Jamie didn't attack you."

Ashton glared venomously, and Margot nodded at Eric before turning her attention back to Ashton.

"Even if it were the truth, Ashton, why would you still have any drugs in your chambers after you've been expressly forbidden from having them? And it is my understanding that the drug cannot kill people, or is there more to this drug than you've told us in the past?"

A few people on the right side of the room started shifting to the left despite the glares from their fellows.

"Besides," Margot continued. "One of Jamie's complaints is that he can't speak to his dragon even though he wants to. He has stated here, before us all, that he wishes to communicate with Marisol, but he is still unable to do so. Unless Arion releases that hold immediately, all of us here will be forced to assume that you are deliberately harming the Queen dragon."

"I am doing it for Jamie's safety," Ashton began, but the council members booed him, even the ones on the right. Ashton glared, then gestured to Jamie. "Fine, if that is what he wants, then he shall have access to his Marisol."

"Not just Marisol," Jamie said, feeling emboldened. "I want full access to all dragons, like I usually have. I don't want Arion interfering in my relationships with any dragons."

He knew that he would be freeing up Arion to potentially harm other dragons, but he needed all of his abilities if he was going to properly fight a war. Ashton scowled.

"So be it."

Suddenly a wave of sound crashed over Jamie and he flinched as he struggled to make sense of everything. Then he felt a nudge from Marisol reminding him to look strong, and he straightened as the noises in his head sorted themselves into different dragon voices and soon all he could hear was Marisol.

Ashton gestured to Jamie. "You see, he barely has control over his abilities. What we need is a Queen who can rule herself, and a partner with the skills to handle his Queen. In this last hatching, we were granted such a Queen. I know many of you feel loyalty to Jamie because he has partnered with a Queen, but he is no longer the only Queen on campus. May I present Derek and Jettie."

Very cautiously, two figures, one human and one newborn dragon, emerged from the door leading to the chamber and made their way down the aisle. There was a soft exhalation as everyone admired the new Queen. Jamie grit his teeth. This was exactly what he had hoped wouldn't happen. Ashton was playing the second Queen card quickly, before the council members had a chance to defect.

"If you want to follow Jamie, I don't blame you," Ashton said. "He is, after all, a Queen, and no matter how strange their ideas are, they are special dragons who deserve protection. But if you remain, you will also be serving a Queen, a Queen who has already demonstrated a maturity beyond her age. When she hatched, she didn't even attack her partner. Instead, it was Marisol who attacked Derek. Marisol clearly is unable to control herself."

Jamie knew Ashton had made a mistake the moment he mentioned Marisol attacking, because suddenly the crowd grew hostile.

"Marisol attacked because I was not in communication with her," Jamie said loudly, and Marisol seconded that thought for everyone to hear. "When a dragon is deprived of human partnership, they revert to their initial violent state. And it was only Marisol's good parenting that led to the lack of a fight, her good parenting, I might add, that Ashton tried to compromise at every step."

Once again the crowd was on his side and even Derek seemed to agree with what he was saying, even though he was standing at Ashton's side. Jettie looked happy at being the center of attention, Jamie noticed, just like Marisol had as a child. He hated Ashton and he distrusted Derek, but Jettie was an innocent and he found that he rather liked her. She was, after all, his daughter in many ways.

Ashton shook his head. "Lies, but you are all wise enough to see through them. Let us end this now. If you are loyal to this unstable child, then go your separate way. We do not need traitors on this campus. And if you are loyal to your council head and to your Queen, then remain and be rewarded."

The council members dispersed, but Margot remained. She gestured for Jamie to mount Marisol.

"You will need to lead them to your safe haven," she said, "and I do not trust Ashton alone with you anymore."

Jamie was grateful for her concern as he climbed on Marisol's back and rejoiced in the sense of connection he felt with her. Outside, nearly four hundred dragons with riders were waiting for him. Some of them were council members, but most were regular students, faculty, staff, and residents of dragon canyon who were tired of Ashton and prepared to help in the war. Jamie sent a message to all of them to follow. He would still have to check each one individually before allowing them into the hatching ground and he dreaded doing so with such a large number, but he couldn't risk allowing spies into his base. He wondered if the island would expand to allow this many new-comers, and he wondered about food. Marisol told him not to worry about food, that the island would take care of them, but there were no large animals and such a large number of dragons would require a great deal of meat.

He led his army to the hatching grounds and then sent each dragon through in groups of three, the most he could scan at a time for their loyalties. Only two failed his test and they hissed before leaving the group. Alan was one of them and for a moment Jamie wondered if he had been forced to help with Jamie's captivity just as Mike had, and if he was planning to rescue Jamie himself, but there was that fogginess around his dragon's mind and he couldn't read Alan's true intentions. With memories of his betrayal in mind, he sent Alan away.

He exchanged greetings with some of the dragons and riders he knew: Amar and Nikki, of course, and Emma, his doctor, and Eric, and a few teachers from his first year. When everyone was finally inside, Marisol sang her song and they entered the hatching ground.

Jamie gasped. The island was enormous, and had sprouted

huts all along the vast beach to accommodate the new residents. What was even more amazing was what had happened to the clearing where the eggs had been. Instead of eggshells and emptiness, there was now a vast herd of cattle roaming the much-enlarged clearing, and the clearing was surrounded by a sturdy metal fence to keep the animals in. They certainly wouldn't have to worry about food, not for a long while. He wondered if they were real cattle or illusions, but they had to be real. How was the magic of the mountain able to create new life out of nothing?

He landed and immediately Scott pinned him to Marisol and began kissing him.

"You did it, Jamie," he whispered. "We have our army."

CHAPTER TWENTY-TWO

Accommodations

T he new council met almost immediately, and Scott didn't have time to give his Jamie the love and attention the boy deserved. But there would be time for affection, now that Jamie was freed. He was amazed at how many dragons had entered the island, and even more amazed at how the island had adapted. A thick mist had rolled in, blocking everyone's view, and when it left the island was so large he couldn't see the end of it and the clearing at the top held cows for the dragons to feed on. All of his worries seemed to fade away, and that was even before the enormous influx of dragons into the hatching ground in seemingly endless groups of three.

At first Scott and the others thought it would just be council members, but soon students came pouring through, then faculty and staff, and even simple dragon partners who lived in the dragon canyon and worked nearby but still followed Tarragon politics. Scott knew that Jamie was checking all of their loyalties and he was impressed, because it took over an hour for all of the nearly four hundred newcomers to enter the hatching ground. As soon as the council members landed, they greeted Scott and began planning where to house everyone and how to organize the huge group that was entering the island.

They mostly talked among themselves, but they did include Scott and made sure to ask his advice whenever possible, and he was grateful. It was refreshing talking to people who respected his role as the Queen's mate, and all of the people who had followed did. But he was also clearly out of his league and the council was more than prepared to take over where his skills were limited. There were people to be housed, students to be re-assured, an entire society to settle. People needed to know where to go and what to do, and the council skillfully settled matters al-most before all of the dragons had finished entering.

By the time Jamie joined them, the council was already send-ing out messages to various dragons and partners, and with Jamie to instantly communicate with every dragon the mes-sages became easy and everyone was told where to go. Within a few hours, as the moon began to settle in the sky, everyone was in a hut and their dragons were settled on the vast mountain that had appeared in the middle of the island near the clearing. Soon, even the council members decided everything was settled for the day. New meetings would start first thing in the morning to prepare the war, but for now, everyone would rest up and con-serve their strength.

As everyone settled into their huts, Jamie and Scott held hands and returned to their tent, the tent they had stayed in all summer. It was winter now, and Scott had used padding and extra blankets to pile up on their sleeping beds. Jamie sighed at the sight of it and squeezed Scott's hand.

"I would like nothing more than to get into bed with you."

Scott squeezed his hand suggestively, but Jamie tensed.

"Not tonight," he whispered in a voice shaded with shame. "Not after everything that's happened."

"Jamie," Scott said. "No matter what that man did to you, I still love you. Nothing will change that fact."

Jamie hung his head and released Scott's hand, plopping down on one of the sleeping bags and tucking his legs under his body.

"He didn't do what you're thinking. He didn't enter me. He wanted me to invite him," Jamie said in a voice full of disbelief and scorn. "He honestly thought I would want him and he was prepared to wait. But Scott," and his voice caught. "If I had been left there, I might have wanted him. That drug, it made me feel things. Things I can't explain. If Mike hadn't rescued me, I might have wanted him to do things to me."

"Hush, Jamie, it didn't happen," Scott said, perching beside Jamie and rubbing his tense back. "And you aren't responsible for what your body feels when you're drugged."

But the words hurt to say. So Jamie had felt something for Ashton when he was drugged? Did he feel aroused by Ashton, even though he knew Ashton was an enemy? Did he feel more aroused by Ashton than he did by Scott? The thought cut him to the core and he tried not to think about it. He would just imagine that Jamie had felt ordinary arousal when Ashton touched him, and not worry whether Ashton had tapped into some level of arousal that Scott had yet to find. He bit back his jealousy and stroked Jamie's back in what he hoped was a reassuring manner. Jamie was too tense, and his head was still lowered in shame. But as Scott touched him, his head began to rise as if Scott were erasing some of Ashton's poison from his body.

"I couldn't contact Marisol," Jamie continued. "I was afraid she would go into her mating flight."

Scott gritted his teeth. So Jamie had been so aroused he was worried about the mating flight. Ashton would pay for making his Jamie so vulnerable and then taking advantage of him like that. He didn't want to know more, but it seemed that talking about what had happened was like letting the poison out of a wound: Jamie needed to expel everything that had happened in order to heal properly. Scott would suffer, but he would let Jamie talk.

"He touched me, Scott, he stroked me and touched me and it felt so good. I've never felt anything like it."

Scott's hands clenched into fists for a moment but then he forced himself to continue stroking Jamie's back. This had to

151

come out sometime, and besides, it wasn't any worse than what Scott had done to Derek. They had both cheated on this relationship, only Scott had enjoyed his fling and Jamie had been drugged and unable to refuse during his. But why did Jamie have to enjoy it so much?

"Every day he came to me, but it was better after he stopped giving me the drug. It didn't feel so good. It was just my body reacting; I didn't enjoy it at all."

Scott was grateful for that, at least. Jamie hadn't enjoyed Ashton; he had only been caught up in the drug.

"When Mike came to rescue me, I thought it was Ashton for a moment and I wanted to die rather than face him another time. The eggs had just hatched, I had been in Marisol's mind again, and I thought he was going to push me into a mating flight. I would rather die than have him win the mating flight, Scott. We have to come up with a plan."

"We will, Jamie," Scott said. "And now that you're away from him physically, he's much less likely to win. Physical contact is important in winning the chase."

"But he's been so close to me for so long," Jamie murmured, his eyes closed as if he were envisioning his imprisonment. "How will I ever be free of him?"

"Hey," Scott said, shaking him gently until his eyes opened and focused on Scott, "You're with me now, not with him. I know it must have felt like forever, but you're free now. You have an army behind you, and more will come once the other nations arrive. You are free and you will fight against Ashton. You will never have to succumb to him again, do you understand?"

A tear streaked down Jamie's cheek. "I understand," he murmured. "But it's so hard to believe."

"Maybe this will help," Scott said, caressing Jamie's face and pulling him forward for a kiss. Jamie hesitated, then allowed himself to be drawn forward.

Scott's lips landed on Jamie's softly and Scott tried to imprint all of the love he felt for Jamie in that single, chaste kiss. Jamie murmured against him and opened his mouth, allowing Scott to enter his mouth and let his tongue trace his contours. Scott caressed his back underneath the layers of shirts and sweaters Jamie wore, and soon he was pulling off layer after layer to expose Jamie's beautiful body. Jamie flinched when the last layer came off, but he didn't try to stop Scott.

Scott removed his own shirt and Jamie pulled away from their kiss long enough to admire his body with a soft exclamation and a quick kiss on the center of Scott's chest before his lips returned to Scott's. Scott reached for Jamie's pants, but Jamie shifted his hips out of reach. For a moment Scott wondered if Ashton had scarred the boy and made him terrified of intimacy, but then he remembered that Jamie had said Ashton hadn't entered him. Still, Jamie was no doubt frightened at the thought of a man touching him, and Scott was hurt and angry on Jamie's behalf that Jamie was uncomfortable with being naked around another man. It had taken weeks to ease Jamie into being used to intimacy the first time Scott had seduced the boy; he didn't relish the thought of repeating it.

"No," Jamie said. "I don't want Marisol entering her mating flight, not yet."

"As you wish, Jamie," Scott murmured, relieved that it had nothing to do with fears of intimacy and only had to do with the practical matter of keeping Marisol from being affected by strong lust. He was, however, a little disappointed that he wouldn't get to enjoy all of his Jamie after dreaming about him for over a week. He wondered how long it would be before Jamie felt ready for complete intimacy, and how long before the mating flight took place. Not until after the war, he thought grimly. Marisol couldn't be allowed to mate until after Ashton ceased to be a threat. But until then, he could still enjoy his Jamie.

Scott's tongue left Jamie's mouth and traced along his cheekbones to his earlobes as Jamie sighed in pleasure. Scott nibbled on his earlobes before kissing his way down Jamie's neck, feeling as always like a vampire as Jamie arched his head back to give Scott full access to the sensitive skin. Scott sucked and kissed him with abandon, eventually moving to one of Jamie's favorite spots: his collarbone. Jamie exhaled sharply as Scott's lips closed over his collarbone and began working their way along its length. Scott's hands, meanwhile, had moved up to Jamie's chest and were fondling his nipples, which were hard in the cold air and perfect for playful squeezes.

Jamie was out of breath in moments, even before Scott lowered his mouth to his nipples and kissed each one soundly before moving back to his collarbone. Jamie's belly was quivering and his pants were tenting, and Scott backed off a little. He didn't want to send Jamie into the mating flight either, but he did want to let Jamie know that Ashton wasn't the only one who could arouse him. He, Scott, could do an ever better job without a drug to help him.

Scott pushed Jamie onto the sleeping bag on his belly and began massaging his back with firm strokes. The boy was tense at first, but as Scott's strokes continued to be soothing and only mildly arousing, he relaxed into the massage. Scott was happy; he wanted to pleasure Jamie without arousing him further and risking a mating flight. He stroked Jamie's back, feeling knots of tension and working on them until they dissolved into nothingness. Jamie would need to drink water after this, he thought idly. He was giving his lover a deep massage that must be at least slightly painful because of the pressure he was putting on certain spots, but Jamie was letting out sighs of relief and pleasure and none of pain.

When Jamie's back was completely loose and the boy lay limply on the sleeping bag, Scott kissed the nape of his neck and lay down on top of him, cradling him. Jamie snuggled into his body as Scott pulled a blanket over them. Jamie needed water so he wouldn't get a headache from the massage, but it could wait. For now, they were together. Tomorrow would come the hard part of making their revolution a reality.

CHAPTER TWENTY-THREE

Queen Dragon

D erek returned to classes almost immediately after the
first-year exam because his injuries healed so quickly,
and he was joined by all of the other students who had
been at his hatching grounds. Marisol's hatching grounds, he
corrected himself. She was the mother. It felt strange to have
a dragon whose mother's partner was Jamie and whose father's
partner was Scott, but he was getting used to it. It just drew him
closer to Scott, after all. Ashton had told him all about the mating flight on his second day as Queen and the first thing he had
asked was whether Scott and Narné could be in his flight despite
being Jettie's father. Ashton had looked annoyed and responded
that the dragons didn't recognize incest the same way that humans did, but there were other reasons Scott wouldn't be invited
to participate.

It had to do with the council meeting Derek had attended, he
knew. A third of the council had left that day, along with a large
number of students and faculty. In fact, when Derek's classes
started up again, Mr. Ferrin was nowhere to be seen and instead
they took their lessons from a new teacher, a man who lacked
all of Mr. Ferrin's warmth and enthusiasm. Even Ashton seemed
to have reservations about the new teacher, but with Mr. Ferrin
gone there were few options.

Derek wondered where everyone had gone, and suspected
they had fled to the hatching grounds where Scott had been after

the first year exam. He sometimes wondered what would have happened if he had stayed, or if he had left with the others, but he was happy on the campus. He had been given a room right next to his father's, and Ashton stopped by to see him at least once a day, usually more. In fact, Ashton was due to arrive any minute now as Derek paced in his richly decorated home and waited. Jettie was in her private dragon chamber, dwarfed by its massive proportions even though he knew she would soon grow to fill the chamber. For now, though, she was just a little thing and she could barely hop up on her dragon bed. Derek had arranged a ramp to make it easier for her and while she scoffed at needing the ramp, he knew she used it whenever he wasn't around.

There was a knock at the door and Derek opened it with a grin. Ashton was there, with a man who had red hair like Jamie's and wide brown eyes. Derek instantly disliked him, but he invited them both in. As usual, they went to check on Jettie first and she squealed when she saw Ashton, who always rubbed her eye ridges in just the right way. She had tried, once, to explain to Derek how to rub them properly, but had given up and simply said that only Ashton knew how to do it.

Ashton rubbed her and examined her.

"Is she eating enough? She hasn't grown much since yesterday. How many scales has she lost?"

"Just two," Derek said, wondering if she was supposed to be growing faster.

She was visibly larger than yesterday; surely that was fast enough. But he had heard tales that Marisol had doubled in size nearly every day when she was first hatched, and she had grown to full size in a matter of weeks. Jettie, on the other hand, was growing at the same pace as the other dragons and probably wouldn't reach full size for months. Ashton seemed disappointed in this, but there was nothing Derek could do about it.

"She's growing quickly for an infant," the other man said, and

Derek began to have warmer feelings about him. Maybe he had judged too quickly.

"But not quickly enough," Ashton said. "The sooner she has a mating flight, the better."

Derek shivered. Ashton had told him all about the mating flight, of course, and told him that Scott wouldn't be allowed to participate, but he didn't know who the other eight participants would be. He trusted Ashton, of course, since Ashton had set him up with Scott in the first place and that had turned out well, but he was still a little frightened by the thought of the mating flight.

"Your bond with her is good?" Ashton asked, turning to Derek.

"Of course," Derek said, beaming. He felt Jettie pressing against his mind, seconding that thought. "Jettie agrees."

"Yet you don't get lost in her thoughts. You've learned how to separate yourself from her very well, and very quickly."

"I did get lost in her at first," Derek said, remembering his first night when he had dreamed he was a dragon only to wake up and find himself a human. He knew that some of the boys got lost in their dragon's thoughts and emotions during the day, but that had never happened to him. He was able to distinguish easily between his own thoughts and Jettie's thoughts, and all of his teachers thought that was a good thing. "But I've learned to keep us separate."

"Well, Alan?" Ashton asked, turning to the other man. "What do you think?"

"She is a queen, but not a Queen," Alan said, and Derek could almost hear the capitalization in his words.

Derek stiffened as though he had been insulted. He didn't understand the distinction, but he knew it was significant and he knew his father wanted a Queen with a capital Q. Scott had said he had bonded to a Queen, so who was this stranger to say otherwise?

"I thought as much," Ashton said in a weary tone. "Thank you, Alan. You may let yourself out."

As soon as Alan was gone, Derek put his hands on his hips and glared at Ashton. "What exactly does that mean? Jettie is a Queen, you can tell by her coloring."

"She will lay eggs, yes," Ashton said. "And she is what I need. You are what I need. Don't worry about that, my son. But she is not the same as Marisol, and the dragons will sense the difference."

"What do you mean? Because she isn't growing fast enough? Is that it?"

"No," Ashton said. "Because her bond with you isn't the same as the bond between Jamie and Marisol. Tell me, does the world seem any different to you now that you're bonded?"

Derek frowned and looked around. "No, except that I have a dragon in my head sometimes."

"With Jamie, all of his senses became heightened and he gained a dragon's ability to see, hear, smell, taste, and feel things that no human ought to be able to sense. He entered Marisol's world. In your case, Jettie entered your world. It's a small difference, but an important one. The dragons regard Jamie as one of their own, but they regard you as a human."

"What does that mean?"

"Nothing, for now," Ashton said. "But they might be more willing to obey Jamie than you, at least until your mating flight. And because Jettie entered your world instead of you entering hers, she will develop at your pace: slow. And we need this mating flight to happen quickly."

"What can I do to speed it up?" Derek asked.

He hated feeling like he was disappointing his father, especially when it was something he had no control over. If he could jump into Jettie's world, he would, only he didn't know how. And he suspected that the time for such a thing had passed, that it was only possible when the initial bond was being formed. He wondered what the world was like for Jamie, viewing it with a dragon's senses. Were his senses always heightened, or just sometimes? And how had his initial bonding been different than Derek's? He knew that fighting was a typical part of the process and he had heard that Jamie came back from his first year exam on the brink of death; did that have anything to do with it? Did you have to almost die in order to see the world as a dragon did? If that were the case, then Derek was glad he hadn't gone through that ordeal even if it would have made his father happier. He valued his life too much, and he was pleased that his dragon hadn't felt compelled to attack him. He had still been injured, sure, but Jettie was intelligent enough to recognize that he wasn't a threat.

"You can do a few things to hasten the mating flight," Ashton said. "Keep feeding her as much as possible and brushing her for loose scales twice a day, and pay attention during your classes. During your free time, try to get as close to her as possible. Share your every moment with her. Don't worry about losing yourself in her mind, just let yourself sink into her."

"But that's exactly what the teachers say not to do."

"They have different goals," Ashton said with a dismissive shake of his head. "Your goal is to get close to your dragon, not distance yourself. Can you do this?"

"Of course," Derek said, pleased that all of Ashton's requests were perfectly reasonable and doable.

"Good boy. I will see you tomorrow, then, and hopefully Jettie will be larger."

Jettie swatted at him playfully. She was annoyed that he was disappointed in her growth, but he gave such good eye ridge rubs that she wasn't actually angry. Derek felt the same way, though his reasons were different. He was upset at having disappointed his father, but thrilled beyond belief to have captured so much of his father's attention.

"Oh, Derek," Ashton said as he was leaving the room. "Have you learned her ability, yet?"

"Not yet," Derek said.

All dragons who could speak telepathically had a special talent, but it sometimes took years before their riders figured out what that talent was and Derek was afraid it might take that long for Jettie. He knew Ashton was eager to find out and so was he, to be honest, but Jettie had shown no traits out of the ordinary yet.

"Well, keep looking," Ashton said, then he vanished into the dragon canyon.

Derek closed the door and returned to Jettie, brushing her scales and hoping that at least one would fall off. None did, but her russet coloring shone brilliantly in the crisp winter air. She was truly a beauty.

"Do you know what your ability is, Jettie?" Derek asked, as he sometimes did.

I am me, she replied. *I do not know what makes me different from the others.*

He sighed. She gave the same answer every time. He returned to the living room and sank down in a chair with his homework. Only one week left until winter break. He wondered if Scott would be back by then, and he wondered again why everyone had left to follow Jamie. He thought of Alan and the man's proclamation that Jamie was a Queen while Derek was only a queen. What did it take to enter the dragon's world? He closed his eyes and tried to imagine himself as a dragon, tried to push his way into Jettie's mind, but she politely pushed him back out. She didn't care that Ashton wanted him to find a way in, she had decided that his mind was not welcome and she wouldn't allow him entrance.

"Please, Jettie," he said aloud. "Let me in."

You would not survive, she said gently. *Leave our bond as it is.*

Derek grumbled to himself, but he trusted her. In truth, he didn't want more of a bond. It was hard enough living with a dragon pressed against his mind all the time. He didn't want to live in a dragon's world with dragon's senses, and he pitied Jamie. A little. He sighed and turned his mind to Scott, as he had been doing lately. He wondered what Scott was doing, and how Scott was handling his exile. As he thought of Scott, his hand began creeping along his body and he let himself take what pleasure he could in his memories of the man.

CHAPTER TWENTY-FOUR

New Love

Somehow in the madness of getting everyone settled for their first night in the hatching ground, Mike was ignored and ended up with no place to sleep. Even though the magic of the hatching grounds had seemed to create a small hut for everyone that would be staying on the island, there was none for him. He wandered for a little bit, looking for an empty hut and finding only occupied ones, before heading back to the new council a little embarrassed at being left out. Perhaps the island hadn't realized he would be staying.

As he headed back to the council, which was beginning to break up for the night, he saw Kale by a large tent, one of the same tents that had been on the island over the summer, and he thought that perhaps there was a tent for him and that's why the island hadn't created a hut. He went over to Kale, knowing he looked a little depressed and forlorn but trying to appear confident.

"How many tents are there?" he asked, looking around at what was the original encampment.

"Just mine and Scott's," Kale replied, then he hesitated and looked around. "Why? Do you need somewhere to sleep?"

Mike flushed, and Kale nodded. "You're welcome to stay with me. I have an extra sleeping bag."

"I would like that," Mike said softly. He hadn't expected such kindness from Kale, or from anyone here. After all, they all knew that he was Ashton's pet. The new council that had formed here had been dismissive of him from the start and he didn't blame them. They probably thought he was a traitor, even though he was the one to rescue Jamie and make all of this possible. Kale seemed to understand, though. Mike followed Kale into the tent and stooped as he entered, climbing onto the sleeping bag that Kale pointed to.

Kale sat cross-legged on his sleeping bag just inches away and Mike followed suit, knowing that Kale wanted to talk to him before they went to sleep. He was a little nervous, and also was starting to worry about going to sleep. He hadn't brought anything with him. Most of the people who had accompanied Jamie had been given enough time to pack their most valuable belongings, or at least a change of clothes. Even the council members had had time to go to their quarters and grab a few things before following Jamie. Ashton hadn't chased them, after all: the dragons wouldn't have allowed it. But he had run out of Ashton's rooms with nothing, not even clothes to give Jamie. All of his stuff was either in Ashton's room or in his room and he hoped it would still be there when he returned. He worried that the remaining people would rummage through the rooms of those who left and take the valuables, even though there was no real need since everyone in Tarragon society was taken care of. But there were several personal items that Mike would be heart-broken to lose, and he was worried that someone might intrude on his space and steal or break them.

At the moment, though, he was only worried about what to sleep in, and what to wear tomorrow. He didn't think anyone would notice if he wore the same outfit two days in a row, but they would notice soon enough if that were all he wore, and especially if he were wearing it to sleep in as well. Perhaps he could borrow from someone else. Perhaps Kale, since Kale was around his size.

"How are you dealing with everything, Mike?" Kale asked, reaching out to take his hand. "I know everything must be up in the air for you right now."

"You have no idea," Mike said dryly.

He knew thinking about clothes was his way of avoiding thinking about the main problem, Ashton. He had betrayed Ashton and the sting of that betrayal went to the core of his being, even though he knew he had done the right thing.

"I have some idea," Kale said. "I ran away from him once too, remember? But I can't imagine what you're going through now. Do you want to talk about it?"

Mike studied Kale. Kale was right, he did know what Mike was going through.

"Why did you leave Ashton?"

"He asked me to sacrifice my life."

"And you wouldn't do that for him?"

"Well, not exactly," Kale said, shaking his head and looking at the ground in shame. "I would have done it for him. But I wanted to say goodbye to my dragon first and when Vestis realized what was going on, he flew me to safety until Eric talked some sense into me and got me to realize that I shouldn't kill myself just because Ashton wanted it."

Mike was silent for several minutes as he thought about Kale's story. So Kale had felt the same instinct to obey Ashton, even to the point of putting up with pain and sacrifice. Mike wouldn't have agreed, he knew. He hadn't even been able to stand seeing Ashton sleep with another person without his loyalty snapping. Kale had been a far better pet than Mike ever had, and Mike was both happy and inexpressibly sad at the same time. Happy that he had never gotten so strongly pulled into Ashton's spell, but sad that he had failed Ashton and hadn't been able to give Ashton the kind of obedience Ashton deserved.

"He was sleeping with Jamie," Mike finally said. "I couldn't stand it. I couldn't stand knowing that he had lied to me when he said I was his one and only. I couldn't stand the thought of him touching someone else, anyone else. He made me agree to let him pursue Jamie during the mating flight and that would have been okay, but not before. So when I realized what he was doing to Jamie, that he was using the drug on Jamie, I snapped. I had to act, I had to get Jamie and me out of there."

"You did the right thing, Mike," Kale said, still holding his hand but now stroking it softly. It felt good to be touched so gently. Ashton was much more forceful with his caresses.

"I know," Mike said. "But I still feel lousy."

Kale drew closer until he was sitting beside Mike, their thighs pressed against each other. Mike leaned his head into the crook of Kale's neck. Kale was so different than Ashton, so respectful.

"You'll get over Ashton," Kale said confidently. "You'll find someone else. You won't be his pet forever, not now that you've stood against him."

"What about you? You still wear his collar."

"It won't come off until a sacrifice is made," Kale said slowly, and then explained about blood sacrifices and the mountain's mist.

Mike went stiff with fear as Kale explained how someone had to give their life in order for the collar to come off, and how the council mostly knew what was going on, how most of the council had also worn the collar. He felt a little better when Kale said that there had to be genuine affection in order for the collar to be worn in the first place, since it meant that Ashton did have feelings for him, but he felt betrayed beyond words that Ashton had intended to use him as a sacrifice and nothing more. But then he remembered Margot's words on the evening they had gone to the girl's campus – she had told Ashton to keep this one, meaning Mike, and Ashton had agreed. Did that mean that Ashton was planning on sacrificing someone else? It had to be Kale, Ashton had to be planning on sacrificing Kale and keeping Mike alive. It warmed his heart a little that Ashton hadn't wanted to kill him, but he was still chilled at the thought that Ashton had initially chosen him with the intention of killing him.

He was also chilled by Kale's description of Arion killing the human's dragon. He would never let harm befall Eraxes. He reached out to Eraxes for comfort and felt his dragon's shock and disgust at what Kale was saying. None of the dragons knew about the dragon sacrifices, Eraxes assured him, or else they would have put a stop to it a long time ago regardless of the mist.

"So all this time, he was planning on sacrificing me?" Mike asked.

Kale had wrapped an arm around Mike's shoulders and Mike was still cradled against his body, and it felt nice to be held this way and told the truth, both things that were rare with Ashton.

"He probably thought he could get away with a blood sacrifice and not your life," Kale said. "Or he thought he could kill me. But yes, that's why he chose you as his pet."

Mike shivered and snuggled closer to the man. He smelled refreshing, like the pine needles from the forest and also like the dark depths of the water nearby. An intriguing combination. He pressed his face against Kale's neck to inhale the scent and realized he was kissing Kale. To his surprise, Kale kissed his forehead in return. Mike lifted his head so they were eye-to-eye and he saw hunger there, and sympathy. Mike winced. The hunger he could deal with, but not the sympathy.

"Please don't feel sorry for me," he said.

"It's just that I know what you're going through, and I know it isn't pleasant," Kale whispered. "I had Eric to help me when Ashton turned on me, and I want to be here for you."

"How did Eric help you?"

"He talked to me," Kale said. "But I can do more for you, if you want."

There it was, out in the open. Kale was offering himself to Mike. Mike knew his cheeks were bright red by the heat he felt in them. Mike had often thought of Kale, and not always in a chaste way, but here Kale was offering himself and willing to let Mike take advantage of him. But Mike didn't want to have him under these circumstances, not when Kale was trying to help him forget Ashton.

"I do want you, Kale," Mike said, noticing how Kale's eyes suddenly sparkled. "But not like this, with Ashton in the middle. I want you without Ashton."

"Then forget Ashton. He's your past, anyway. Let me be your future."

Mike smiled at how quickly Kale was willing to disregard Ashton after the long conversation they had just had about the man. Kale was really trying to win over Mike, but he didn't know he already had. Mike leaned forward and kissed Kale on the lips, and it felt as though a spark lit between them. Kale grabbed the back of his head to keep him in the kiss and aggressively pushed his way into Mike's mouth. Mike let him, too surprised by his forceful actions and too turned on by the actions to stop. Normally he was in charge aside from Ashton, but he could already tell that Kale was going to be the dominant one in this relationship.

Their kiss seemed to last forever, and as they kissed Kale pulled him down until they were lying together on the sleeping bag, which provided minimal padding against the hard earth below. It was a bit uncomfortable, but the kissing more than made up for it. And even though it was cold outside, their tent felt like a sauna because the sexual heat was so intense between them. Mike began peeling off his clothes as Kale did the same, and once Mike whipped off his pants he realized that Kale was naked beside him. Kale was incredibly handsome, with shaggy brunette hair that looked as though it had been weeks since he had gotten it cut framing his square-cut jaw and deep-set brown eyes, but it was his body that really drew Mike's attention.

Kale's entire upper body was tan, as if he had spent the summer without a shirt, and several scars ran from his back to his chest, no doubt from his hatching. Right at his waist, however, his skin turned pearly white and Mike adored the tan line dearly, especially as it drew his gaze to the mound of brown curls that barely hid the cock beginning to rise. Mike had always thought of himself as well-endowed, but Kale was even more impressively built and Mike's mouth went dry at the thought of having that cock inside him. It was not as big as Ashton's, he was pleased to note, because Ashton had sometimes torn him and their sex was often more painful than pleasurable; Kale was the perfect size.

Kale was examining his sudden nudity as well and after a moment examining each other, Kale pulled him close for another kiss and pressed Mike back on the sleeping bag, straddling him so their cocks pressed against each other. Kale let his hips grind against Mike slowly as pressure built between them and Mike gasped for air. His cock was on fire and they were only rubbing against each other. What would the rest of the evening be like? Kale continued to kiss him passionately, possessively, and let his hands travel along Mike's body freely. Mike, for his part, could do little more than clutch Kale's back and his hair, urging him to continue what he was doing because it felt so good. They continued for what felt like hours as Mike grew harder and harder, and then his balls began to tighten and he knew he wouldn't be able to take much more of it but he wanted to cum with Kale inside of him.

"Inside," he managed. "I want you inside."

Kale was panting and out of breath but he pulled them apart and let one hand travel from Mike's cock downwards until he was parting Mike's cheeks. Mike worried about the lack of lube, but as Kale's cock rubbed against him he realized there was more than enough precum to ease the entry. Mike tried to calm himself and took a deep breath. He didn't want to cum with the penetration; he wanted to enjoy himself. Kale pressed against him slowly and Mike winced. Kale stopped immediately.

"Did I hurt you?"

"No, faster, faster," Mike panted.

Kale grinned and pressed harder until he popped through to Mike's body. Mike arched his back and bore down on Kale, surprising the man, who must have expected Mike to want to take it slower. But Kale seemed ready for anything and he entered Mike quickly until he was fully seated in Mike's body. He leaned his head against Mike's chest, his own chest heaving, and then began a long pull outward. Mike cried out and soon they were caught up in a rhythm better than anything Ashton had ever given him, because Kale continued to watch him and alternated his strokes when he saw Mike wince with pain or gasp with pleasure. Mike gave himself fully to the pleasure and let Kale take complete control of his body as he had never done with Ashton, and he was richly rewarded as Kale lovingly penetrated his body.

It seemed like hours before Mike's balls started to tighten again and he knew the end was near. Kale was gasping for breath and so was Mike, the two of them sharing their breath between heady kisses. Kale leaned forward against Mike and thrust hard, and Mike tipped over into bliss, his body spasming as everything within him seemed to spill outward. Kale cried out as Mike felt something wet splash against his insides, and then Kale leaned against him in contentment. They stayed that way for several long moments, panting for breath as if they had just run a marathon, evidence of their pleasure all over their bodies.

Finally, Kale got up and grabbed a towel that he used to clean up Mike and himself. Once they were clean, he unzipped his sleeping bag and gestured for Mike to get in with him. Mike obeyed, and Kale wrapped him up in his arms. Mike wouldn't have to worry about getting cold, he thought drowsily as the remnants of their pleasure began to send him into a blissed out sleep. He kissed Kale's hand and let himself fall asleep, safe in the arms of his lover.

CHAPTER TWENTY-FIVE

Reconnaissance

J amie sighed. The new council had been meeting all morning and had just taken a break for lunch, finally. He hadn't anticipated how time-consuming it would all be, and how many steps were involved in preparing everyone. The council had organized everyone into huts the night before, but this morning they had organized everyone further, going around and getting everyone's name, their dragon's name, their occupation, and whether or not they were willing to be in the actual fighting or if they were simply escaping Ashton and lending their support in other ways. Only about a third volunteered to be in the fighting, which surprised Jamie, who had expected everyone who left to be prepared for battle. But perhaps he shouldn't have been surprised, since after all the group included students too young to fight and also doctors and other professionals who really shouldn't be fighting as they were more valuable off the field.

Emma was in charge of the doctors and she was already arranging part of the beach into a makeshift hospital where she planned to heal any injured dragons or humans. She already had a few customers, since two of the students who had joined them came from traditional hatching grounds and had emerged injured from the first year exam. Jamie was impressed that they were willing to risk everything and join him, but he knew the thought of a rebellion was an exciting prospect and they probably hadn't thought everything out fully. He was heading over to the hospital now to check on them, since he wanted to make sure the hospital was ready for action when the fighting started.

No one knew when the fighting would start, or how it would happen. They didn't know if it would be best to emerge from the hatching grounds as a unit and attack, or if they should try to surround the campus and cut off their supplies in a siege. They would need a good deal more dragons to carry out that plan, but more were on their way. And they hadn't yet decided what Jamie's role would be. After all, he needed to clear every dragon who entered the hatching grounds but if there was mass retreat and all the dragons tried to enter the hatching grounds at once, Jamie would be overwhelmed and he might let enemies into their base. So far he had discovered that once he allowed a dragon access, that dragon could reenter the hatching grounds far more easily, with almost unconscious approval from Jamie. He would be able to let in nearly twenty at a time if they were already approved. But they were talking about armies of a thousand or more, and couldn't take the time for Jamie to scan them by twenty every time.

It was a difficult situation and what most of them were really hoping for was a quick end to the hostilities, a single pitched battle that ended the war quickly and with as few casualties as possible. That would be the best for both sides. Jamie knew the doctors were hoping for the same, but were apparently preparing for the worst as he saw the vast area that had been designated the hospital.

Emma was sitting on a tree stump sipping tea, which she must have brought along with her and used her dragon's breath to heat up. Jamie waved and headed towards her. She was still his favorite doctor after saving his life, and from what he had seen in Eraxes's mind about the drug, she was the one who had discovered that Ashton was drugging Jamie and Marisol and had been the one to tell Mike to put an end to it. She waved in return and gestured for Jamie to join her on a nearby fallen tree that provided a perfect bench.

"How are you doing, Jamie? I want to get a full physical as soon as you have time," she said. "I want to make sure you're healthy after your captivity."

Jamie winced. He didn't like anyone bringing up his long week and a half as Ashton's slave. It was humiliating and shameful that he had been so helpless to everything Ashton wanted, and he knew that everyone assumed Ashton had raped him even though Ashton hadn't. Everyone looked at him with pity in their eyes and he wanted to tell them that nothing happened, but he couldn't, because something had happened. Just not what they thought.

"I'm fine," he said. "I had food and water."

Emma tsked. "I'd still like to see you. You've been under so much stress, it can't be good for you, and being separated from Marisol on top of everything else, well, it can have physical effects. But let's not talk about that now. Did you need something?"

"I just wanted to see how everything was going here."

"We're organized. Most of the doctors came here, leaving just enough to be able to handle the injured on campus. We all would have come, but we are responsible to all dragons, even those we disagree with, so we chose a group to stay behind. I'm glad I came, though," she said. "The island here is surprisingly nice."

"It is, isn't it? It wasn't anywhere near this large last time I saw it. Marisol said it adjusts based on our needs."

"I just hope we're not using the mountain's magic unnecessarily," Emma said. "The mountain renews itself through blood, and we don't need to be making another sacrifice so soon after the attack on Kale."

Jamie was silent, but he thought of killing Ashton on the mountain and wondered if that would appease the mountain. For a time, probably, but then another sacrifice would be needed, and another. There had to be another way for the mountain to protect them and continue its magic without relying on blood and sacrifice. He was a little surprised that Emma knew about the sacrifices, but perhaps Kale had told her or she had overheard Kale talking. Doctors knew many secrets on campus, but rarely let them slip.

"It's good to see that Kale is well," Emma said, as if she knew that he was thinking of Kale. "But he needs a haircut. One of the women who came with us is a barber, I believe. You should send Kale to see her."

Jamie laughed. Over the summer when they had been living together, free from Tarragon Academy, his and Kale's hair had grown long and unruly. Scott continued to get haircuts on campus since he still visited, but Jamie and Kale cut each other's hair or just let it grow long. He had grown accustomed to seeing Kale with long hair, but perhaps it was time for the hair to go. He wondered what Mike thought of Kale's hair. He knew Kale and Mike had spent the night together after Mike had been left out of the housing dilemma. There were enough huts for everyone except Mike and the council hadn't even thought of Mike, assuming their work was done when the newcomers were housed. Only Jamie had realized that Mike was left without a home, but when he had gone to offer Mike one of the tents, he had seen Kale inviting Mike inside. He was pleased by their relationship, since Kale would undoubtedly know what Mike was going through right now.

Jamie didn't fully understand Mike's actions, but when he read Eraxes's mind he found only pure hatred of Ashton and he knew that Mike was firmly on their side, no matter his past actions as Ashton's pet. Even though Mike had seen him in chains and refused to help him, Jamie knew he had secretly been planning Jamie's rescue the entire time. It couldn't have been easy, after all, and Jamie forgave him for taking ten days before rescuing him. Jamie would forever be grateful to Mike, and he hoped Mike didn't feel too isolated at the camp. The other council members snubbed Mike, assuming that he was still Ashton's pet and that he had acted out of spite or jealousy, not out of a desire to see Ashton gone, but Jamie knew better. Mike was a genuinely good person who had gotten caught up in Ashton's games, gotten lost for a while, but was now back on track.

He and Emma said goodbye and Jamie meandered through the hospital, greeting the doctors and nurses. They were pleased to see that he was well and he realized that everyone here had been worried about him. It was strange to think that this many people cared about him, but they did. He reached the two injured students, who sat up straight at the sight of him.

"Hi," one of them said, introducing herself as Lydia. "Are you really the Queen?"

"Yes," Jamie said, and lifted his shirt to show off his scars as he was accustomed to doing with the important representatives who came to see him. They were duly impressed and showed off their own half-healed scars, none as impressive as Jamie's.

They chatted about the first year exam and about their dragons, always a popular subject especially among the newly partnered, and then Jamie frowned.

"Why did you come with me?" he asked. "Your dragons can't even fly yet."

It was true, they had been carried to the hatching ground by larger dragons just as Jamie and Marisol had once been carried by Eraxes and Narné.

"Ilsa wouldn't let me stay," Lydia said, gesturing towards her dragon who was hopping around outside the hospital area. "She said you were our Queen and we had to stand by you no matter what. She said you were one of them, one of the dragons, and all dragons were loyal to you."

"I wish all dragons were loyal to me," he said. "But unfortunately a lot of them stayed."

"Their dragons are loyal, though," Lydia said confidently. "They just don't want a war, I think. They want you and the other dragon, Arion, to work things out peacefully."

"How do you know this?"

"I can hear echoes of the dragons," she said shyly. "Sometimes when I close my eyes I can hear voices that I know aren't mine or Ilsa's, and they're so strange I know they must be dragon voices. They talk about you a lot, and how you need to be protected, but they also talk about Arion and how he needs to be obeyed. They sound confused a lot of the time."

Jamie considered. He could hear other dragons, but only when he concentrated and he could only dig so far into their minds. He couldn't hear what they said to each other, though. Lydia had a very valuable gift, one that might come in handy in the future.

"Thank you for telling me," Jamie said. "It's nice to know that the dragons at least respect me."

"They do," Lydia assured him with glowing eyes. "Much more than the other queen."

"You mean Jettie?"

"Yeah, the one that Derek partnered with. He's so lucky," she added with a sigh. "Not that I'm disappointed with Ilsa, of course."

"What do the other dragons say about Jettie?"

"They adore her, but they never talk about Derek. They do talk about you, though. It's like you're a fellow dragon or something, and he's just a human."

Jamie thought of the gifts he had received when he bonded with Marisol, and he thought of how bonding with her had radically altered the way he viewed the world. He barely noticed it anymore, the over-saturated world that seemed to exude emotions in addition to color, the sharp tang of scents wherever he went, the incredibly complex tastes he had started to experience. They were part of his world now, and rarely even fazed him at all. They were normal, just as they were normal for Marisol. He had wondered if Derek would undergo a similar shift, but apparently he hadn't. Jamie couldn't help but feel some relief at that – Derek may have a queen dragon but he wasn't a true threat to Jamie. The dragons would still prefer Marisol to Jettie.

"Thank you, Lydia," Jamie said. "I may come back to talk to you. Which hut are you in?"

She gave directions, and then he left to head back to the council. Lunch was almost over and he wanted to grab a quick bite before rejoining the meetings. At least Scott was there to keep him from getting too bored, he thought. And now he would have news to give to the council, good news, about how the dragons viewed this war and how they viewed him. He needed all the help he could get.

He was headed down the beach when Scott ran up to him, out of breath and gasping for air.

"Jamie, something's happened," he said. "You need to come quickly."

CHAPTER TWENTY-SIX

A Stronger Bond

Derek brushed Jettie and was pleased when three scales fell off. He kissed her forehead and shared a happy thought. She was just as delighted as he was that she was growing a little faster than she had been. He had been feeding her more and brushing her more, as Ashton had recommended, and he had been trying to lose himself in her thoughts even though his instructors taught the opposite. Still, he couldn't get lost in her mind no matter how hard he tried. There was a firm wall between them that wouldn't budge, and he had the distinct impression that Jettie didn't want it to budge. Whenever he tried too hard to get lost in her thoughts, she would gently scold him and remind him that the relationship they currently had was enough for her, and should be enough for him as well.

He couldn't explain to her why he needed to impress Ashton so much. She knew, partially, but she couldn't really understand it. She didn't understand the need to impress a father figure, since the relationship between dragons and their parents was much different. Technically she knew who her father was, but she had no real feelings for him aside from a small level of affection and that was mostly because Derek had feelings for Narné's partner. He had tried to explain his desire to impress Ashton, but she just ended up shaking her head and accepting his seemingly irrational need. She wasn't complaining, since she got extra food and attention, but Derek knew that she didn't fully understand.

He was just about to leave for his classes when someone entered the dragon chamber. Derek's heart leapt – but it was Alan, not Ashton. Ashton usually visited in the evening, not the afternoon. Still, Alan was close to Ashton so perhaps he was here on Ashton's behalf. He shook Alan's hand and wished it were Ashton and they were greeting with a hug. Ashton had shown only limited physical affection towards him and Derek knew they were still warming up to each other. After all, Ashton had only been in his life this semester and they had only become close in the days since the hatching.

Alan was carrying something but keeping it hidden as he approached Derek, who craned his neck to see what it was. Alan's cloak kept it concealed, and Derek gave up with a shrug. If it were important, Alan would show it to him. He trusted his father's friend. Alan went over to Jettie and examined the scales on the ground.

"Three scales today. That's good improvement," he said, scratching Jettie on her eye ridges. Derek could feel his little dragon's pleasure at the scratching as she turned her head into Alan's caress. Alan wasn't as good as Ashton at rubbing her eye ridges, but he was close. "Have you made any progress strengthening your bond?"

Jettie hissed and pulled her head away. Derek knew she was starting to get annoyed at Ashton's insistence that their bond be strengthened. She was satisfied with their bond, Derek was satisfied, so why was Ashton still trying to push the issue? He could feel her thoughts loudly in his head, but he wasn't losing himself in her thoughts the way the other students did. He could clearly identify her emotions as being separate from his, and he wanted it that way.

"I think our bond is set," Derek said. "We're both happy with it. I know she might not grow as fast, but I don't think it's even possible to change our bond at this point."

Alan sighed. "It is possible. Are you going to continue trying?"

Jettie hopped over to him and butted her head against him. *Tell him no,* she said in an irritated voice. *I know you want to make him like you, but perhaps Ashton will like your strength.*

Derek took a deep breath. Perhaps she was right. Perhaps doing everything Ashton said wasn't the best strategy, and he should show some backbone. After all, Ashton was sure to appreciate strength in his son. He would stand up to Alan, and perhaps Alan would report his strength back to Ashton.

"No," Derek said. "Our bond is fine the way it is."

Alan shrugged and came over to Derek, one hand cradling whatever it was he was holding and the other extending to grasp Derek's shoulder. Derek allowed the touch just as Jettie had done earlier. Then his other hand whipped out a long dagger and he stabbed Derek in the belly.

Derek stared at the dagger in his flesh, not quite believing the extraordinary pain his body was experiencing. This had to be a dream. Alan would never hurt him.

Alan drew the blade out and Derek stumbled and fell. Jettie roared and knocked Alan away before nuzzling Derek.

"I'm sorry, Derek," Alan said. "But I am in charge of making sure your bond is strengthened, and the only way to strengthen your bond if you won't try is through blood. Jettie has the power to heal you, but only if she strengthens the bond between you. If she doesn't, then you'll die and she will die as well. It's up to her, now."

Derek gasped. It felt as though he were choking and his mouth filled with blood. He spat it out and clutched his belly, which was gushing blood. He tried to put pressure on it and stared at Jettie, silently asking her if Alan's words were true.

I can save you, but it would kill you, Jettie said in a state of near panic. *You cannot survive the full bond.*

Alan stared at them. "No one will come to help you, not even Ashton. He has given me permission to do whatever I deem necessary to strengthen your bond. Either you bond, or you die."

He turned his back and left the room. Derek felt hot tears streaming down his cheek as he coughed up more blood. He was being left to die and Ashton wasn't going to come and rescue him. If he had just gone with Scott, this wouldn't have happened. Scott! What if Scott came to save him? Surely Scott would be able to carry him to a doctor, since no doctor would risk Ashton's anger and come here to save him.

Jettie, he thought. *Summon Narné.*

She hopped next to him. *I already have, and the Queen,* she said, nuzzling him. *Stay strong.*

He tightened his grip on his belly. He knew you were supposed to put pressure on injuries like this, but he didn't know how much good it was actually doing. Blood continued to seep out and he was beginning to see stars amid the darkness circling his vision. He pressed against Jettie in his mind. He could tell that if he just broke through the wall dividing them, he would be able to share in Jettie's strength and survive this. But she had said he wouldn't survive breaking through the wall, and he trusted her. What other choices did he have, though? Was this what Jamie felt like when his bond was formed? Despite himself, he felt sympathy for Jamie and he knew that he would never look at him the same. Jamie had gone through this same ordeal and survived, Derek told himself. He would survive as well.

Derek's head sank into the floor and his grip loosened as loss of blood made his body harder to control. His head sank into a pool of blood and he knew from Jettie's panicked cries that he was going fast. He wondered what would happen to her if he died. Would she survive without a human? He didn't think so. How could Ashton approve such a thing? Surely it wasn't so bad that he wasn't bonded as strongly as Jamie. Was it really worth losing Jettie?

His mind began to grow dark, and then he heard a loud roar, far louder than Jettie's cries. Crimson covered his vision and for a moment he thought it was blood, but then he recognized Marisol towering over him. He flinched. Was she going to kill him as she had tried to do before? She shoved her muzzle into his body and knocked him flat on his back, exposing his injury as a spurt of blood splattered across her nose. Then she licked the injury, slowly, and dread ran through him. She was going to eat him. She had been prepared to eat him before at the hatching grounds, but now she was really going to do it. He tried to brace himself.

Then he noticed that Jettie wasn't fighting Marisol but rather welcoming her and nuzzling up to her. Wouldn't Jettie try to stop Marisol from eating him? Marisol withdrew her muzzle and Derek noticed that the blood had stopped flowing from his injury. Did her saliva have some sort of magic in it? It didn't matter, though; he had lost too much blood. He wouldn't recover without a doctor. Marisol scooped him up in one claw and scooped Jettie up in her other, then flapped her great wings. They were aloft, and the pain from his injury was unspeakable as Marisol's hard scales pressed directly on the wound. He felt as though his entire body would burst into a bloody mess. He coughed and knew he was still bleeding internally when blood came up. He needed a doctor, fast.

Marisol carried them up over campus, but his vision was starting to fade again. He was barely aware of her singing a song as mist closed over them, and then they were landing. Hands were on him, and something was being jammed down his throat. Suddenly breathing was much easier even though it felt like a tube was threading all the way down his throat. He was given an injection of something that made everything go numb and he was deeply appreciative. Doctors poked and prodded him, cutting him open in places and stitching him up in others, all while he lay there barely awake. He was aware of Jettie nearby, sending him strength and encouragement. The wall between them was intact, he was pleased to see. They would have the same bond as before, the type of bond they were both comfortable with.

As he lay there, he began to see familiar faces and wondered if it was the drugs pumping through his system or reality as Scott and Jamie appeared before him. It must be reality, he figured, because in a dream only Scott would have appeared. The tube was taken out of his mouth and he became more aware of his surroundings. He was on a beach, and while it looked like the same beach from the hatching grounds, this one was enormous and filled with huts. It must be somewhere different. There were doctors all around and Jettie was being kept from his side, forced to watch from the sidelines. As soon as his thoughts began to clear, he sent her a message of reassurance and her frantic hopping ceased.

"Are you all right, Derek?" Scott asked. "We came as soon as Jettie called us. What happened? How did you get injured?"

Derek remembered Alan holding the dagger, Alan with the dagger plunged into his gut, Alan walking away to leave Derek to adapt or die. All with Ashton's approval. But Ashton was his father. How could his father do such a thing? It didn't make sense. Maybe Ashton was possessed. Maybe he was under a spell. Because there was no way his own father would let him be attacked and then leave him to die.

"I don't know," Derek said, not wanting to acknowledge what Ashton had done.

"You don't remember?"

Derek knew his cheeks were on fire. "That's right."

Jettie's growl was audible even from the distance she was at. Tears filled Derek's eyes and he looked away from Scott and Jamie, ashamed at what his father had done.

"No," he whispered. "I do remember. It was Alan. He attacked me and left me there because Ashton wanted him to. He wanted Jettie to heal me so our bond would be as strong as Jamie's and Jettie would grow faster."

He couldn't look at Scott or Jamie, and instead fixed his attention on the smooth fabric making up the floor of the open-air tent he was in. Jettie made a sound of distress and he looked at her instead. She took several steps closer to him, her russet scales shimmering in the setting sun, but she kept her distance as the doctors commanded. Finally, he looked at Jamie and Scott. They both looked horrified, but not surprised.

"Marisol healed you," Jamie said eventually, when the silence had become uncomfortable. "Dragons can heal humans and it helps form a bond between them. Since Marisol already can speak to all riders and has that bond, she was able to heal you without affecting your bond to Jettie or her bond to me."

"So if Jettie had healed me, our bond would have strengthened? Alan didn't lie?"

"No, he didn't lie," Jamie said, looking as if he had swallowed something unpleasant, "But he didn't understand the truth. Jettie says that you wouldn't survive the type of bond established by a healing. Alan just refused to listen."

"How could he?" Scott asked, speaking for the first time. He seemed genuinely upset and he reached out to squeeze Derek's hand. Jamie's eyes flashed with jealousy but he made no move to stop Scott and Derek was grateful. He needed loving contact right now more than anything, after being betrayed by his father. "How could Ashton risk harming the one thing that was giving him authority? How could he harm his own son?"

"He probably realized that Derek couldn't just replace me, not according to the dragons," Jamie said. "And that made Derek disposable. Ashton is ruthless; we know this about him. But even I never would have guessed he would let his own son die."

A group of men and women approached and Jamie cursed. "It's the council," he said. "They'll need to be told what happened, why we left so suddenly. I don't think Derek's ready for them, though. Scott, why don't you stay with Derek while I deal with the council?"

Scott agreed and Jamie left to intercept the group. Scott ran his hand over Derek's brow and wiped the tears from his eyes.

"It's all right now, Derek," he said in a low croon. "You're safe here."

Derek shivered and clutched at Scott's arm, needing the reassurance of his physical presence. Scott would never hurt him or betray him. But he had thought the same of his father, and Ashton had turned on him. Would there come a day when even Scott would turn? He turned his head away from Scott and tears began to flow again. If Scott turned against him, he wasn't sure he wanted to live.

CHAPTER TWENTY-SEVEN

New Trouble

J amie flung himself down on the sleeping bag and rolled over on his belly. Scott was still with Derek, trying to calm the boy, and despite everything, Jamie couldn't quell the faintest hint of jealousy at the thought of them together. He shut his eyes and reached out to Marisol, who was communicating with Jettie and reassuring the young dragon. Marisol sent him a brief mental hug and he wrapped himself in her love. He was still getting used to having her in his mind after so many days without her.

He had barely gotten used to being out of that cell when everything had happened. Scott running up to him, yelling that Derek and Jettie were in trouble. Jettie had reached out to Narné first, but Marisol soon afterwards and as soon as Marisol saw what was happening, she took to the air without waiting for Jamie's permission or approval. Not that she needed it, since as soon as he realized what Alan had done he would have sent her anyway. She was the only dragon who could possibly rescue Derek and Jettie. Anyone else would be attacked by Arion, but not even Arion would dare attack Marisol. Even the dragons who stayed with Ashton believed that Marisol was the rightful Queen and wouldn't allow anyone to harm her.

Jamie had been swept into her mind as soon as she took off and he shared the rescue with her, gazing in shock as she saw Derek huddled on the floor clutching his belly in a pool of blood and Jettie hopping frantically nearby. He had tasted Derek's blood as Marisol licked him and used her saliva to start healing the wound, just as she had done with Jamie's wounds a year ago in his first year exam. Jamie couldn't ignore the similarities: the boy crippled with fear and agony, the infant Queen dragon nearby unable to help save his life. Jamie had been far more grievously injured, but Derek was still near death due to blood loss as Marisol carefully picked him up in her talons to carry back to the hatching grounds. She had to carry Jettie as well, since the little queen couldn't fly, and it was a good thing Marisol was considerably bigger than the other dragons or else she wouldn't have been able to carry both.

When they arrived back in the hatching grounds, Jamie had managed to detach his mind from Marisol's and tell Scott and the council members who had gathered what had happened. He and Scott had run to the hospital to take care of Derek and Jettie and the council had called a hasty meeting to assess the new situation.

And now Scott was with Derek, alone together, at least if you didn't count the doctors, and Jamie was trembling with fear, adrenaline, and jealousy. He sighed heavily and pushed himself up from the sleeping bag. Then he took a deep breath and left to talk to the council. They were waiting outside his tent and he was glad he hadn't taken longer. Luckily, they seemed to understand that he needed a moment to recover, because none of them commented. He told what had happened, and what Derek had told them.

"If he's desperate enough to send someone to attack his only queen and his own son, then he must realize we have the upper hand," Eric said, looking at the rest of the council members for agreement. Even though the council members were all technically equal, Eric was the youngest and the newest and was used to having his ideas shot down, Jamie knew.

"But do we?" a woman asked. "What does he expect us to do that he's so afraid of?"

"Whatever he was trying to accomplish, he couldn't have expected this to happen. Jamie, what was the reaction when Marisol showed up?"

"Arion was furious," Jamie said. "Arion was guarding the room and if any other dragon had tried it, they would likely be dead. But there were other dragons around and Arion couldn't attack Marisol in public like that, so he had to let her pass. Ashton's not going to make that mistake again."

"He should have known Marisol would come," the woman said. "It had to have been a trap. Is Derek loyal to us, or is there a chance he's a spy?"

"I don't know," Jamie said. "His loyalty has always been up in the air. But I think he was truly shaken by what Alan did and I think Scott can persuade him to join our side."

"Will you be okay with that?" Eric asked, watching Jamie keenly. "Will you be okay with having another queen here, one that your boyfriend has had sex with?"

Jamie flushed. His jealousy rose to the surface but he reminded himself of everything that Derek had just been through. Derek and Scott were talking, nothing more, nothing to be jealous of.

"I would rather have him on our side than acting against us," Jamie finally said.

The council members relaxed and he realized that if he had rejected Derek, they would have been on his side. They would act to serve and protect him, even if they lost an advantage. It was an odd feeling having such loyalty from people he barely knew.

"But we have to act quickly, while the campus is still in disarray," Jamie continued. "Ashton will try to cover it up, and make it seem like we kidnapped Derek against his will. We have to get people there to tell the truth."

"We do have some people there," one of the council members said. "Not all of us came with you. If you can get in touch with their dragons, they can start telling the truth and weakening Ashton's hold on his people."

"Of course," Jamie said. "Who?"

They listed four council members and it was a simple task to reach out to their dragons and illustrate what had just happened. Their dragons were shocked and appalled and promised to send the news on to their riders. They also sent news that Ashton was summoning foreign leaders to his aid. Jamie wouldn't be the only one with an army, it seemed.

He related the news to the council and they didn't seem surprised.

"Our forces will arrive sooner than his. We'll need to make this a quick battle, and a decisive one. We need to kill Ashton and replace him as soon as possible," a woman said. She eyed the men on the council. "You should start considering who will lead your academy now, so there isn't civil war after we get rid of Ashton."

"Scott will lead," Jamie said. "He is the Queen's mate, after all."

"He's too young and inexperienced," one of the men said. "We'll respect him as an equal and perhaps in time he can rule the council, but right now he's still a student and doesn't fully understand the intricacies of Tarragon society worldwide."

"So teach him," Jamie said. "One of you will be a regent and teach him what you know, and then step down when he's ready."

"That would be best," another council member said. "We don't want a power struggle to weaken us further. We'll need to stand strong after Ashton is removed or else Tarragon society might fall apart."

The men in the council talked a little longer, then the eldest nodded his head. "We will discuss this further in private, I believe, and tell you which of us will act as a regent for Scott until he is mature enough to lead. But right now, we need to focus on our strategy. The campus will be weak without Jettie, and we believe it is time to strike."

"Now?" Jamie asked, his heart accelerating rapidly. "But our army isn't here, it's just us."

"Not an attack, but a protective shield around the airspace above the hatching grounds. Right now we are limited. If we wish to come or go, we have no idea what's waiting on the other side of the mist. If Ashton has any sense at all, he'll post his army over the hatching grounds and simply kill us as we leave. But if we secure that airspace, then we will be able to come and go freely, and you'll have an easier time checking our loyalties before letting us in."

"That would be a good idea," Jamie said slowly. "But do we have enough dragons to do it?"

"We believe so. Ashton won't attack until his armies arrive. The most that would happen is a skirmish, and we have enough dragons to deal with anything he could send our way. Besides, if the worst happens, we can always retreat into the hatching grounds."

Jamie nodded. "Then let's do it."

The council members seemed to have the plan already set up and Jamie wondered if they had just been waiting for his permission before starting, because as soon as he approved, they dispersed and went in very specific directions. Eric stayed behind, however, and Jamie was grateful. He didn't understand how this war would work. He was in charge of everything, technically, but he, like Scott, was still a student and the council members had far more experience than him.

"We worked out a plan with Kale," Eric told him. "They'll be putting it into place now. Soon we'll control the airspace over the hatching grounds and no one will be able to enter unless they go through us."

"Kale helped with this? When?"

"This morning," Eric said. "You may have noticed that some of the council members were absent from the morning meeting."

Jamie hadn't noticed and scolded himself. There were only nine council members, how could he not notice that they weren't all present? But they were so intimidating and they all seemed to blend into each other aside from Eric. It was hard to keep track of who was who and where everyone was. He was just glad they were there to handle the details of the attacks, and he was glad Kale was here with his experience at the White House. Kale would know what to do to secure the airspace without endangering the dragons.

"Alan was your bodyguard for a while," Eric said. "How much do you know about him?"

"Not enough, clearly," Jamie said with a scowl.

He couldn't believe that Alan would do something like this, not when he was the only person on campus who had known Jamie's parents and from what he had said, been friends with his mother. He had been shocked when Alan had been part of his kidnapping earlier but he had assumed that, like Mike, Alan could do nothing to rescue him. But this was an intentional attack on another person and their dragon. This was completely different and it revealed something chilling about the man that Jamie had been totally unaware of. Marisol was still unable to read Alan's dragon's mind due to the fogginess around his dragon – his dragon's gift – and he now suspected that Ashton had been counting on that when he sent Alan to be Jamie's bodyguard. Alan was loyal to Ashton, completely, despite his seeming friendship with Jamie's mother.

"It seems like he's one of Ashton's hit men," Eric said. "We've always known that Ashton has a few people that he uses to take care of problems, but we've never known who they were before."

Jamie was silent. Take care of problems. His mind fled to his parents and the problems they had posed. His mother had been a part of Tarragon society but no one knew she had a dragon, and his father had been an outsider. Jamie knew his mother had a dragon, which meant that by marrying his father, she was breaking a rule. Looking back to his conversation with Alan when they had first met, he realized that Alan, while he had seemed friendly enough talking about Miranda, his mother, had

very little to say about his father aside from a few empty plati-
tudes. It was almost as if he didn't approve of the marriage, or he
didn't want to talk about Jamie's father with Jamie. What if – and
the thought filled Jamie with horrifying clarity – what if Alan
had been the one to kill Jamie's father?

He didn't think Alan was responsible for his mother's death;
Alan had shown too much remorse for her death. But he hadn't
seemed to care for Jamie's dad at all and the thought that Jamie
had allowed his father's potential killer so close to him for so
long was sickening, but now that he had thought of the possibility he couldn't get it out of his mind. He pressed a hand to his
forehead and sat down on the sand.

"Is everything all right?" Eric asked, reaching out to touch his
shoulder.

"Do you think – is it possible that he could have killed someone?"

Eric was silent for a while as if trying to figure out why Jamie
was asking, then he nodded as if putting the pieces together.

"Your parents. It is possible, Jamie. Their deaths happened
under suspicious circumstances, and there may have been council involvement. It was before my time on the council," he added.
"I'm sorry."

A tear ran down Jamie's cheek. He stood up and went back
into the tent, brushing Eric aside.

"Tell me when I'm needed for the army," he said, then closed
the zipper and collapsed onto the mound of blankets and pillows
for the second time, this time in tears.

CHAPTER TWENTY-EIGHT

Old Loyalties

Scott stroked Derek's hand as the boy drifted in and out of consciousness. He knew Jamie was jealous, but there was nothing else to do. Derek needed someone he trusted right now, and Scott was the only one who would do now that Derek's faith in his father had been shattered. Scott couldn't believe that Ashton had allowed an attack on his son, no matter how ruthless Ashton was. Especially since Derek was bonded to a queen. He looked out the tent where Jettie was now curled up and asleep like her partner. It just didn't make sense for Ashton to resort to such a desperate measure.

He must have been counting on Jamie's jealousy to prevent Jamie from rescuing Derek, Scott thought. Because otherwise Ashton had to have known that Marisol would come in and rescue the little queen and her human partner, and he had to have known that Arion wouldn't be able to stop the large Queen dragon. It was nice to know that Arion wasn't bold enough to attack Marisol, he supposed. But if Arion had so much as raised a claw against the Queen, the other dragons – all of them – would have turned on him and Ashton and Ashton's war would have been over. Ashton could hurt Jamie, but never Marisol.

So why had Ashton done it? Perhaps Ashton had given Alan free reign to do whatever the man deemed necessary without knowing the specifics. That might make sense; if he didn't realize attacking Derek was an option, he wouldn't know to forbid it. Because now that Derek was here, with the rebels, Ashton's position was far less stable than before and he had almost no credibility with the other dragons. He would have a hard time convincing anyone to remain on his side after attacking his own son and a queen dragon.

Unless, of course, he lied. Scott sighed. Ashton would have no problems weaving a tale about how Marisol had swooped in and kidnapped Derek and Jettie, and the remaining council would believe him, and that would be that. No retaliation, no repercussions. As much as Scott hated to admit it, this event might even make Ashton's position stronger if the man played it right, and Ashton seemed to always know how to play to his audience.

Derek murmured something nearly inaudible and his eyes opened. He seemed surprised to see Scott, then he shifted and winced and it seemed like he remembered where he was and why. A pained expression crossed his face and Scott squeezed his hand.

"How do you feel?"

Derek licked his lips. "Thirsty."

Scott stood up and got a doctor's attention, and soon several nurses were helping Derek sit up as he drank some water. He grimaced and spat it out on the sand beside his bed and it was heavily tinted with blood. Scott was alarmed, but the nurses reassured him that it wasn't new blood. Derek drank some more until the nurses stopped him, then remained propped up on several pillows as the nurses examined his rapidly healing injury.

It was deep and would leave a scar to go with his other scars, but it was healing quickly due to Marisol's saliva. All dragon saliva had healing properties but only on the person they had a bond with and Scott was impressed that Marisol was capable of healing other people. It was a good thing, too, or else they would have lost Derek. And Jettie, he thought, glancing over at the russet pile of scales who was unwinding from sleep with a wide yawn. Both Jettie and Derek were precious and Scott would be heart-broken to lose either of them, but he would mourn Derek more because he knew Derek better. Derek was elusive and multifaceted, and manipulative as often as he was sincere, but Scott felt drawn to him nonetheless and he was grateful that Marisol had been able to rescue him from certain death.

As soon as the nurses left them alone again, Derek looked at him, at their hands that were still clasped together, Scott's covering Derek's.

"Where's Jamie?" he asked.

"Busy with the council," Scott said. "Don't worry about him. He'll do everything in his power to protect you."

"Why?"

Scott was a little taken aback by the direct question, though he knew why Derek was asking. After all, Derek and Scott had slept together and it was no secret that Derek still had feelings for him, even though Derek seemed to have given up on those feelings in favor of friendship.

"Jamie is a good person, and he wouldn't let anyone get hurt the way you were."

"And I'm a valuable asset in your war, right?" Derek sounded dejected and pulled his hand away from Scott. "That's the only reason everyone's being nice to me, isn't it? Because I'm valuable?"

Scott grabbed his hand and his shoulder and leaned forward until they were nearly touching noses.

"You are valuable, Derek," he said. "But you are not an asset. You are a person, and a truly special one at that."

"My own father was willing to let me die," Derek said, casting his eyes down. "What do you want out of me that I won't be able to give you?"

"I want you to survive, and be happy," Scott said.

Derek laughed. "See? I can't give that to you. I won't be happy without having you, and you aren't available."

Scott leaned back, aware now that the nurses were watching him like hawks and would report his closeness to Derek back to Jamie. Derek had a point; he wasn't available. He couldn't be available because he was already promised to Jamie. But that wasn't a reason for Derek to despair.

"You will find someone, Derek, I just know it. You're too wonderful not to. And until you do, you have Jettie to take care of. Isn't she enough, for now at least?"

"She's enough for me," Derek said, meeting his gaze defensively for some reason. "Is she enough for you?"

Scott didn't understand what Derek meant by the question but he nodded. "She's incredible. You have no idea how rare it is to have two queens when we haven't had a single queen in decades. And you survived the bonding, which is rare. You and she are a perfect match just the way you are."

Derek relaxed a little. "Then you accept her? And our bond? You don't want anything more from us?"

"What more could I expect? Whatever relationship and bond you've developed is unique to the two of you and I wouldn't change it for the world."

A smile lingered around Derek's lips. "I do love her a lot. Ashton made me feel like I wasn't doing something right with her, like I had made a mistake when I bonded with her and I should have done more."

"He's a fool," Scott said with a wave of his hand. "Your bond isn't like Jamie and Marisol's, and it shouldn't be. Every dragon and rider have a different, unique bond and they should."

"I don't know what her gift is," Derek said.

"You will eventually," Scott said, knowing that Ashton had probably hounded him for that information as well. He hadn't really imagined what life must have been like for Derek after returning to the campus but it must have been hellish with the one person he wanted to impress demanding things he just couldn't give.

"And I don't want to fight him," Derek said, squeezing Scott's hand. "No matter what he did, he's my father and I won't fight him."

"You won't have to," Scott said, mentally filing that away under important information to tell Jamie – later. He didn't blame Derek for not wanting to fight against his father but Derek had to be accepting of the fact that Ashton was going to have to pay for his crimes, and he might have to pay with his life. Scott took a deep breath.

"Derek, we're going to war with Ashton. People might die. Ashton might die."

The boy shivered. "There's no way for peace?"

"No."

"I don't want you to kill him. Please, Scott, promise me that you won't be the one to kill him."

Scott sucked in some air. He didn't want to kill Ashton but he knew that Ashton was going to have to die for Tarragon society to move forward. Someone would have to kill Ashton. But hopefully it wouldn't be him. He didn't know if he could make this promise to Derek, though, because if they were fighting and the chance came to kill Ashton, Scott knew that he would have to take it, promise or no. He didn't want to be the one to kill Ashton, but if push came to shove, he would be willing to strike the final blow and bring justice back to Tarragon society.

His silence must have gone on for too long because Derek lowered his eyes again and released his hand.

"I understand," Derek whispered. "You can't promise me. He's going to die, and you might be the one to do it. I could never forgive you if that happened."

"I don't know if I could forgive myself if I killed another person," Scott said honestly. "No matter who that person was."

"At least we agree on that," Derek said with a faint smile.

Scott took his hand again and Derek didn't protest.

"Look, Derek, I would offer to take you back to campus but you aren't safe there. Will you be okay staying here, with us, knowing what we're planning on doing?"

"I won't betray you, if that's what you're asking," Derek said in a sharp voice. "But yes, I'll be all right here. Just don't expect me to join in the celebration when it's over."

"I doubt I'll be in the mood for celebration either," Scott said. "Maybe we can spend that evening together and reflect on the past."

He hadn't meant it suggestively but from the suddenly speculative gleam in Derek's eyes he knew Derek had interpreted it as such, and it seemed like too much trouble to explain himself. But all he meant was that it might be nice being with someone else who wasn't celebrating the death of another human and his dragon when this was all over. Any death was serious and ought to be mourned, even one's enemies, and he knew Derek would need special support because it would be the father he still cared for, despite what that father had done. They would be good company for each other without anything sexual happening between them.

And, of course, there was always the chance that they would lose, that Scott would be killed or captured by Ashton, that Derek would be killed or captured. Scott tried not to think too hard on it but it was there. Jamie had already been captured and it had changed him in dozens of little, almost unnoticeable ways that Scott doubted even Jamie was aware of. Jamie was jumpy, and fearful, and avoided physical contact when possible. Nothing obvious but it was there and it made Scott's heart ache because he knew he should have prevented it. He should have taken Margot's warning more seriously and prevented Ashton from ever getting his hands on Jamie.

But the past was the past, and all Scott could do was ensure that it never happened again. The mating flight hung heavily over his head and he knew Jamie was worried about it as well.

If Ashton won the mating flight, would the dragons currently supporting the rebellion once again side with Ashton because he was the proper Queen's mate? It was a question Scott didn't want to know the answer to but he knew Jamie fretted about it just as much as he did. And now Derek's mating flight was an issue. Whoever mated with Derek would have power and authority, though second to Marisol's mate, but it would still be a potential challenger. Scott was just glad Ashton couldn't fly in his son's mating flight, but he knew Ashton would have plenty of his men ready to take his place. He thought of Alan, who had been slated to be in Jamie's mating flight, and shivered.

Derek lay back down in his cot and seemed to drift off to sleep and Scott brushed a strand of hair back from his sleeping face. He was so beautiful, but he also looked so much like Ashton. If they did succeed and Ashton was killed, would people target Derek as well? The boy had some protection because of his queen dragon, but Scott would have to make sure that Derek was protected as well. He didn't want anything happening to such a fine young man. When he was sure that Derek was sound asleep, Scott informed the nurses that he was leaving and headed towards his tent where Jamie would be waiting.

Jamie would be disappointed that Derek wasn't joining their cause, but hopefully pleased that Derek was recovering well. And Scott knew that he needed to return soon so Jamie wouldn't be too jealous. Jamie had been under so much stress lately, he didn't need jealousy on top of everything else. Scott glanced back at Derek as he left and the boy had rolled over on his side with one hand resting on his cheek where Scott had stroked him. Scott sighed and began preparing himself to deal with Jamie.

CHAPTER TWENTY-NINE

Skirmish

K ale insisted that he be part of the group leaving to secure the airspace around the hatching grounds. He had been trapped in the hatching grounds for over six months now and while the hatching grounds had expanded dramatically in the past few days, there had been hardly any space to fly for months and he was hungry to be on Vestis, free in the air again. Mike came with him, and he was a little worried but didn't try to stop his new lover from coming. Instead, he had smiled at Mike and kissed his hand when Mike announced that he would also come with the group. It would be wonderful to fly together with Mike, despite the dangers. Since both of their dragons were male, they could never be in a mating flight together, but simply being at each other's side would be a wonderful feeling.

Kale hopped up on Vestis, carefully avoiding his blue dragon's long spines and watching the green dragons with some envy, as their dragons didn't have spines along their backs. Marisol had short spines that were easy to navigate, and Jamie mounted her with no trouble. Only the blue partners had difficulty getting on their dragons, but it didn't stop anyone. They would ride out of the hatching grounds together, and then the dragons would leave their precious human cargo at strategic points along the mountainside to guard against human attackers while the dragons kept the air clear. The humans would stand watch for twelve hours, then be replaced, but the dragons could remain for days. Dragons, though they enjoyed sleeping, did not need to sleep once they reached maturity.

Once they were all mounted and ready to fly, Kale looked over at Mike and met his smile. They were finally acting against Ashton, and it felt wonderful. Jamie gave the command to take flight as he flung his arm forward, and the entire beach seemed to take to the air. The dragons flew in perfect formation, speaking silently to themselves to arrange the best, strongest positions for each without bothering their humans for input. When they reached the limit of the hatching ground, mist circled them and then they were flying over a mountain with no lake in sight. Kale breathed a sigh of relief that there were no dragons waiting for them, and he felt a grin break out over his face to be flying over Mount Tarragon again.

While half of the dragons remained airborne, the other half deposited their humans along the various trails to the hatching grounds. Since the first year exam was over, there was no reason anyone would be on the trails except to sneak into the hatching grounds. Kale and Mike sat at the back of the dragons and waited in the air, since they were considered the most vulnerable to attack. When the first dragons returned to the air without their partners, the second half, including Vestis and Eraxes, soared to the ground.

Kale and Mike had been given the actual trailhead where the path to the hatching grounds split off. That was their territory to protect. They had been given this area because it was in the center of the protected area and no one should be able to get to them unless the outer ring was taken out, and if that happened, their dragons could carry them to safety. Everyone seemed to recognize that Kale and Mike were likely to be Ashton's targets and even though they grudgingly allowed them to participate, they were also trying to protect them. Kale was grateful, but knew they were being overprotective. Ashton wouldn't bother with them when he had Jamie to deal with, and dragons in his skies. He would be focused on the other men, not petty revenge.

With Kale and Mike safely tucked away at the trailhead, Vestis and Eraxes took up their positions at the back of the dragons once again. Kale watched his dragon fondly and shared his excitement with the dragon. They were both giddy at being free and outside of the hatching grounds, able to fly wherever they wanted. True, Vestis had to fly in formation and technically couldn't do whatever he wanted, but the possibility was there and that was enough for both of them.

"How does it feel to be back here?" Mike asked, no doubt observing Kale's pleasure.

Kale beamed and took his hand. "Wonderful. I know there's danger, but being free like this after so long is a gift."

Mike traced his thumb along the top of Kale's hand and looked up at him through his lashes. "You know, we're not likely to see anyone for some time."

Kale laughed. He pulled Mike close and kissed him thoroughly as Mike melted against him. Mike's hands stroked his back, then wandered lower to grip his ass and bring him closer to Mike's own hips and growing hardness in his groin. Kale let him; it felt amazing to know that Mike was turned on by this and that Kale had finally found someone who loved him, truly loved him, unlike Ashton. But when Mike's hands tried to slip under his waistband, Kale reluctantly pulled away.

"Not here, or now," he said gently. "Even if we are safe, we can't let our guard down."

"I just wish this were all over," Mike said, lifting a hand to tug at the collar around his neck. "I wish I had never met Ashton and met you instead."

"Without Ashton, we never would have found each other," Kale said, wishing it weren't true but knowing it was. He had come to the campus to save Jamie originally, but his plan had quickly become saving Mike as well. He didn't know if he even would have noticed Mike if the man hadn't been Ashton's pet. It was sheer luck that Kale did notice Mike and developed feelings for him, because those feelings had blossomed into something miraculous.

Kale thought of his life before returning to campus, his busy but empty life as the President's bodyguard. He had always had things to do, people to protect, reasons to stay single. It was dangerous falling in love, after all. He had learned that the hard way after Ashton. He had loved Ashton so deeply, and Ashton had betrayed him utterly. So when he ran away, he had closed his heart off and vowed to only care about people who deserved his trust. He had to care about people in order for his dragon's gift to work and as a result he did care about the President and several other members of government, but he never loved anyone. Now, though, he loved again and it was a wonderful feeling, as though something that had withered in his soul were being reborn.

His dragon gift allowed him to sense danger to people he cared about and he didn't sense any danger to Mike immediately, but he could sense an edge of danger as if something were brewing in the future. It wasn't surprising, given the situation they were in, but he wanted to make sure that Mike was never in any danger. He would do anything to protect Mike, no matter what. The edge of danger spiked, and Mike pointed at the sky.

"There're here," he said, and Kale's head whipped around to look at the airborne dragons.

Jamie had sent forty dragons to secure the airspace, and it looked like Ashton was matching him dragon for dragon. The enemy dragons looked to be carrying humans and they dipped down to the ground to unload their passengers just as Jamie's dragons had done. Kale looked to Jamie, the only person still astride his dragon. He was at the far back of the dragons, even behind Vestis and Eraxes, and he pointed forward and yelled something inaudible from their position on the ground. Jamie was leading his troops into battle. The dragons surged forward. The goal, Kale assumed, was to prevent the enemy dragons from unloading their partners because the dragons wouldn't be able to properly fight with humans on their backs.

As soon as the dragons surged forward, Marisol and Jamie

faded into the mist as they had agreed to do once the battle started. All of the dragons had insisted that Marisol be protected during the actual fighting, and Jamie had reluctantly agreed. No one wanted to risk the Queen's life in a mere skirmish. Kale knew that Jamie was following the progress of the battle, though, through the other dragons' minds using his gift and he was briefly jealous of such a powerful gift.

The dragons met in combat in the air and the enemy dragons successfully held them off while the rest of the humans dropped to the ground. The enemy dragons were all green, making it easy for their partners to slide off them when the dragons were still several feet from the ground. Then the real fighting began, and Kale watched in awe.

The dragons attacked each other violently, slashing with claws and biting each other with bared teeth, but though blood visibly spurted from some injuries, the dragons seemed to draw back from killing each other. If a dragon started to withdraw from the field, the other dragons let it go without any follow up attacks. Kale knew that the dragons forbid killing other dragons but he hadn't expected it to extend to war. He couldn't see what was happening on the ground but the danger he sensed was growing stronger and stronger. He suspected the enemies had breached the outer ring and were making their way to Kale and Mike.

"Mike, we need to hide," he said as the danger seemed to peak.

He grabbed Mike and pulled him into the woods behind a thick tree just as three men strode into view. They were unfamiliar men: Ashton's men.

"They wouldn't be stupid enough to leave this spot unguarded," one of the men said. He had blood splattered on his shirt and carried a similarly blood-stained sword. All members of Tarragon society were proficient with swords and Kale was grateful that they were using swords instead of guns. With swords, they might stand a chance.

"There's no one here. Maybe the cowards ran, like the last bunch," another man said. His clothes and sword were clean, but his face looked like he had just gotten his nose broken and his fists were bruised like he had been in a fistfight. Kale didn't envy whoever had been on the other side of those fists.

"Search the area, then let's move on. You know the song, Lee?"

The third man nodded and Kale's heart went cold. They knew the song to the hatching grounds. That meant someone who had been invited to the hatching grounds had been a spy, or else they had tortured the information out of someone on the mountain. It didn't matter too much, since Jamie would just deny them entrance, but if Jamie were constantly being bombarded with requests to enter the hatching grounds and had to constantly judge who was worthy or not, he would be unable to do anything else. This was a very dangerous development and one he needed to tell someone about immediately. But first he and Mike had to survive, and get rid of these goons, if possible.

Kale reached for his sword in its sheath around his waist. They were all armed with swords, and perhaps he could take out the men with Mike at his side. Mike was a teacher, after all, and had to be better than most if he was responsible for teaching. But then Kale remembered that Mike was the history teacher, not the fencing teacher. There was a good chance Mike hadn't even touched a sword since his days as a student. Kale looked over at Mike and gestured to his sword. Mike went pale, and Kale inwardly swore. The man would be of little help getting the jump on these intruders.

The three men wandered off to search the area and Kale relaxed. They weren't looking in the right place. He turned to Mike and gestured for Mike to remain absolutely silent, not that Mike needed the reminder. Kale needed to figure out how to prevent these men from singing the song, or at least how to persuade them to move on from this area. It was too dangerous to try to move away from their current hiding spot, since they would inevitably make noise and draw the men's attention, but they were partially exposed and couldn't hide forever.

He was just coming up with a plan when there was a whooshing sound and something sharp penetrated his arm. He stared at the dart in confusion for a several long seconds, not understanding what was happening, then there was another whoosh and Mike grunted. Kale saw a dart in his arm. The sense of danger skyrocketed and Kale nearly collapsed from the pain. Or he thought it was the pain. He pulled the dart out of his arm and saw Mike do the same. Not thinking clearly, he staggered out to the small clearing with the firepit and fell to his knees. He caught sight of a cloaked figure moving through the trees. He had been darted and as his limbs started to go numb, he realized that he had been poisoned as well. He collapsed on his back, staring up at the sky. He could see the dragons fighting overhead and then, to his shock, he saw Vestis drop like a rock out of the sky, followed shortly by Eraxes. A large dragon lazily flew down after them and Kale wondered if that dragon were on their side or Ashton's.

Blackness was starting to shroud his vision but he fought it. He could see Mike collapsed on the edge of the woods by the tree they had hidden behind. He worried about Vestis. The dragon wouldn't die after dropping out of the sky like that, but he would be knocked unconscious and injured, possibly even severely injured. Dragons were nearly invincible but a drop like that would surely do damage. He looked around, trying to find the cloaked figure that had darted him, but there was only silence and the screaming sense of danger. Blackness covered his vision and he was left with fear for several long minutes before he succumbed and the blackness veiled his mind.

CHAPTER THIRTY

Sacrifice

Mike slowly regained consciousness. He was standing up, bound to a post of some sort, and someone was squeezing his hands and whispering his name over and over. Someone was tied to the other side of the post, back-to-back with him, and they were trying to get him to wake up. He turned his head as far as it would go with the post in the way and saw Kale's dark eyes fixed on his.

"Mike, are you all right?"

"Yeah, I think so," he said hoarsely, his voice not working properly.

He looked around. They were in a clearing on the mountain. At the other end of the clearing were Eraxes and Vestis, but his heart clenched as he noticed that both dragons were not only unconscious but staked to the ground by thick chains crisscrossing their bodies in a web of steel that would surely prevent them from moving. Their heads and necks were stretched out and exposed and Mike wondered why.

"My sacrifices have awoken," a new voice said, and Mike flinched at the familiar tones. Ashton.

He turned his head to see the man approaching in his dark robes with the crimson dragon on them. Never had they looked more imposing, or more ominous. He looked like a sorcerer about to perform some dark spell on his unwilling victims, and Mike knew that wasn't far from the truth. Ashton strode arrogantly until he stood directly in front of Mike, then he ran his hand down Mike's cheek. Mike struggled to look strong, but he couldn't fight the fear threatening to suffocate him. A tear escaped, and Ashton brushed it away and kissed his lips lightly.

"I would have given you everything, pet," he said so softly Mike doubted Kale could hear it, even though they were bound so close together. "But now I must take something away from you."

He moved until he was in front of Kale and Mike struggled to be able to see what was going on. He could just see the edge of Kale's face and Ashton's body when he twisted his head, but the pole and his position prevented him from seeing what was really going on. Ashton whispered something to Kale, and Kale went rigid; Mike could feel it in his hands, which were still grasping his. Kale squeezed his hands tightly and Mike returned the gesture. He didn't understand what was going on, except that Ashton had called them sacrifices and Kale had once said that Ashton had asked him to sacrifice his life. Were they going to be killed to satiate the mountain's need for blood?

Ashton stepped away from both of them and pointed to their dragons. Arion flew down out of nowhere and perched on top of Vestis.

"No," Kale cried. "No, Ashton, you can't do this!"

"It is already done," Ashton said, and he made a slashing gesture with his hand.

Arion lowered his jaw around Vestis's throat. The dragon was still unconscious and didn't fight. Mike tried to reach out to Eraxes to see if he could help Vestis somehow, but Eraxes was unconscious as well. Arion couldn't really be about to hurt Vestis. Dragons couldn't kill other dragons; it was forbidden. Mike's jaw dropped as Arion's teeth pierced Vestis's delicate throat and blood began to flow. The blood was absorbed into the ground instantly rather than pooling, and Arion clamped his teeth further.

Kale screamed and Arion shut his jaws all the way and then yanked, ripping out Vestis's throat. Kale's scream doubled in intensity and the post they were bound to quaked with his efforts to free himself. Mike felt numb as he watched blood seep from the gaping wound in Vestis's throat. Arion swallowed the flesh from Vestis's neck and let out a roar. A scattering of scales fell from his body and he seemed to increase in size as Mike watched, as if the flesh of another dragon had given him strength and size. Mike tore his eyes away from Arion to look at Ashton, who had his eyes closed with a smile of pleasure on his face. He looked younger, somehow, as if he had lost a decade from his life, and Mike wondered if the dragon flesh had done that as well.

Kale's hands scrabbled against his own as Ashton seemed to come back to reality and fixed his gaze on them. He glanced at Mike briefly, but his attention was on Kale. He drew a blade and went up to Kale. Mike craned his neck to see what was going on. Kale went absolutely still with fear and he grasped Mike's hands. Mike couldn't see what happened but there was a whoosh of air and Kale tightened his grip and let out a gurgling cry. His breathing sounded as though he were underwater and after a few seconds, his hands grew sticky. Mike could just make out blood running down his neck. Ashton had slit his throat. He trembled as the reality sunk in. Ashton had slit Kale's throat. Kale's grip on Mike's hand loosened and the blood that had seeped to his hands dropped to the ground, absorbed instantly by the hungry mountain. Kale was dead.

Ashton approached Mike with a blade crimson with blood. Blood was on his hands as well as Ashton reached out to pull at the collar around Mike's neck. It didn't come off, and Ashton sighed.

"I had hoped to spare you, pet," he said. "Despite your treachery, I had hoped you could be reformed. You have so much potential. I want you to know that I have never cared about anyone the way I cared about you. But the mountain demands more, and we must give it to her."

"No," Mike said weakly. "I'll be your pet, I'll do everything you ask. I'll tell you Jamie's plans and how to enter the hatching ground. Just don't hurt Eraxes."

Ashton shook his head. "I'm afraid it's too late for that, pet." He stroked Mike's hair with a blood-soaked hand and Mike shivered as Kale's blood was streaked through his hair. Kale was dead, and his murderer was right in front of him, yet all Mike could think of were ways to survive, not ways to get revenge. But what options did he have? He was tied to a post, unable to move, and his dragon was equally tied up and unconscious.

Marisol, he thought suddenly. If he could reach out to Marisol, perhaps she could come and put an end to this. Someone had to pay for Kale's death, after all. But he needed to buy time.

"I love you," Mike said, choking on the words that were so close to being true. He had almost loved Ashton. If he were honest with himself, he had loved Ashton for a time, but he didn't like to think about it. It was nothing compared to what he felt for Kale, only now Kale was dead and Mike's life was empty. He would fill it with revenge, but he had to buy time.

"Let me help you," he continued. "Let me tell you what I know and then sacrifice myself to the mountain."

While he spoke, he reached out to Marisol. She was instantly in his mind. She had felt Vestis die, he realized, and was already on her way with Jamie and several council members. There were already dragons nearby, he saw, but they were unlikely to act without the Queen present.

Ashton stroked his cheek and left a trail of Kale's blood.

"Such a good pet you are," he murmured. "Fine, tell me what you know, but understand that your death must happen. The mountain must be appeased."

Mike told him what he knew of Jamie's plans in halting, slow language as if he were too terrified to speak quickly, and Ashton didn't seem to realize that he was stalling. He couldn't think on his feet fast enough to lie convincingly so he told the truth and hoped that his betrayal wouldn't harm his allies in any way. He reached out to Marisol to warn her that he was spilling their secrets and she sent a reassuring thought that it was okay, that he should do whatever it took. So he continued, as slowly as possible, with tears and hesitations, to tell Ashton everything about Jamie's army and their plans.

Ashton listened keenly, sometimes comforting Mike when he broke down into tears, sometimes wiping those tears away with fingers wet with Kale's blood, and when he did that Mike had to fight the urge to vomit. His lover's death was being rubbed against his body and he could do nothing but betray the cause his lover had fought for. Every drop of Kale's blood that touched him was a reminder of the betrayal he was engaging in, the selfishness he was showing. His tears were real, as were his stuttering breaths that delayed his speaking, but he was determined to keep Ashton interested for as long as possible.

But he had to run out sometime, and when he did Marisol was nowhere in sight, nor were the other dragons she had said were nearby. Ashton kissed him lightly on the lips and told him to stop talking, that his time was up. Then Ashton turned to Arion.

"No," Mike cried, just as Kale had done. "Kill me, but don't kill Eraxes."

"You realize he'll die without you," Ashton said.

"Then kill me first, as the law requires."

"The law," Ashton said spitefully. "A ridiculous law. Do you know what happens when a dragon consumes living dragon flesh? You gain strength, spirit. You regain your youth. I have lived centuries because of this. But the fools on the council refuse to allow it because they feel it is barbaric. How much more barbaric is feasting on the flesh of living dragons than providing a human sacrifice every decade? They've never complained about the human sacrifice, but for some reason they draw the line at killing dragons who are doomed to die anyway."

Mike felt tears fill his eyes. Not only was his death not going to avenge Kale's, but he was going to be helping Ashton by giving him strength and youth. He had wondered about Ashton's age and his seeming fitness, but he had never questioned it before. People partnered to dragons often lived a century, sometimes more if the bond with their dragon was good. He had never imagined that Ashton was multiple centuries old, or that he used dark magic to maintain his youth.

Ashton raised his hand and made a slashing motion, and Arion perched on top of Eraxes. Mike screamed. Arion fixed his jaws on Eraxes's throat. Suddenly three dragons appeared out of nowhere and shoved Arion off Eraxes, knocking him to the ground and pinning him there. Arion hissed and Ashton went pale. Three council members stepped out of the woods surrounding the clearing.

"What is the meaning of this, Ashton?" one of them said.

Mike recognized them as council members loyal to Ashton, but they didn't look loyal now. Their dragons were keeping Arion flat on the ground and two of the council members came up to Mike and began untying him and Kale.

"You know what this is," Ashton said. "The mountain was not satisfied with one sacrifice, so Mike must die as well."

"You aren't attacking Mike," the council member said. "We understand the fickle nature of the mountain, and we accept it. But you are attacking a dragon, which violates every law of our society and the dragon's society."

"An oversight," Ashton said. "His dragon would be dead as soon as he died. Why not get the killing over with sooner rather than later?"

"We heard what you said, Ashton," the council member said. "About your youth and strength. Have you truly been killing and eating dragons all these centuries?"

Ashton's eyes flashed with rage. Mike was now untied and he immediately turned to Kale, who was now being cut down. Oddly, there wasn't a lot of blood on Kale's body. In fact, if it weren't for the slit throat, Kale would have looked almost like he were sleeping. Mike cradled his body and sank to the ground, stroking Kale's long hair and whispering words of love that he hoped passed into whatever afterlife Kale believed in. He knew he was still in danger, and that these council members could decide to kill him at any minute, but at least they wouldn't kill Eraxes first. That much was clear.

The council members flanked Ashton, who was staring at the member who had spoken with sheer loathing on his face. Arion was still pinned to the ground, but he had stopped fighting, almost as if he were waiting for a signal.

Ashton lunged and stabbed at the council member with the blade he still carried, but the council member leapt out of the way just in time. At the same moment, Arion roared to life and knocked the other three dragons off him. The dragons scrambled to get him back under control but now that Arion was in the air, he had the advantage. Ashton had the advantage now, too, since he was the only one with a weapon. Even though the other three members circled him, they looked wary and fearful and Mike knew they would rather run and pretend this hadn't happened than stay and fight. He stood up on wobbly legs and rested Kale's body on the ground beside him. He would join in the fight. He might be unarmed, but he had his lover to fight for and unlike the council members, he wouldn't run away no matter what.

He reached out to Marisol a final time and instead of a response, he heard a roar and looked up to see Arion being plucked from the sky by the larger Queen dragon. She slammed him into the ground, knocking him unconscious. Jamie and Scott leapt off her back, each holding a sword. Reinforcements had arrived.

CHAPTER THIRTY-ONE

Justice

Jamie was helping the council put the finishing touches on their first attack, due to begin the next day, when Marisol received a cry for help from Mike. At first he was only marginally aware of the plea, but in seconds he lost himself entirely in her mind and saw the entire image as Marisol was seeing it: Mike had managed to project what he was seeing and feeling to Marisol and it was so powerful it had drawn Jamie in as well. The scene was horrifying. Kale was dead, and Mike was about to die. Their dragons were helpless and were being killed first. Mike was tied up and unable to do anything but talk and stall until Marisol arrived.

As soon as Jamie regained control of his own body again, he related what he had seen to the council. In minutes, they agreed that half the council should accompany Jamie, Scott, and Marisol. Since Arion seemed to be killing dragons even though it was forbidden, Narné would remain. Narné wasn't too happy about that decision, but everyone knew that if any dragon was going to get killed by Arion, it was Narné, who had beaten Arion in Jamie's mating flight. Jamie and Scott were given swords and the council members prepped them for battle. Jamie hadn't fought with a sword all summer and had been behind the other students when he started back up in the fall, but he was decent. Ashton, on the other hand, was a master swordsman, so the goal was to avoid fighting him head on and instead look for ways to get the dragons to do the fighting.

Marisol informed him that several dragons had witnessed Arion about to kill Eraxes and stopped him from doing it, and they were now fighting. Jamie urged her to fly faster and in moments they were at the clearing on the mountain. Arion was pinned, but even as they watched he flung off the dragons keeping him down and started soaring around to attack them. There were two dragons chained to the ground and one of them, Vestis, Jamie saw with horror, had his throat torn out. He fought the urge to vomit. He had been expecting to see it yet the reality of the scene was far more gruesome that he had imagined. Marisol roared in fury and snatched Arion midair in her talons before slamming him into the ground, hard. So hard his head bounced against the ground and Jamie knew he was unconscious. Jamie and Scott leapt off Marisol's back and he looked around for the council members who were supposed to have accompanied them. Had they betrayed Jamie? Where were they?

They are gathering others, Marisol said. *We must take care of Ashton ourselves until they return.*

Jamie gulped. He saw Mike standing beside Kale's prone body and he had to fight tears. One person had already died in this conflict. He couldn't allow anyone else to die. Jamie had known, of course, that war meant death, but he had never really understood the reality of it. Every life lost was precious. He had never expected it to be someone he cared for, someone he had spent all summer with, laughing and joking and pulling pranks on. He and Kale had grown close over the summer and now Kale was gone forever. Ashton would pay dearly for this.

There were three council members and Mike circling Ashton, and now Jamie and Scott. Only Jamie and Scott were armed, and the council members looked like they would rather run than fight but Jamie hoped they stayed. They would provide a good distraction so Ashton didn't focus all his attention on Jamie or Scott, who were unlikely to hold him off in a serious attack. Ashton looked calm and in control, his weapon held ready and pointed at Jamie.

"Are you sure you want to do this, Jamie?" Ashton said. "I would be happy to talk to you and listen to your concerns."

"You killed Kale," Jamie said. "I think the time for talking is over."

"A sacrifice to the mountain," Ashton said with a shrug. "And not the only one who will be required to sacrifice his life today. The mountain requires another before she is satisfied."

"Or maybe she just didn't get the person she wanted," Jamie said, thinking of what Kale had said about Ashton wearing the collar once. The mountain was protecting them against Ashton, after all, would it be that unbelievable that the mountain wanted Ashton's blood and no one else's?

Ashton laughed. "You think to give her my blood? It will be a long time before that happens, little one. But if you don't want to talk, then we won't."

Jamie stiffened and raised his weapon as Ashton raised his. Marisol growled low in her throat. The three council members backed away until they were at the edge of the clearing. Their dragons took up positions behind Marisol, who was still standing on top of Arion. He knew Marisol wanted to pick him up and carry him to safety, but he needed to face Ashton and with Scott at his side, he had a chance. He glanced over at Scott to make sure Scott was all right, since he hadn't spoken, and Scott nodded at him.

Ashton lunged without warning and his blade scraped along Jamie's left arm, piercing the skin before Jamie whipped up his blade to block it. He hissed in pain but Ashton wasn't done, while he was in close quarters he elbowed Jamie in the gut and Jamie nearly fell to the ground. Scott was after him in an instant, wielding his sword with far more grace than Jamie. Jamie sucked in air and tried to stay out of their way while he recovered. His arm stung, but he couldn't leave Scott to fight his battle for him. As soon as he could straighten and lift his sword, he dashed out and tried to attack Ashton. He hit air instead, and again Ashton's blade sliced across him, this time across his right thigh. Scott again distracted Ashton with a skilled blow as Jamie backed up for a moment to recover.

Scott could hold his own against Ashton, he noticed, but Ashton's back was open while he fought. Jamie tried moving to Ashton's backside to attack but Ashton kept sidestepping to keep both of his opponents in view. It was seemingly impossible to get a blow in. Jamie winced as Ashton's sword flashed across Scott's chest and the fabric of his shirt ripped open and blood began to flow. It was the first time Ashton had struck Scott, and Scott bit back a pained cry with a look of determination on his face. Jamie tried to get a strike in, but he seemed to make it worse whenever he tried to enter the fight. Instead, he circled and forced Ashton to be on guard, giving Scott a slight advantage over the man despite Ashton's superior sword skills.

Marisol roared as Scott finally pierced Ashton's defenses and sliced through the man's sword arm. Ashton winced but kept going without even glancing at the injury. Then Marisol's roar grew in volume and she hopped off Arion, distracting Jamie, who suffered a minor cut on the back as a result. Marisol was in the thick of the fight in an instant and grabbed Ashton in one clawed hand and Scott in the other. She released Scott as soon as he stopped fighting, but continued to hold Ashton, who squirmed and demanded to be let loose.

"This isn't a fair fight, Jamie," Ashton called. "You can't call your dragon in to win your battles for you."

"I didn't tell her to do anything," Jamie said honestly.

I obey no one, Marisol said so that everyone could hear. *I am the Queen, and all must obey me.*

Jamie shivered at the absolute command in her voice. He had never heard her like this before. Then he noticed the other dragons arriving. They were all council members. All of the council members, he realized soon, men and women, loyal to both Ashton and Jamie. Margot landed first and stood a few yards from Ashton. Marisol regarded her seriously with eyes that were almost entirely black.

"As acting head of the council," Margot announced, "I call this meeting to order. We are here to discuss the fate of Peter Ashton."

Jamie let out a sigh. So they were going to talk some more, and as usual, Ashton would get his way. He could feel that Marisol approved of this meeting, however, even though he couldn't figure out why. The council had been a disappointment every time he had met with them and he saw no reason for that to change.

Mike approached Jamie and Scott, and he must have had the same feelings because he looked highly skeptical and disappointed. He also still looked shell-shocked and terrified, as if afraid that someone would kill him at any moment. Given what Ashton had said about needing another sacrifice, he probably had good reason, but Jamie would not let anything happen to him even if it meant that the mist would fade away and stop protecting them. Mike was covered in blood, from his hair to his hands, and Jamie wondered if he had held Kale while the man bled out. He knew they had gotten close over the past week or so, and it hurt him to see Mike in so much pain.

"Margot," Ashton said. "You are not acting head. I'm right here."

"You renounced your position when you killed and ate a living dragon," she said sharply, and the council members nodded in agreement.

"You have no proof of that," he said desperately.

"We saw it," one of the council members who had been at the clearing from the start said. "We hid and saw Arion eat Vestis, and we heard Ashton talk about the purpose of eating dragon flesh."

Mike went rigid beside Jamie and Jamie knew he was wondering why the council members hadn't tried to stop what was happening or save Kale's life. Jamie was wondering the same thing. If they had witnessed it, and they must have, because there was no point in lying, then why hadn't they tried to save Kale? The whole council was corrupt, not just Ashton. Getting rid of Ashton would get rid of the main problem, but the council would still be full of the men and women that Ashton had hand-chosen for the positions.

"Enough, Ashton," Margot said. "The dragons will decide your fate. It is in the hands of Marisol. She is our Queen, and she will decide what happens to you."

Marisol nodded her head regally before speaking so everyone could hear her. *I have consulted with all of the dragons about Ashton's fate. For his crimes, he and Arion will sacrifice their lives here on the mountainside.*

Margot nodded once. "Then it is decided. Ashton will sacrifice his life, and Arion will be killed afterwards, as should happen in a sacrifice."

"This is ridiculous," Ashton said. "This dragon is a child, full of a child's need for petty revenge. She was friends with the other sacrifice and her actions are those of revenge, not sanity."

I based my decision on the will of all dragons, Marisol said in a surprisingly calm voice. *No dragon believes that you should live after what you have done to our kind.*

"Arion thinks I should live," Ashton said. "He's the one who committed the crime, not me. Why am I the one to pay the price?"

He would never dream of killing a living dragon without your words to poison him.

"Enough, Ashton," Margot said. "Marisol's word is final. Prepare yourself."

"Wait," he cried. "I have a son. I have a dragon. I have things to live for!"

"You should have thought of that earlier," Margot said.

She approached Ashton, still held tightly in Marisol's claws, and tied his hands. Then she led him to the post where Mike and Kale had been tied and fastened him there. When he was fixed in place and unable to move, she took his sword from the ground and brought it to Jamie.

"You are the Queen," she said simply. "This is your duty."

Jamie stared at the sword, then at her. "What am I supposed to do?"

"Slit his throat," she said. "Marisol will take care of Arion."

She took his hand and wrapped it around the hilt, but he continued to stare at the sword in shock. When the council had shown up, he had assumed that they would take over and finish the job for him. Even earlier, during the fight, he had assumed that Scott would win the battle for him. He had never imagined that he would be the one to kill Ashton. He looked at Ashton and noticed a gleam in Ashton's eye, as if Ashton had spotted his weakness and his unwillingness to kill.

"Come now, Jamie, you see how barbaric this all is," he said. "Untie me. Remove me from the council, banish me, if you must, but surely you can't kill me. You shouldn't have to carry the weight of my death on your shoulders for the rest of your life."

Jamie hesitated. He knew he shouldn't be persuaded, but banishment had its advantages. But no, Ashton would only try to strike back wherever he went. He would never leave Jamie and Scott alone. If Jamie banished him, he would be seeking revenge at all times, never satisfied with life outside the academy. Worse, he might take to killing dragons for sport because he wouldn't be bound to the laws of Tarragon society.

"Kill Arion, if you must," he said, sounding slightly more desperate as if he could tell that his words weren't having the desired effect. "Leave me without a dragon. But don't take my life."

Jamie grimaced. The man was willing to sacrifice his dragon just to live a little longer? Jamie would do anything for his dragon, even die, and the thought of abandoning her was terrible. Ashton deserved to die, and Jamie had to be the one to do it. He looked at Margot as if for permission and she nodded her head and gestured him forward.

"You had feelings for me," Ashton tried again. "When we were together, I know you felt something. I gave you more pleasure than you had ever known. How can you possibly want to end that?"

Jamie flushed and his hand wavered. It was true, but it was having the opposite effect. He wanted to shut Ashton up so Scott wouldn't find out about it, so no one would find out about it. He stepped closer to Ashton and raised the blade to the man's neck. He would have to press hard to cut through the skin, and slash with all his strength so it was a clean stroke and a quick death. There had to be better, more painless ways of killing people but perhaps this was part of the ritual of sacrifice. Jamie took a deep breath. Ashton went deadly silent and appeared to be holding his breath. Then the man spoke one last time.

"Tell Derek I love him."

Jamie wavered again, but he knew he had no options now. He couldn't delay anymore or give Ashton any more chances to say things to change his mind. He pressed the blade and pulled it across at the same time. The flesh was tough, but gave way at the last instant and the sword nearly decapitated Ashton it went so deep. Blood splashed onto Jamie's face and clothes and he backed away quickly, kneeling and vomiting. When his belly had emptied itself on the ground, he looked back to see almost no blood on the body; the mountain had absorbed it all.

He heard a commotion and looked to see Marisol ripping Arion's throat out, only she spat out the dragon flesh rather than eating it. Arion's blood vanished into the soil as well. There was a clinking sound and Mike gasped as his collar fell to the ground, then faded into the earth. The collar on Kale's neck also faded into the ground.

Margot stared at the places where the collars had been in shock, then looked back at Ashton's body. Jamie couldn't bring himself to look back at the body. His stomach was still flipping in his body and he knew the sight of the corpse would be too much for him. He had killed someone. He stared at the blood on his hands, blood that hadn't been absorbed into the mountain. He was a killer. Would Scott still love him after he murdered a man in cold blood?

CHAPTER THIRTY-TWO

Aftermath

Derek flinched as a large party of dragons returned to the skies with Marisol and Narné at their head. He already knew that his father was dead. Jettie had informed him, gently, of the dragon's decision. Marisol had shared what Ashton had done with all the dragons and requested their advice in how to deal with them, and because Ashton had brought death to the dragons, the dragons had insisted upon death for him. Jettie and a few others had pleaded for mercy but they couldn't stand up to the near unanimity of dragons who were horrified that Ashton and Arion had violated the most essential rule of dragon society and killed other dragons.

Derek was trying to come to terms with his father's death. He felt empty, hollow, but in a way that he had been all his life. His father had always been an absence and this was nothing new, but before he had always been filled with hope that his father would suddenly discover him and realize that he loved Derek. Now there were no chances left; Ashton would never love him. He had failed as a son and it hurt more than he could put into words or explain to Jettie.

He sat on his cot and tried to imagine what his life would be like now that Ashton was gone. Always before he had lived with the goal of impressing Ashton. Everything he did had that one ultimate goal. He played sports, played music, made friends, became popular, did well in school, everything so that Ashton would notice him. What was he supposed to live for now?

"Derek?" a familiar voice called, and he looked up to see Scott approaching. "We're moving everyone back to campus as soon as possible. I offered to fly you and Jettie back. Is that okay?"

"Yeah," Derek said. "I hear you won. Good job."

Scott winced. "The cost was high. Too high. Kale is dead, Ashton is dead, and Jamie's in a state of shock. How are you handling things?"

Derek staggered to his feet. His whole body felt heavy and not just because he had been lying in bed the past day. He felt beaten down and worn out. But he didn't want Scott to know how depressed he was feeling.

"I'll be fine," Derek said.

"Derek, I want you to know... The last thing he said was that he loved you."

Derek looked up at Scott in surprise. He wouldn't have expected that, not after Ashton had just tried to kill him. But maybe he hadn't known what Alan had been going to do, maybe Alan acted on his own and Ashton hadn't approved. That had to be the case if Ashton had loved Derek. No father who loved his son would try to kill that son just to get a stronger bond.

Tears welled up in Derek's eyes as he sniffled. Ashton loved him. It was more than he could have hoped or dreamed and he only wished Ashton could say it to him in person, or that he could have heard it firsthand instead of through Scott. A strange lightness flitted into his heart and relieved some of his depression. Somehow, he had done something to please his father before his father's death because Ashton loved him. He hadn't been a total failure as a son. He didn't know what he had done, but Ashton wouldn't waste his last words on someone he didn't truly care for. But he still wanted more; he was still used to living in order to please Ashton. Ashton might be gone, but the need to please him remained and would likely remain for some time until the reality of the man's death sunk in.

Scott grabbed Derek's waist without a word and helped Derek out of the medical tent towards Narné, who waited nearby. The doctors and nurses were packing everything up and moving with a haste that surprised Derek. He supposed they weren't sure how long the hatching grounds would continue to support them now that they no longer needed the protection. The sky was littered with dragons leaving the grounds as people who had just left their lives days or weeks ago to join the rebellion now returned to the campus.

Scott helped Derek onto Narné's back and then hopped up behind him. Derek tried not to read anything sexual into the way Scott held him but it was hard not to, since they had been intimate together and this was an intimate embrace. Scott's face was pressed against his, their cheeks touching, the entire front of his body pressed against Derek's back as Narné gently lifted into the air. Jettie was finally big enough to fly by herself but Narné kept a careful eye on her in case she grew tired and he needed to grab her midair. It would still be a while before Derek could ride Jettie, but he was pleased that she didn't need to be carried anymore. She was a queen dragon, after all, and deserved to be able to fly on her own.

Derek felt his breathing even out in time with Scott's as they flew and he relaxed against the older man's grip, wishing Scott felt about him the way he felt about Scott. If only Jamie weren't in the picture. Jamie ruined everything, and there had to be some way to get Scott to see that. Perhaps that could be his reason for living, Derek mused. Now that his father was gone, he needed some purpose in his life and perhaps he should devote himself to catching Scott permanently.

Scott shifted against him and Derek leaned his head back against the other man, enjoying the embrace as they left the hatching grounds and were suddenly above Mount Tarragon. The weather was colder and Derek shivered. Scott rubbed his arms and tightened his grip. Then they were spiraling downward with several other dragons and partners over the medical building. Derek had hoped to be released to his dorm where he and Scott could spend some time alone, but this would have to do. He could make it work. They landed and Scott hopped off first and then grabbed Derek's waist and lifted him off.

Derek clung to him for a long moment after his feet hit the ground, staring up into his eyes and wondering if he dared kiss Scott or if that would be too sudden. Scott stared at him in return with a flicker of something in his eyes, but Derek couldn't tell what. Desire, maybe. Fear, perhaps. Hopefully not disgust, but Derek really didn't think so. Derek decided against the kiss and instead leaned forward to hug Scott. Scott relaxed into the hug almost immediately and buried his head into Derek's neck.

They hugged for a long time beside Narné while Jettie pranced around them, happy because Derek was happy. Scott seemed to need the hug as much as Derek did and Derek tried to let go of his sorrow and confusion and instead enjoy the feel of Scott's powerful body against his as it once had been. He wanted more from Scott, but he could sense that Scott was not in the mood for romance. Scott was mourning his friend, Kale, and even though Scott had said that Jamie was in shock, Derek could tell that Scott was in shock as well.

A dragon's roar went up nearby and Narné stiffened, then leapt into the air with a deafening response. Scott's body stiffened and he pulled away from Derek. His lips were parted and his eyes were dilated, and he looked flushed and aroused. Derek smiled and started to lean in for a kiss but Scott placed a finger on Derek's lips.

"The mating flight," he said. "It's started. I have to go."

He dashed towards a dragon that was just landing. Before its rider could slide off the dragon, Scott was climbing up behind the rider and ordering the dragon to take him to the dragon canyon. The rider and dragon obeyed and took off. Narné was already a small speck in the sky he had flown off so fast.

Derek stared at the dragon carrying Scott in shock for a moment, then looked at Jettie.

What happened? he asked her.

Marisol has entered her mating flight, Jettie responded. *Narné must win the mating flight or else Scott will no longer be the Queen's mate.*

Derek scowled. Always, Jamie was getting in the way. Now Jamie's mating flight was ruining what could have been a perfect time for Derek to worm his way back into Scott's heart while Scott's defenses were low. He would just have to wait and see what happened, and hope that Scott didn't win the flight. He did feel some sympathy for Jamie because he was a little frightened of the mating flight himself, but he resented the fact that it brought Jamie and Scott together. If Scott didn't win, Jamie might have an uncomfortable mating flight, but Derek would get what he wanted for once. And wasn't it time for Derek to get something, anything, after all this time waiting?

"Excuse me," a gentle voice interrupted his thoughts.

Derek looked up to see a beautiful man in his thirties approaching the bed where Derek was settling in. He had cropped blond hair and smooth blue eyes, and a creamy complexion with only a hint of wrinkles around his eyes that made him look approachable and friendly. Completely different than Scott, but Derek found himself entranced.

"I wanted to express my condolences," the man continued, sitting down in a chair near the bed where Derek was now seated.

"Thank you," Derek said, unsure what else to say. He knew he was avoiding thinking about the loss of his father and it kept hitting him in different ways, but he had forgotten that other people would be affected by it, too, and not everyone would be glad to see Ashton gone.

"I was a friend of your father," the man continued. "You can call me Chris. He was the one who invited me to join the council."

Derek sat up a little straighter. A council member. That was someone important, not someone he should be swooning over, no matter how beautiful he was. And a friend of Ashton. A thousand questions filled his mind as he suddenly saw a way to get to know Ashton even after the man's death. Ashton might be gone, but perhaps Derek could still find out about who he was, and how Derek could live up to his expectations. Because he had lived all his life wanting to please Ashton, and that impulse was too ingrained in him to stop with Ashton's death.

"Did he ever talk about me?" Derek asked shyly, glancing down at his hands before looking back at Chris.

Chris smiled. "Frequently. He had big plans for you, Derek. He was very proud of the man you have become."

Derek was filled with pride, though it was tempered somewhat by the knowledge that he had failed Ashton by not bonding with Jettie properly. Ashton had even been willing to let Alan kill him to achieve that higher level of bond. But Ashton said he loved Derek. He fingered the bandage on his stomach where Alan's blade had entered him and Chris must have seen the motion because a look of anger crossed his features.

"Alan acted rashly, and without Ashton's permission, Derek. Ashton would not have let you die."

That didn't seem to fit with what Scott had said, but Derek couldn't think of a reason why Chris would lie. Or why Scott would lie, for that reason. But he wanted to believe Chris, wanted to believe that Ashton hadn't wanted his death, so he did. It was easier that way, and his love for his father wasn't shaken to its core if Ashton hadn't ordered Alan to nearly kill him.

"Why aren't you in the mating flight?" Derek asked and couldn't hide the bite of jealousy in his voice. Scott had dropped everything to be in the mating flight; he couldn't imagine why a handsome man like Chris – and a council member no less – wouldn't be involved.

"I'm not interested in Jamie," Chris said. "But Ashton did ask me to be in your first mating flight, Derek, and if you allow it, I would like to honor his request."

Derek flushed. Being in his mating flight meant potentially having sex with him. Chris was asking to have sex with him. He studied Chris more carefully and found that he was nothing but attracted. Chris's friendship with his father just made him more desirable. He was a little older, maybe, but not too much for Tarragon standards. Derek liked that he wasn't interested in Jamie – that was a major plus on a campus where everyone seemed obsessed with Jamie. And Derek wanted to learn more about his father and Ashton's plans for Derek's future. He wanted to live up to his father's dreams for him.

"I would like that," Derek said, still blushing.

Chris smiled and reached out to take his hand and Derek let him. His touch was soft, his hand gentle as he stroked Derek's palm with his thumb in a very sensual manner.

"Your father said you had his ambition and drive, and you would be ready to lead someday," Chris said. "I want to help make sure you are ready when that day comes."

Derek's mouth widened into a smile of pride at the thought of his father saying that about him. He thought he had leadership potential as well. It might be a problem with Jamie seeming to be the leader on campus, but maybe they could split leadership or maybe Derek could start another school somewhere else. He knew Scott and Jamie had talked about opening other schools to allow more people in Tarragon society to survive into adulthood. He could easily imagine Jamie remaining here while Derek went off on an adventure to found something new and exciting, a new place for students to come and learn and bond with their dragons. Jettie bumped against his mind with excitement and he knew that she was up for the challenge as well.

Scott would stay with Jamie, Derek suspected, but perhaps Chris would come with him. Perhaps Chris was exactly what he needed. Someone new who could woo him and love him as he deserved to be loved without splitting his affection with Jamie.

Someone who could guide him on the path his father had laid out for him. Derek's smile stretched into a grin at the possibilities before him and Chris shared his smile with a glint in his eyes. He looked satisfied, probably because Derek was interested in him. It must have been a risk coming over here and telling a stranger you had feelings for him and wanted to be in his mating flight, but Derek was grateful that he had. Thanks to Chris, Derek now had a view of the future that was full of hope and possibilities, and he was eager to get started.

CHAPTER THIRTY-THREE

Mating Flight

Scott's mind was racing as he urged the poor dragon he was riding to greater speeds on his way to Jamie. Part of his mind was with Narné, of course, as Narné searched for the Queen in the skies above the academy, but the rest was broiling with doubt and fear. What had triggered the mating flight?

After killing Ashton, Jamie had collapsed to the ground and barely been able to stand. He had been in tears and unable to speak or do anything. Scott had gotten him settled in their bed in dragon canyon before returning for Derek, his other delicate charge, but Jamie had been in no state of mind for a mating flight. If anyone but Scott won this flight, it would shatter Jamie completely.

He shouldn't have left Jamie alone, Scott realized with the perfect clarity that comes with hindsight. He should have stayed at Jamie's side. Jamie needed him after what had happened on the mountain. But Derek had needed him, too, and he had told Derek that he would be there for the man after everything happened. He couldn't leave Derek alone to deal with his father's death any more than he could leave Jamie alone, and in this case, Derek had won out. No matter how much Scott regretted it now.

But what was the trigger? Last time, Jamie had gone into the mating flight because he and Scott were about to have sex. Jamie was in no mood to have sex now, and there was no one besides Scott that Jamie would even consider having sex with – he hoped. He still remembered Ashton's words about giving Jamie pleasure and he remembered how Jamie's hand had wavered as if that were the truth and that stung deeply. But Ashton was dead now, and surely none of his minions were bold enough to act with his body still warm.

The dragon he was riding finally arrived at the empty dragon chamber where Marisol had been only half an hour earlier and Scott leapt off and thanked them, then dashed to the bedroom where dozens of men were gathered. He shoved his way to the front. At first they resisted, their eyes dilated with desire and only partially aware of what was happening in this world due to their bonds with their dragons, but when they realized who he was they grudgingly let him through. Jamie was on the bed, held down by five men who were caressing him and whispering things to him. Jamie was naked and clearly aroused.

Scott took up a position by Jamie's head, where he had been in the previous mating flight, and leaned down to Jamie's ear.

"It's all right, Jamie, I'm here."

Jamie's face, which had been twisted in pleasure and fear, relaxed somewhat and the tension seemed to melt out of his body. Scott wanted to shout at the other men to leave, to stop touching his lover, but they were circumspect in their touches and Scott knew the importance of touch during a mating flight. Besides, if he did kick everyone out, no one would consider this a fair mating flight and they might not respect him as the Queen's mate. No, he had to win this the proper way. He leaned his head against Jamie's and shut his eyes to connect with Narné.

Narné flew in hot pursuit of the young Queen, who was having quite a time with her pursuers. She had left them all behind but kept flitting back to them as if to encourage them to keep coming, and each time she returned the mass of dragons surged forward in an attempt to catch their prize. But soon, her speedy chase had winnowed out all but three dragons: Narné and two others who could keep up with the swift Queen. She soared into the clouds and dove down to the forests, and Narné saw how her altitude changes slowed her down. If he could catch her on one of her dives, he would win her. The other two dragons were struggling to keep up and seemed confused by her rapid and unexpected plunges, but he was ready.

On her next swoop, Narné dove with her and reached out to grab her just as she breezed by them. His claws struck flesh and he clutched her, strengthening his grip until he had her in his grasp. She shrieked in surprise and readjusted herself. Her neck wrapped around his sinuously and her lips pulled back. There was blood on her teeth. Arion's blood.

Spooked, Narné let go for just an instant and Marisol kicked him away and continued on her plunge, then soared up again and continued her race. Back in Jamie's room, Scott cursed himself for letting go. The blood had been a shock, but not enough of one to let go of the Queen. Now the other two dragons had seen one way to catch the Queen and would likely imitate it, and his chances of winning had dropped. He needed all the speed and strength he had to win this flight.

Back out in the open air, Narné waited for the Queen's next dive and managed to catch her again. She was growing tired now and slowing down, but the other two dragons were hot on his tail. He had just arranged Marisol in his grasp when, to his surprise, one of the other dragons attacked him and tried to tear him off Marisol. It was strictly forbidden to attack another dragon during the mating flight, especially when that dragon was already attached to the Queen, and Narné recognized the scent of one of Ashton's men in the dragon who was now clawing at Narné's back and wings.

In the bedroom, a man leapt onto the bed with Jamie and positioned himself at Jamie's entrance as Scott struggled to focus on reality instead of his dragon-blurred vision. He would not allow anyone else to touch Jamie, and what this man was doing went against all regulations and laws of them mating flights. But even so, if this man managed to penetrate Jamie, he would become the next Queen's mate.

Scott stood dizzily and tried to ignore the doubled sensations of dragon and man as he shoved the man off Jamie. The man fought and clawed at him just as his dragon was doing to Narné. His nails pierced Scott's chest and Scott hissed, but kept forcing the man back off the bed, always keeping one hand on Jamie so the contact between them wouldn't be broken. Once he got this man away, he would have to enter Jamie quickly, never mind any gentleness, to ensure that the mating flight ended soon.

The man attacked him again and again until Scott finally punched him in the nose and he fell backwards off the bed with a cry. In the sky outside, the attacking dragon reeled backwards and Narné took the chance to enter his Queen just as Scott entered Jamie.

Jamie's eyes were closed and he looked terrified, but Scott leaned down and kissed his cheek.

"It's me, love, you're safe now."

Jamie kept his eyes closed but his body lost some of its tension as Scott began pulsing into him in time with the dragons. Scott was barely aware of the other man now, or the other men in the room with them standing witness to the mating flight. He was with Jamie, and that was all that mattered.

Jamie's eyes opened for just a moment and Scott saw lust there, but fear as well and he kissed Jamie's forehead to reassure his love. Then Jamie's eyes closed again as if Jamie had just been checking to make sure it was Scott and not someone else, and he reached up to encircle Scott's shoulders with his arms. He moaned softly as Scott continued thrusting deep into him, driven by the fires in their own bodies as well as their dragon's desires.

Scott could hardly tell what was human emotion and what was dragon; the two blended together in perfect harmony until it was all one heartbeat of thrust and withdraw, thrust and withdraw, with Jamie writhing in pleasure below him and Marisol trumpeting hers. He was blended with Jamie now, as they always were during sex, their emotions running together and Jamie's sensations as clear to him as his own. It had taken several minutes before the connection formed this time, but now that they were fully locked onto each other the sensations were incredible, human and human and dragon and dragon, all mixed into a single awareness of bliss beyond anything Scott had ever experienced.

Jamie was panting and arching his body in time with the thrusts, his nails biting into Scott's skin as he couldn't control his moans now. Scott was having trouble controlling himself and knew he was growing erratic. He could feel Marisol's exhaustion along with her growing pleasure and knew this incredible moment couldn't last forever, but he stretched it as long as he could, glorying in the feel of his lover and his dragon all together in his awareness.

Then a trigger went off deep within him and he exploded, and felt Narné explode as well. The two of them clung to their lovers as Jamie and Marisol weren't far behind and the connection between the four of them echoed with the power of their orgasms, wrapping around each of them and shaking them to their very roots. Then the link faded and Scott was only Scott again, exhausted and battered and sore.

He pulled out of Jamie gently and Jamie finally opened his eyes and kept them open. A hesitant smile tugged at Jamie's mouth as if he were afraid of what Scott would think of him and Scott kissed him. Then Scott turned to the other men in the room, all council members, along with two female council members who were bonded to male dragons and had taken part in the mating flight.

One of the men who had been at the hatching grounds and was loyal to Jamie stepped forward and placed his hand on Scott's right shoulder.

"You are the Queen's mate," he said, then returned to his position with the rest of them.

One of the women pushed forward.

"You are the Queen's mate," she said, also returning to her position.

One by one, all of the men and women in the room acknowledged him as the Queen's mate. All except one, who sported a swelling black eye and a scowl. It was the man who had attacked Narné and Scott mid-flight and broken the rules. Two council members held his arms to prevent him from leaving, and once everyone had acknowledged Scott as the Queen's mate, they turned to Jamie, still naked on the bed and looking increasingly embarrassed.

"This man interrupted your flight," one of the council members said. "It is up to you to decide the punishment."

Jamie went white and Scott knew he was thinking of Ashton and killing Ashton. But he didn't think the council members meant killing the man. Jamie was silent, though, with a vague look that meant he was consulting with Marisol. The others waited, no doubt also noticing that Jamie was conversing with his dragon. Then Jamie nodded.

"He is to be stripped of his title and removed from the council, but kept on campus," Jamie said. "We will keep a close eye on him until he has proven his loyalty to the new order."

"You can't do that," the man protested. "Ashton named me to this council decades ago, I won't let some kid remove me on a whim!"

"This is our Queen," one of the council members said in a shocked tone. "Not some kid. And his word is final."

The council members bowed to Jamie and shuffled out of the room, leaving Scott and Jamie alone. As soon as the door shut behind them, Jamie's eyes filled with tears and he was in Scott's arms. Scott held him tight and rocked him.

"That was too close," Scott said. "I'm sorry for that. I will never let that happen again. I'll never leave your side again."

"Yes, you will," Jamie said wearily. "You'll have to. But you'll come back, won't you? You won't ever abandon me, no matter what?"

Scott thought of Derek and how he had neglected his duty to Jamie in order to be with Derek. He needed to resort his priorities. There were plenty of people who could take care of Derek, even though he enjoyed Derek's company and genuinely liked the man. But he was the only one that could take care of Jamie. He had to stop putting other people before Jamie, because Jamie needed him. And truth be told, he needed Jamie. No one else made him feel the way Jamie made him feel, like his heart was open and shining for the first time.

He had hesitated at the sight of blood on Marisol's teeth and he shouldn't have, and he knew that hesitation was eating away at Jamie's self-confidence. Jamie had killed someone and would be feeling vulnerable. It was Scott's duty – and pleasure – to reassure him.

"I will never abandon you," he said, brushing his lip against Jamie's forehead. "No matter what happens. I am bound to you not by Tarragon laws but by love, and that will never change. Now that we're free, nothing will ever get in our way again."

Jamie hugged him with a strength that surprised Scott, and he returned the hug in kind. Then he ran a finger down Jamie's bare shoulder.

"We need to clean off and get you dressed, sweetheart. Care to join me in the shower?"

Jamie smiled shyly and stepped out of the hug, pulling his hand in the direction of the bathroom. Taking that for a yes, Scott grinned and followed.

CHAPTER THIRTY-FOUR

Looking Ahead

J amie stood on the balcony overlooking the dragon canyon. Marisol and Narné were curled around each other in the immense chamber and he ought to be curled around Scott in the same way, but he needed air to breathe, and space to think. The events of the past few days kept replaying in his mind in horrifying clarity and he knew it would be a long time before they would fade and he could move on. Kale, lying dead on the ground with Mike clutching his body. The feel of Ashton's flesh giving way under his sword as he executed the man. And Scott hesitating, drawing back during the mating flight.

The last one stung the most. Scott had pulled away from him when he needed Scott the most and it had almost ended in disaster. Another man had almost slept with Jamie. Scott had accepted Jamie quickly, but that hesitation had been there. And even when Scott entered him, there hadn't been that instant connection between their minds that there usually was. In fact, Jamie had needed to open his eyes to confirm that it was actually Scott and not a stranger on top of him because he couldn't feel Scott's mind. But then everything had clicked into place and they had become one.

Scott accepted Jamie now, even though Jamie had killed a man, and Jamie knew he shouldn't resent the fact that it had taken Scott a few moments to accept that fact about Jamie. But his hesitation had come at just the wrong moment, when

Jamie was feeling so vulnerable and lost and in need of someone strong to be there for him. He knew the world didn't revolve around him, of course, but surely Scott at least could take his feelings into consideration and be there for him the way he needed. He loved Scott, absolutely, but he knew it would be a while before he felt truly safe with Scott again.

There had also been a tenderness in Scott's mind towards Derek when Scott and Jamie had become one and shared each other's minds and emotions. Jamie knew that Derek was a threat, and now that Derek was partnered to a queen, that threat was even greater. He had talked to the council members about starting a second school so that more members of Tarragon society could survive into adulthood and perhaps it would be best if Derek were sent to the new school, far away from Scott. Mike would probably also go, Jamie reflected. He doubted Mike would want to remain at a place with so many bad memories.

The new school couldn't be too far, of course, because the mist would have to protect the school and no one knew how it operated or what its range was, but the council had suggested that a school in nearby Spokane might be possible. Derek was from Spokane, so it was natural that he would go there. However, Jamie would have to be careful not to allow any of Ashton's men at the new school. They wouldn't be under Jamie's watchful eye and they might reinstate the same policies that Kale had given his life to fight. Jamie would have to be very careful that Derek didn't try to take over the school and take over his father's place on the council as well. Perhaps Mike could help with that.

It would be a careful balancing act, but one he was willing to accept in order to get Derek away from Scott. He would handpick the people to send to Spokane and perhaps go himself to set up the school, and then keep an eye on them through his Queen's gift of communicating with all dragons. It would be a strain, but it would work.

Jamie let out a sigh and fingered the edge of the platform where rough rock met sleek interior. Marisol was letting out little snorts every time she exhaled and a reluctant smile crossed Jamie's face. She had forgiven Narné for his hesitation and was sleeping quite soundly; now it was time for Jamie to do the same. Although perhaps without the snorts. He returned to their bedroom but didn't get into bed yet. Instead, he walked to the mantle and picked up the snowglobe there.

It was still broken, of course. Nothing could make it work again, just as nothing could bring his parents back. And now he had witnessed two more deaths and been the cause of one of them. He fingered the globe and stared at the house before setting it back down. Ashton had been responsible for his parents' deaths. Ashton was now dead. Justice had been served. He ought to be happy, but instead he felt sick, sick to his stomach at what that justice had entailed. His stomach flipped and he bolted for the bathroom, reaching it just in time as his dinner spewed back up and into the toilet.

As he knelt by the toilet helplessly, a hand patted his back and he glanced up to see Scott with a look of sympathy on his face. When his stomach was empty and stopped flipping around, he wiped his mouth and stood up, a little dizzy.

"It's okay, Jamie," Scott said. "I'm here now. You're not alone."

But he felt alone. Scott had abandoned him not once but twice, first when he had been handed the sword to kill Ashton and again during the mating flight when Scott had hesitated. And there was so much danger in the world right now.

No one had been able to find Alan, so he was still a threat somewhere out in the world. Many of Ashton's minions had vanished from campus. Somewhere out there, they were gathering, but they were leaderless for now. He just had to make sure that Derek didn't become a figurehead for them, willing or unwilling.

And something needed to be done about Mike. Jamie winced. Jamie had been in a state of shock after killing Ashton, barely able to stand or understand what was happening, but even in his altered state he had recognized that Mike was far worse off than him. Many of the council members still didn't trust Mike and paid him no mind, but Jamie knew he would have to be handled very gently to make sure he mentally survived what had happened. At least his connection to Eraxes was intact. Jamie had worried that Ashton would try to cut off people's connections to their dragons with his last breath, but it seemed that not even Ashton was that spiteful. Or perhaps Ashton just hadn't thought of it. The latter seemed more likely, as Jamie doubted there was any level Ashton wouldn't stoop to in order to hurt people.

Thoughts of Ashton brought back the inevitable memory of killing the man, and he wondered again why he had been the one to do it. He shut his eyes and buried his head against Scott, who held him tightly and stroked his back. He wondered about Margot especially, and why she had insisted that Jamie be the one to kill Ashton. Her actions had always seemed strange, as if she had ulterior motives; after all, she had both helped Jamie and refused to take sides in the conflict. He didn't know her game, but she was still in charge of the girl's college and he knew she had also participated in the sacrifices that had taken place every decade. Even though she hadn't killed the dragons first, she had still killed people to placate the mountain and the thought chilled Jamie.

At least there would be no more sacrifices. Margot had explained that normally after a sacrifice, the collar would fall off and be held in storage until the mists began to thin again. This time, however, both collars – and there were only two collars, she assured him – had vanished completely. Margot explained that she believed it meant the mountain didn't need any more sacrifices. Jamie had to agree. Ashton's blood, bitter though it was to spill, had seemed to satisfy the mountain and he hoped the mountain would never need blood again.

Jamie sighed. He would worry about Margot later, when he had more energy. Right now, he was exhausted and still reeling from the mating flight. He hadn't meant to enter the mating flight and in truth, he hadn't. Marisol had. She had been holding back for days, resisting the urge, and as soon as Scott had tucked him into bed and he began to relax, she had relaxed as well. Her relaxation had led to her emotions running high and soon she could barely keep still, and Jamie had awoken to her frightened but triumphant cry as she launched herself out of the window.

He had been terrified, since Scott was nowhere nearby and the room had almost immediately filled with people, including some he could sense were loyal to Ashton. But he was in no position to object, as Marisol's lust had quickly overtaken him. Even when Scott showed up, the flight hadn't gotten much better and he knew it would remain one of the most harrowing flights of his life, far worse than his first because it came on the heels of such a traumatic event. He didn't know what he would have done if Ashton's men had been successful. He might not have been able to live with himself. And Scott had nearly lost him.

He pulled away from Scott, feeling a surge of resentment and fear.

"I need to brush my teeth," Jamie said weakly.

As he rinsed out his mouth and brushed his teeth, Scott hovered in the doorway. When the taste of vomit was finally gone from Jamie's mouth, Jamie turned to Scott and hugged him tightly.

"I can't forget," he whispered. "It's all so real."

"It's all right now, Jamie," Scott said. "I won't ever leave you again."

Jamie was silent. He knew that Scott loved him, and had accepted him despite what he had done to Ashton. But what if something else happened, something worse? Was there something that would make Scott turn away from him forever? Jamie shivered. He didn't want to find out. He wanted to bask in Scott's love forever and never worry about the possibility that he might one day be forced to do something that Scott couldn't live with.

"I'm sorry I hesitated," Scott continued, clutching him tight. "It was surprise, not fear. I could never be afraid of you, no matter what happens. My love for you is absolute and unconditional, Jamie. I am yours forever."

A tear ran down Jamie's cheek. This was exactly what he needed to hear. He thought of meeting Scott, how nervous he had been when he first confessed his love to the man. He thought of how betrayed he had felt when he learned that Scott had been assigned to seduce him, but how that had changed when he learned Scott's reasons for wanting to seduce him. He thought of his first mating flight, how frightening and confusing it had been but how Scott had been there for him regardless of the consequences. He thought of Ashton's machinations and attempts to keep them apart, but how Scott had continued to fight for their love. He thought of the summer they had spent together in pure happiness, the semester that had just passed in relative quiet until the end. Scott had always been there for him; one minor hesitation wasn't enough to throw out all of the unconditional love Scott had always shown him.

Jamie felt a gentle push from Marisol and was surprised that she had woken up. He felt a little guilty that his emotional distress had woken her, but she didn't seem to mind. Instead, she was reminding him that Scott and Narné were his mates by law and by love and that he loved Scott as much as Scott loved him. Jamie nodded. He did love Scott; he was just afraid that Scott didn't love him. But if Scott's words were true – and he had no reason to doubt their sincerity – then there was nothing holding him back. Scott accepted him, Scott loved him, and nothing would prevent him from embracing his love and sharing the future with him.

Cautiously, Jamie smiled at Scott and kissed him on the lips. Scott kissed back, matching his chaste kiss. Jamie could see the relief in his eyes and realized that Scott had been just as frightened of losing him as Jamie was of losing Scott. Well, that fear could be laid to rest now and forever. From now on, Jamie vowed, he would love Scott with all of his heart and he would trust Scott to do the same. He snuggled into Scott's arms as Scott stroked his back and kissed the top of his head.

"I love you, Scott," he said.

"I love you, Jamie," Scott replied.

Life would continue much as it had before, Jamie realized: with fear, with hesitation, but now, unlike before, there was an overarching love that negated everything else that stood between them. As he inhaled the warm, musky scent of his lover and felt Scott's powerful arms enfold him, he thought of the future and wondered what it would hold for them.

ABOUT THE AUTHOR

Elizabeth James

Elizabeth James hails from Portland, Oregon and spent many hours of her childhood tucked away in the Gold Room of Powell's Books, reading science fiction and fantasy masterpieces and hidden treasures. She writes romance with strong elements of science fiction and fantasy as a result, focusing on LGBT characters.

THRALL OF DARKNESS

Thrall of Darkness was founded because there is a shortage of good, quality literature featuring gay protagonists that does not reduce gay characters to stereotypes or dismiss them as secondary characters. Every story seeks to challenge the status quo by focusing on gay characters and combining drama, action, and sex into an addicting blend of fun-filled narrative.

You can find more information on Thrall of Darkness novels and short stories at thrallofdarkness.com.

BOOKS BY THIS AUTHOR

Demon Season

Taylor just wanted to bond with a regular demon during his first demon season, but instead he ends up with the prince of demons, an incubus! He fights through his fears of intimacy while battling past enemies as he and his demon come to a new understanding.

A Vampire's Desire

Kairos takes a job in an ancient vampire house knowing nothing about them and their society, and immediately falls in love with his boss, a powerful but cold vampire. As he tries to get closer, threats from a rival house threaten to tear them apart.

Dragon Tamer

Luke has heard dragons all his life and when a dragon summons him to raise her dragonlings, he runs away to help her. But the world he enters is fraught with danger and he knows little of the outside world. As the dragons begin dying off and dragon tamers like him become scarce, a rival tribe kidnaps him and everything he knows is thrown into question.

Sagent

Gabriel is a sagent, a sex agent, at the start of his career, but he is already scarred by his previous agency. When he is sent on a dangerous mission to the underbelly of Destiny, everything starts to fall apart. Isolated from his agency and not knowing where to go, Gabriel must choose between returning to safety and Destiny, or staying and forging his own path.

First Prince

Wren is the beautiful yet rebellious first prince of Fontain, forced to move to the Imperial Palace as part of a treaty. Upon arriving, he receives a frigid welcome and realizes his stay will be fraught with danger. When he finds romance in an unexpected place, he realizes that his life may not be as dire as he imagined and pleasure can be found where it is least expected.

Prisoner Of Love

When Prince Tristan is captured in battle, he fully expects to be tortured and killed. But the torture turns to erotic pleasure as he learns that his enemy, Prince Ryan, is in love with him and has been planning his capture with meticulous care for years. Will Tristan hold firm to his principles, or will Ryan's forceful seduction overpower his senses?

Dark Offering

Nightmares are a nightly occurrence on the planet of Ylse, and they're strong enough to lure humans to be fed on by the creatures who haunt the night. Jarl is charged with risking the night to feed the colony. He comes across one of the creatures offering peace. Is the creature sincere or is this just a new way to lure the humans to their deaths on this inhospitable planet?

Bride Of Albis

Sam and his small crew of space-faring traders have their usual routine permanently shattered when they are kidnapped by pirates. Sam makes a deal with the head of the pirates: he will be sold as a slave in exchange for the freedom of his crew. But when he discovers that the pirate lied and sold his crew as well, he vows vengeance.

Seeking More

Seeking More is a collection of eight contemporary gay romance stories that range from the deeply emotional to action-packed, from hapless MFA students to couples on the brink of a new relationship. Each story is focused not only on steamy romance, of which there is plenty, but also on character development and an emotional connection between reader and character.

Eve Of Eternity

Sabine is a young woman searching for her identity while fleeing the powerful man trying to steal her heart and mind. She's almost under his control when she is kidnapped by a man with conflicting loyalties and a mysterious past who claims to kidnap her in order to rescue her. Will she break free from the men around her?

Treacherous A Dragon's Love

In the middle of the final battle against the great dragon Arostrath, a woman appears bound in golden chains. The King claims her as his reward but the youngest son has an unusual fondness for her that could cast the kingdom into ruin. Will his love for the beautiful and strange woman destroy the kingdom, or does her mystery hide the answer to all of their prayers?

www.ingramcontent.com/pod-product-compliance
Lightning Source LLC
Chambersburg PA
CBHW020054180626
46812CB00006B/2324